They were following a trail to the dawn of time....

FATHER EDDIE FITZSIMMONS, the priest. His search for the grave of Eve was his last, desperate attempt to restore faith lost in a world ravaged by suffering.

BRAXTON HICKS, the reporter. He didn't buy this regression theory, but he did want to help his friend. Besides, it could be the story of a lifetime.

KATHY SULLIVAN, the woman. Troubled by unanswered questions about her past, she soon discovered that under hypnosis her mind opened the door to something much more incredible... and dangerous.

ZELDA ROOTE, the hypnotist. Her skills could regress Kathy into the unexplored territory of mind and memory—but could she lead them to the place they sought?

FRANK GUNTHER, the guide. He thought he was leading a group of tourists on a sight-seeing safari—then he discovered what they were hunting, and he moved in for the biggest kill of his life.

DOG BASSETT, the hunter. He knew rich folks would pay big money for the wild animals he dodged the law to kill. Then he realized the bones of the world's first woman would bring him one hell of a bounty.

EVE OF REGRESSION

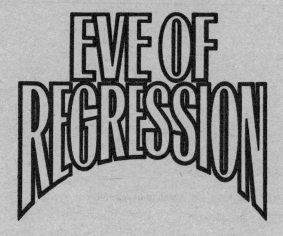

EVE OF REGRESSION

JOHN ARTHUR LONG

WORLDWIDE. ®

TORONTO · NEW YORK · LONDON · PARIS
AMSTERDAM · STOCKHOLM · HAMBURG
ATHENS · MILAN · TOKYO · SYDNEY

EVE OF REGRESSION

A Worldwide Library Book/January 1988

ISBN 0-373-97055-2

For my sister, Gerri, who
helped show me the wonder to
be found in books before I
was old enough to read,

And for my brother, Roger, whose
heart belongs to the wilderness.

With special thanks to
Ken Robinson for first
suggesting we take
a tent safari through
Hemingway's Africa.

We shall not cease from exploration
And the end of all our exploring
Will be to arrive where we started
And know the place for the first time.
Through the unknown, remembered gate
When the last of earth left to discover
Is that which was the beginning...

—T.S. Eliot
Four Quartets

Prologue

DARKNESS HAD FALLEN, and deep in the savannah, under the sparkling arch of the star-filled African sky, a lean, tall, muscled Masai warrior worked at his task. Streams of sweat dripped down the man's body and glistened in the firelight, for the work was hot and arduous. A short distance away the warrior's constant companion, a towering giraffe, looked on while the man labored, oblivious to the sounds that filled the blackness beyond the light thrown by the fire he had built.

The Masai's purpose was to craft and forge a new spear. He did not enjoy the task, for those of his tribe did not do this work. Iron forging was for other tribes, not for the noble Masai.

Still, he knew it must be done. He had thrown the sacred stones and the message was clear: The spear must be created. There was no choice, for he was Twamba, a man who from birth had been set apart from the others. A man who could walk among the things of nature and hear their whispers. And as he grew, he had learned to listen to the secret voices around him. And he had learned to follow, as he was following now.

So he forged a spear. And after it was crafted, he would carve the sacred symbols into it. And he would bless it in the ceremony that had been taught to him long ago by another who had followed the voices of nature that speak to those who learn to listen.

Unseen in the darkness but not far away, rose a great bluff. Twamba knew the place well. He had been there often. It was a place where once the great God had spewed forth his anger in a violent tongue of fire, and strange twists of frozen stone now stood in irregular caves and overhangs. It was a special place. A place that brought the old and weak of the savannah to it for refuge, as if in response to some great instinctual urge.

The stories told of how long before Twamba was born, and even before his father's father was born, the animals had been coming to this place. Those who knew of such things believed it had been so before the great God erupted in fiery wrath and changed the face of the land forever into such a wild and desolate place.

It was said that a great river had flowed across the land, leading to what was a holy place for the sacred spirits who live always, and that creatures seeking refuge followed the moving waters to their source. The tale told that it had always been so, not just for the animals but for the early ones from the beginning of time.

And now, though they came seeking refuge, seldom did the creatures of the great plains leave. The secret caves and hollows where the weak and infirm sought shelter became their final resting place. A great graveyard for the beasts of the savannah.

Twamba knew it to be a place of death, but still he came often to the bluff to help animals that might possibly survive. For not only was he a mighty Masai warrior. The tall giant had also been blessed with the gift of knowledge about special herbs and was a renowned man of medicine, healing where it was needed.

However, even Twamba moved with caution in the place of mystery, for though it was a refuge for the weak and old, one breed of animal came to this place not to die but to survive. A wise warrior must be wary of these animals for they were without hearts of feeling and prowled over the jagged stone floors and precipices in great numbers.

At night they lurked among the shadows, hugging the rocks. Occasional glimpses of their snarling faces could be seen, then only the shine of their eyes reflecting out of the darkness.

They were hyenas. Carnivores. With their strange, almost crippled, stunted bodies and eerie, mocking cries, they still had the strongest jaws of any beast alive. They would attack a living animal if hungry enough. But mostly they waited. Waited to fulfill their special role in nature's carefully balanced plan as scavengers of the dead.

This night the hyenas peered out from the shadows over the dark plain to where the tall Masai labored by his fire. Raising their heads, they screeched and howled mockingly at the strange sounds and sights the warrior created, not understanding this intrusion at the border of their domain.

And they were not alone. Even Twamba did not understand why he forged the spear. He only knew that while moving among the ancient petrified formations in the wide, open-roofed cavern that could be found beyond the stone wall, he had seen an opening he was certain had never been there before. It was a large, gaping crevasse near the base of the tree that stood at the center of the open ground.

Finding the opening, out of which the spray of a warm mist rose, was disturbing to the Masai, and sensing it was a sign to be heeded, he had traveled a short distance beyond the bluff to sit and throw the sacred stones. That was how he had come to know he must forge the spear.

Having finished the task, the tall Masai held the weapon high in the firelight to examine his craftsmanship. Then, satisfied, he lowered it to his side. His work was done. He would keep the spear with him, confident that when the time was right, the reason for its coming into being would be made clear to him.

Until then, the matter would not be of concern to him. It was enough that he had followed the urges that came to him, for he had learned that to do so always gave him a feeling of great peace.

One

AS SHE STARED out of the little girl's frightened eyes, Kathy Sullivan tried desperately to summon the strength to scream. Or to take control of the child's movements. But as always, the ability to do either eluded her, and the dream that had tormented her sleep so many times before went on.

As she watched the events unfold through the eyes of the child, an agonizing terror clawed at her, yet she was helpless to intervene. With a disturbing double vision and a growing horror she watched the dream, all too aware how it would end. This nightmare that she knew would lead her once more into that searing blaze of fear and heartbreak....

THE DARKNESS CAME when the old one ceased to be. It came during the time of light, rushing at them and clamping down on their senses until they felt enveloped within a black grief. And now, something in the darkness led them on. The old one must be taken back. Only then would the darkness end.

They followed the moving water, guided by its rushing sound as it rumbled in torrents beside them. Only in the momentary flashes of fire that cut through the gloom and sliced into the earth could the wide expanse of raging foam be seen as it cascaded past them. Against the direction of this wide current they moved...toward the water's source.

That was the place the old ones had spoken of in guttural vocalizations and sign words. It was there, the old ones had told them, that the great brightness had been lost.

The old one's body was covered with an animal skin and lashed to a crude two-poled wooden sled that some of the stronger men pulled after them. Flowers and herbs adorned the still form being dragged along the ground, and the old one's mate, her head lowered in mourning, moved slowly along next to the death sleigh. Beside her, not understanding the darkness and frightened by the wailing around her, walked the little girl-child.

Consumed by her own loss, the old woman had ignored her daughter since the coming of the darkness, seemingly oblivious to the girl's existence. And yet the little one stayed right with her mother, her tiny fingers clutching frantically at the hide skirt next to her, holding on for dear life to the one person who would keep the terrible fear that surrounded them from rushing in and snatching her away.

The marked warrior led them. The one whose scarred and hardened being seemed never to tire. Holding his great lance high above his head, he urged them on. So long had he been gone, many had not recognized this eldest child when he suddenly reappeared, emerging out of the darkness to join them. And those who did showed their disapproval. Yet now, all followed him, for though he had been cast out after the unforgivable act of slaying his own brother, only he seemed strong enough to lead them through this dark unknown.

A younger male child assumed the task of keeping the group together and comforting the old woman, who staggered under the weight of her grief. It was this woman with the little girl clinging to her that they watched. For she alone had been there. She had seen the source from which the raging waters flowed. It was her reality that shaped their visions. She would know when the journey was at an end. When they had reached the place of the beginning.

And through it all there was a fear of the great beasts that lurked about them. Within the dark they could hear them. And in the sudden flashes of light their shapes could be seen as they stalked around the group. And each time there seemed to be more of them than before.

Then, while Kathy Sullivan felt a heavy sense of foreboding spread through her and prayed for the dream to end, it happened. As she looked up questioningly through the girl-child's eyes, the old woman suddenly stopped moving. The group came to a halt, and though no one spoke, they all knew. She had seen it. The old woman had seen the light.

Then they could all see it. A small, pulsating shaft of white glowing in the darkness far ahead.

After so much darkness, the light seemed to transform them. A new energy surged through the group, and in spite of their fear they increased their speed, prodding each other on. The old one had been right. There was a light. And it beckoned to them. Drawing them on. Pulling them forward. Pulling them back to the source.

The most transformed was the woman. As the ever-increasing glow highlighted her features, she no longer appeared old. Her body was now straight and tall. The pain seemed to dissolve from her face, replaced by a radiance that none of them had ever seen there before.

Finally the group stood within the perimeters of the golden light. The men pulling the death sleigh brought it forward to the very edge of the swirling luminescence.

For the first time the girl-child's hand relaxed, releasing its grip on her mother's skirt. A tiny smile flickered across her face as she stared in delight at the spinning ovals of sparkling white light.

Then, in the midst of the brilliance that surrounded them, the warrior hurled his lance into the ground and dropped to his knees. With a mighty crack of thunder, a bolt of flame knifed through the darkness above and the ground in front of them split open. As they covered their ears against the deafening sound, the death sleigh hovered at the edge of the new crevasse, then slipped forward and was gone.

Instinctively the little girl grabbed at her mother's skirt, but the old woman lunged forward, and the child's fingers closed on air. She screamed in fear, but already her mother had moved into the light and was only partially visible. Then the brilliant vortex closed around her, and she too was gone.

As one, the members of the group cried out. With piercing wails of grief they fell to their knees, humbled by the towering wall of light before them.

All except the girl-child. Her screams were singular. Her loss apart from theirs. She cared not about this great mystical wonder, this threshold that led the way to all that had been lost. Her loss was a child's loss, and she knew only that her mother had disappeared into the light and was gone.

Then a different sound arose from those near the rear of the group. It was a cry of alarm, and those at the front turned to see huge scale-covered bodies emerging from the darkness. The beasts were attacking. As the warrior rose to his feet, rallying the others to defense, only the little girl refused to turn from the light.

Oblivious to the snarls and screeches behind her, she tried to move forward. But the light was a blaze now. A great flaming sword that held her back, blocking her advance.

AND, AS ALWAYS, now that it was too late, Kathy Sullivan was finally able to grasp control. The girl-child's mouth opened to bellow her sorrow, and Kathy heard herself screaming with the pain of irrevocable loss.

Two

SHE WAS AWAKE NOW, held by strong, comforting arms that rocked her softly.

"Shh ... It's all right, Kathy. It's all right."

It was Zelda, of course. The heavyset hypnotist was sitting on the edge of the bed where Kathy had fallen asleep. Once her sobbing subsided, Kathy wiped her eyes and looked anxiously around to confirm that she was, after all, awake, and that this was reality.

They were in the room they had rented at the Norfolk Hotel in Nairobi, and Zelda was there, as always, ready to offer whatever support was needed.

"I'm okay now, Zelda ... really," Kathy said, pulling away slightly in embarrassment as she pushed back disheveled locks of her wavy red hair.

Zelda nodded, patting Kathy's hand reassuringly. "Of course you are. It was the dream again?"

"Yes," Kathy replied, rubbing her face with the back of her hand. "My God, I always feel like such a fool when I wake up, but it seems so real."

"I know," Zelda said. The hypnotist studied the fine features of her client's attractive face to reassure herself that the young woman was, in fact, all right. Then, shifting her considerable weight and smoothing the billowing flowered kimono she wore, she pushed herself up from the side of the bed. "But it's just the way your subconscious is attempting to rationalize what happens during hypnosis. I know it's disturbing, but I'm not surprised that the dream is occurring with more frequency now that we're getting closer."

"Well, it's no problem, really," Kathy said with a heavy sigh, allowing herself to fall back into a prone position on the bed. "I'll just stop sleeping until we've resolved this."

A smile formed on the older woman's face. "Thank God for that strong determination of yours. A lesser person probably would have stopped long before this."

Kathy stared at the ceiling above her. "No, it's not determination, Zelda. It's gotten beyond that now. It's an inner need. I'm not sure I could stop now even if I wanted to."

"Yes, you could," Zelda said firmly, her hands coming to her hips and her voice filled with authority. "We can call this off anytime you decide you've had enough. And I mean that, Kathy."

"Yes, Doctor," Kathy replied with feigned seriousness. "But do you think I'd quit after coming so far...after the commitment Eddie has made to this? Not to mention how much all this has cost you."

"Forget the cost. My family left me more than I could spend in a lifetime. The money is unimportant to me. I've told you that."

"I know, but—"

"No buts, Kathy! The most important thing in all of this is your well-being. Eddie and I are in perfect agreement on that. We're on new ground here. And as exciting as I find that to be, I also know there is always an element of risk in opening the unknown regions of the mind. Don't forget, in spite of what has happened and what we believe, this could still be the brain playing tricks on us—some mysterious mental manipulation we know nothing about.''

"Zelda, we've covered all this. And what just happened was only a bad dream, like always. I'm okay, really. Besides, you don't believe for a second it's the mind playing tricks, and you know it.''

Zelda shook her head, needlessly smoothing the sides of her short-cropped hairdo. "No, you're right,'' she said, the edge of her own conviction in her voice. "I don't. I believe we've tapped into something quite extraordinary. That we're on the brink of a great discovery. But with all of my experience, I can't be aware of what's really going on inside you, Kathy. Only you can. But don't forget, I also know what's motivating you in this. And in spite of what you may hope for, I want to reiterate that the chances of you gaining new information relating to your own mother are just as slim as our finding concrete proof of anything else. So, please...if these dreams are too disturbing, or if you feel it's all too much, we stop! All right?''

Kathy shifted her gaze to meet Zelda's eyes. Fear was in Kathy's hazel eyes, along with doubt and anxiety. The professional in Zelda could see that clearly. But there was something else in Kathy's expression that overrode these negative emotions. An inner determination. A resolve not to be defeated. It was a quality Zelda had recognized from the beginning in this tough-willed young woman. And it was one of the main reasons the hypnotist had decided to undertake their present mission.

"No, we're not stopping, Zelda,'' Kathy said with a clear finality. "I admit I'm open to some ups and downs, but I will handle it, damn it.'' She reached out and grasped the older woman's hand. "If it reaches the point where I can't cope, I'll tell you. I promise."

"All right," Zelda said, bringing up her other hand to cover Kathy's, which she squeezed briefly before releasing her grasp. "That's my girl. In any case, Eddie phoned and he's gone to meet his reporter friend. If all goes well, they should be here soon. He's going to meet us downstairs with Mr. Gunther so we can finalize plans for the safari. Do you think you'll feel up to it, or would you rather wait until later?"

Kathy swung her feet off the bed and arched her back in a weary stretch. "No, I'm fine. Just let me wash my face and at least make some attempt to look presentable. How much is Eddie telling these people, anyway?"

"Well, besides being a writer who can put this all down for us, the reporter is Eddie's good friend, and Eddie said the only way to deal with Mr. Hicks was to level with him right from the beginning. As far as our guide, Mr. Gunther, is concerned, he's been hired to take us on a standard tour safari until we decide to tell him otherwise."

"Won't Gunther sense something's strange after he sees me taken through a hypnosis session? That's going to be a little difficult to hide at a campsite."

"Eddie feels we shouldn't say anything until we have to."

"My impression of Mr. Gunther is that he'll go along with just about anything if the price is right."

"You're probably correct," Zelda agreed, frowning. "I also think you would be wise to keep your eye on him. I don't like the way he looks at you."

Kathy nodded. "I noticed. He practically undressed me with his eyes yesterday when we were making the

arrangements. A lech of the first order. Anyway, let me
get cleaned up before Eddie gets here with his friend.
Braxton Hicks! I still can't get over the name."

"You're certain it's the same as the medical term?"

"Absolutely. Must be some kind of bizarre coincidence. Although I'm sure I'll win the strangeness award
as far as he's concerned when Eddie explains what we're
trying to do." Kathy rolled her eyes and disappeared
into the bathroom, her voice trailing after her. "I mean,
I know what we've already explored and discovered so
far, but sometimes when I step back and think about
how weird this whole thing is, Zelda, I wonder if we all
aren't off our collective rockers."

Zelda shook her head in an unconscious negative response, her hands going to her hips the way they always did when she intended to make a strong point
about something. There was not a trace of doubt in the
hypnotist's voice when she spoke. Hers was the voice of
a woman who not only believed in what she was doing
but was in complete control of her present course of
action. That quietly firm yet authoritative tone had
guided Kathy Sullivan through many hypnosis sessions
in recent weeks.

"The thing to concentrate on, my dear," said Zelda,
"is not doubt, but the fact that we are doing this to find
the truth. Always keep that objective as your goal. Because we are going to find out the truth of this. I promise you. And when we do, all doubt will vanish."

Three

BRAXTON HICKS pulled open the heavy wooden door and, with a sigh of relief, pushed his athletic six-feet-two-inch frame through the entranceway, leaving the sweltering heat outside for the cooler interior of the National Museum. In spite of his unending love affair with Africa, Braxton had never been able to get used to the oppressive heat that enveloped the teeming city of Nairobi for the majority of the year, and he welcomed any excuse that gave him a chance to escape from it—even a mysteriously ominous call from his old friend, Eddie Fitzsimmons.

After crossing the main lobby, Braxton headed down the far side of the first hall, then stopped. Eddie stood several feet in front of him, staring intently into one of several lighted display cases. The small man was dressed in his usual dark pants and black short-sleeved shirt, the clothing hanging limply on his thin body.

A smile formed on Braxton's face when he realized what had so engrossed his friend's attention. Of course Eddie would be at that particular display. Braxton walked up beside the shorter man and glanced into the glass case: staring back at him were the empty eye sockets of a two-million-year-old skull. It was named "1470" and had been found by one of Richard Leakey's teams on the shore of Lake Turkana several years before. Braxton knew that because of his friend's passion for paleontology Eddie had seen the skull innumerable times before. Yet in spite of that fact, his concentration was so complete he wasn't even aware of Braxton until the news correspondent spoke.

"*Jambo*, Father Fitzsimmons," Braxton said in a warm hello. "Welcome back to civilization."

"Hello, Braxton," Eddie greeted, his face lighting up as he became aware of the man who had joined him. "Thanks for coming."

Braxton's smile changed to an expression of concern as he noted how frail the priest appeared.

"No problem." Braxton nodded toward the display case. "Listen, since you're so fascinated with this guy, Ed, why don't you take a lesson from him. The reason he looks that way—you know, with the emaciated cheekbones and all—is because he spent too much time worrying about others and didn't take care of himself. You look like hell, old buddy. You know that? Keep it up and I'll make sure they reserve a special showcase here for you. Homo Erectus Fitzsimmons, late 1900s." Braxton passed a hand in front of the display case. "Put the placard right under the light here. Look good, don't you think?"

The priest grimaced. "Don't I get more than a hello before the lecture begins?"

"I'm afraid if I don't lecture there might not be anyone to say hello to. Do you know how long you've been out this time without reporting back to civilization?"

"I know. I know. Actually, I've been back in Nairobi for several days now."

"Well, whatever you've been doing, it certainly hasn't been eating and sleeping."

The priest ran a hesitant hand through his thinning, sandy-blond hair. "No, I haven't had much of a chance to relax, I'm afraid."

Braxton nodded. "Okay. End of lecture. It's good to see you again, Ed, anorexia candidate or not. What's up? You need more coverage on the home front? If so, you've got it. I'll help as much as I'm able to."

The priest's expression clouded. "I'm not sure anything can help, Brax."

Braxton's eyes narrowed as he studied the man beside him. Actually, the haggard appearance was nothing new. Eddie always looked as if he needed a month's sleep and fifteen full-course dinners. It was the "nothing can help" comment that set off a warning alarm inside the news correspondent. For as long as Braxton had known him, from the early days when they were roommates in graduate school through the years when the priest was sent to administer aid to the Africans, Eddie Fitzsimmons had always had an unshakable faith that mankind could be helped. In fact, it had been Eddie's faith that had convinced a directionless Braxton to do his own bit for humanity, and he had joined his friend on a Peace Corps tour of duty in Kenya. As it turned out, they had both stayed. Braxton, because he fell in love with the country, and Eddie, because he felt that ministering to the needy made a difference. A man like Eddie didn't give up unless something was very wrong.

"What did you say, Father Fitzsimmons?"

"I haven't come for others this time, Braxton. Anyway, not completely. This time it's for me. I need help." The priest attempted a smile. "And who better to turn to than the one person I know who refuses to take life seriously."

"Hey, come on, now. I take everything seriously, Ed. I just don't dwell on it, that's all."

"No, don't sell yourself short, my friend." Eddie looked up at the deeply tanned face of the man next to him. "You have a rare quality to assist yet maintain a certain objectivity; to keep a distance."

"Which also allows one to keep from making any sort of serious commitment in life," Braxton added, squirming under Eddie's analysis. "Anyway, I'll admit you're right. We're both wonderful people. Now what's this all about?"

The priest sighed heavily, glancing away for a moment. "I...I need a vacation, Braxton. How do you always put it? After a week or two out in the open, watching game or staring up at the cloud-covered peaks of Kilimanjaro, everything always seems better? Well, that's what I need. Would you like to come along?"

Braxton's face broke into a grin of pleasure, and he pushed the baseball cap he wore back on his thatch of wavy dark hair. "Are you serious? A safari?"

The priest nodded. "Can you get the time off?"

"Timing couldn't be better. All the news focus is in New York at the United Nations, where the requests for more billions of dollars in aid are being prepared. The most exciting thing that's happened here this week was a native stealing some vegetables at the open-air market and then plowing his broken-down truck into the side of the post office when the police came after him. Exciting news for Nairobi, but hardly the kind of hot item they're dying for me to send Stateside. No problem. I'll tell the home office I'm going out to survey the changing wildlife scene. I've been waiting years for you to take a little time off, Ed. I'm ready when you are.

Let's exchange that black outfit of mourning you have on for a khaki shirt and shorts and move on out.''

The priest hesitated. "Well . . ."

"What? Afraid that baby-white skin on your legs might not be able to take being exposed to the sun? Okay, no shorts. We'll get trousers."

"Actually, there are a couple of things of more importance than clothing to be worked out first."

"Uh-oh," Braxton said with a suspicious tilt of the head. "How foolish of me to assume Father Fitzsimmons would do something for the simple pleasure of relaxation. Okay, what's the catch?"

Instead of answering, the priest turned once again to the display case in front of them. "Bone hunting, as you always called it, Braxton. I want to hunt for his relatives."

Braxton nodded as he, too, gazed at the skull, whose hollow sockets shrouded in darkness seemed to glare out at them. "Ah, yes, the Fitzsimmons obsession. Okay, I have no problem with that. But it's a big savannah. You have a hot lead, or were you standing here hoping old skullface would tell you where to look?"

"No, I think I know where to look." After glancing down the empty hallway, the priest extracted a white piece of paper from his pocket and, unfolding it carefully, handed it to his friend. "We'll start with this. What do you make of it?"

Braxton held the paper closer to the display lighting. The sheet was filled with primitive drawings. His first impression was that they were the work of a child, drawings made in layers, one imposed on top of another and then another. However, on closer examination, he realized there was a mature range to the subject matter. Only the form in which the art was rendered made it simplistic. After a moment he looked from the drawings to the priest.

"Well, if it's a treasure map, I don't think you're going to find the treasure."

Eddie smiled weakly. "You're closer than you imagine, Braxton. The picture is clear. You simply have to know how to read it. Ever seen anything like this before?"

"You know I have," Braxton said, studying the drawings again. "There are some just like it upstairs in this museum."

"Similar in appearance, but not just like this one," Eddie corrected.

"Well, they're Stone Age drawings. What have you got, Ed? A new discovery that you're not sure is authentic?"

"Oh, it's authentic all right, but it wasn't done in the Stone Age. The fact is, this drawing was done by an acquaintance of mine only yesterday while under hypnosis. She has no background whatsoever in anthropology or any kind of study dealing with ancient man, yet this drawing and many others have come pouring out of her." Eddie pointed his finger at the skull behind the glass. "And I have reason to believe that not only are they accurate, but they can point the way to one of his relatives and our most distant ancestor."

The priest took the paper and held it up before Braxton's face. Braxton could see Eddie's thin fingers were trembling slightly, and his friend's voice caught with excitement as he spoke.

"I'm talking about the beginning, Brax. Eve! And the greatest treasure in religious antiquity. If I'm right, these drawings will guide us to the grave of Eve."

"What!" Braxton exclaimed incredulously. He reached over and placed a hand against the priest's forehead. "Nope, no fever. But obviously you've been out in the sun too long, Ed. Will you listen to what you're saying, please?"

"I know what I'm saying. And I know it can't be true. Yet after all I've seen these past few days, a part of me knows beyond doubt that it is true. Not only that, but the entire Eve business is not as farfetched as you may think. Now listen to me. Just recently scientists using a DNA tracer called mitochondrial offered proof that everyone on earth has one ancestor in common."

Braxton arched an eyebrow.

"No, don't give me that look," the priest countered. "I'm talking facts, not conjecture. Scientific proof of one relative common to all. Two biologists named Cann and Stoneking traced the mutation back to a single female who lived somewhere in Africa between 140,000 and 280,000 years ago."

"Eddie—"

"Hear me out a minute, Braxton, please! Mitochondria—or mtDNA as it is called—is only inherited through the mother, and its mutation changes at a known rate. That rate has been traced to a single female ancestor who, it would appear, is the mother of us all. Needless to say, the information has had the molecular-biology as well as the anthropological communities buzzing with speculation. To say nothing of the creationists. The people who did the study refer to this single, African female ancestor as Eve."

"Okay, Ed. You're the expert on this stuff. But speculative biological theory is one hell of a lot different from saying you can find the grave of Eve."

An expression of unwavering determination settled across Eddie's features. "Braxton, I've seen the hypnotic trances. The subject has been through past lives to the very beginning. The proof is there."

Braxton glanced toward the paper in the priest's hand. "You mean the drawings?"

"Yes. But it's more than that. Much more! When regressed, this woman becomes a persona who purports to be the daughter of Eve. And she is obsessed with the grave. She wants to find it! To return to it! To find the grave of her mother. If what she indicates is true, there is an undiscovered gravesite of Eve! Perhaps Adam, also. We're not sure yet. And she appears to be able to locate it. Think of it, Braxton! The grave of Eve! Real. Uncovered. Through some strange quirk of fate, we may have stumbled onto the missing link. The last element that would bring science and religion together. Braxton, it may be real! All of it! Proof at last that Genesis is not poetic allegory but fact."

For several seconds after Eddie finished speaking, neither man said a word. Bathed in the soft glow of the display-case lighting, they simply stood unmoving, looking at each other, until finally, with a shake of his head, Braxton adjusted his cap once again and exhaled heavily.

"Eddie, nobody knows how much you love this ancient-man stuff more than I do. I used to always be stumbling over all the skeleton pieces you kept in our place at school. And don't think I've forgotten all those times you dragged me out to search for bones buried in dried-up river bottoms. But, damn it, hypnotic regression to past lives is crap. I don't have to tell you that. You talk about proof. The proof is that everybody discovers they're really the soul of someone famous. It's tabloid stuff. 'I Was Hitler' screams the headline when a local butcher from Paterson, New Jersey, is regressed and begins to spout German. And this one is really a beaut. Bridey Murphy takes a back seat to this baby. It couldn't be Hester the cleaning lady from nineteenth-century England, or even Joan of Arc. Oh, no. The daughter of Eve, for crying out loud! Sorry, it's bullshit. And I don't care what mutating DNAs indicate, if you believe you can find the grave of the original woman, you'd better turn in your frock and join the *Enquirer* staff.''

"I asked for your help, Brax," the priest said, a look of hurt surfacing in his clear blue eyes.

Braxton pursed his lips tightly and, after allowing several seconds to tick by, shook his head. "Okay, Eddie. You're right. I'm sorry. But you have to admit it's one hell of a leap from a relaxing fun-filled safari to finding the grave of Eve.''

"I'm aware of that. I didn't know how to explain it. I had a lot of trouble coming to you at all. You don't have to tell me I'm not thinking clearly. I'm not an idiot. I've tried to deny it to myself. But every time I watch Zelda guide a regression..."

"Zelda is your friend?"

Eddie shook his head. "No, Zelda is the hypnotist. Zelda Roote.''

"The hypnotist's name is Zelda Roote!"

The priest nodded, hurrying on. "Yes, I knew you'd never let that name go by, but before you make a judgment, let me tell you that she's a wonderful, sincere woman who cares deeply about Kathy and what happens to her.''

Braxton lifted a hand defensively. "All right, I'm trying, Ed. I swear to you, I'm trying. So then your friend's name is Kathy?"

"Yes, Kathy Sullivan. We were neighbors when I was growing up."

Braxton frowned. "I don't remember you ever mentioning a Kathy Sullivan."

"I didn't know her that well, actually. We would talk when we ran into each other, but the conversations were always superficial kinds of things. She was simply the girl who lived next door. Her family always lived next to mine, or rather she and her father did. The mother died because of complications during Kathy's birth. The father seldom spoke to me, although my father knew him. Dr. Sullivan was a withdrawn type. Apparently he never completely recovered from the sudden loss of his wife. And before you say it, I know the death of her mother at her birth could have major psychological implications for Kathy Sullivan in all this, but it still doesn't explain everything, Braxton."

Braxton wrapped an affectionate arm around his friend and guided him back down the hall toward the museum's lobby. "Come on, Ed. Let's walk. I need some air, even if it's hundred-degree air."

A stifling blast hit them as they walked through the doorway and started down the front steps of the museum.

"Look, Ed," Braxton said, squinting in the glaring sunlight as they waited for the traffic to clear before crossing the street. "The fact that it's you telling me this makes a difference. Not much, I might add, but enough. So, okay. You say I can help; I'll do what I can. But how did you get involved in all this? I thought you were somewhere on the Tanzania border helping to distribute relief aid.''

"I was," Eddie replied hurriedly, following Braxton across the street. "Injai came driving into the relief station a couple of weeks ago with the message that a woman named Kathy Sullivan had come to Nairobi looking for me and that it was critical she see me. Well, I had no idea what it was about until Injai informed me that she had said she had been my neighbor. Then I remembered her, of course, and fearing one of my parents had become ill or worse, I came back immediately."

"Little did you realize..." Braxton said with an amused smile.

"Exactly. Kathy Sullivan may have only been a vague memory of the girl who lived next door, but I've certainly gotten to know her quite well in the past few days."

"And what is your assessment?—besides the given that in a far distant life she was the daughter of Eve, of course."

The priest ignored Braxton's whimsical jab, answering with thoughtful concern. "A frightened but determined woman. I've grown to like her a great deal, actually. I wish we had gotten to know each other earlier. She's a sincere, caring person. Just troubled, that's all. And very frightened by what's happened to her. She's very mixed up right now. Uncertain about what's going on. But...we all are."

"And the hypnotist? Ms. Roote. What's the story there? Egomania getting off on mental manipulation?"

The priest shook his head. "No, not at all. I wouldn't be involved if it were anything like that. Zelda is sim-

ply someone who believes in what she is doing. If anything, she can't believe what's come out of her own
hypnosis sessions, yet she's tremendously excited about
it. She sees it as a possible turning point in validating the
very science of hypnosis. That's why she has enthusiastically endorsed my contacting you, Brax. She wants
someone to make a written record of what happens."

Eddie had followed the news correspondent to the
front of a large compound directly across from the
museum. Now, as Braxton headed toward the entrance, taking several Kenyan dollars from his pocket
and shoving them through the window to a waiting
cashier, the priest frowned in confusion.

"Braxton, what are you doing?"

Braxton grinned, accepting his change. "Going in the
Snake House. I love it. Never pass it up when I visit the
museum. And considering the circumstances, it seems
appropriate, don't you think? Come on, Father."

For the first time since they had begun talking, the
priest laughed aloud, and the two of them moved on
through the entrance to the interior of the compound.

The Snake House was laid out with glass-fronted
cages along both sides, which contained a wide variety
of African snakes. In the center of the compound was
a large open fenced-off area of dense vegetation where
various species slithered freely in and around the
greenery. Because of the midday heat there were few
visitors within the compound and it was fairly quiet,
except for the squeals of frightened delight from several members of a Japanese tour group as they moved
from window to window.

"So, you met with Kathy, and she dropped the Eve
bomb on you..." Braxton began, leaning on the rail-
ing that surrounded the center section.

"Along with a few drawings. Her father still lives next to my parents, and once she learned where I was, she saw it as fate's moving hand and she and Zelda came to Nairobi. Apparently she first tried to locate me because she knew I had become a priest. Then, learning of my background in paleontology, she hoped I could give her a rational explanation for what was happening."

"Obviously that hasn't happened."

"No, instead I . . . I've become hooked. I've tried to remain objective, but when she raises her hand to draw her scrawls, my heart races with anticipation. And the terrible part is that I know I'm not helping her the way I should as a priest, and I don't care. I know I should be advising Kathy to turn to the church for solace but, God help me, I don't want her to stop this, Brax. It's as though I've become addicted to it. I have to follow this through to its conclusion. If there is a grave, I must find it! To show you how far gone I am, I've actually formed the habit of referring to the persona that emerges from Kathy while she's under hypnosis as Eve. Not the original, of course. I refer to this one as the Eve of regression."

Braxton nodded. "You said she thought coming to you was fate, Ed. What do you think? You think it's God dealing you a nice hand because you've done so much for others over the years and he knows you like to hunt bones?"

Eddie's expression clouded and he looked away. "You're not pulling any punches, are you?"

"Do you want me to?"

"No. Of course not. Oh, Braxton, I know. There's the rational side of me that knows this is not real. But even if I'm falling into some great religious test of faith and pit of temptation, I can't stop myself. That's why I need you, Braxton. I need your objectivity. I need you to help me find a way to restore my... my faith."

Braxton made no immediate reply, and as the two of them stood silent for a moment, a rustling in the dense vegetation before them suddenly grabbed the attention of the two men. Several small green snakes were intertwined amid the leaves and branches, their bodies still, their unblinking eyes staring blankly outward. Near the middle of the greenery, what had looked like a thick branch suddenly moved, revealing itself to be a large serpent, its skin color a duplication of the surrounding vegetation. The snake's slow, oozing movement forward ceased as quickly as it had begun, and it lifted its sleek, bullet-shaped head to give an openmouthed hiss into the dank air.

"There's a little symbolism for you, Ed," Braxton said lightly, jerking a thumb in the direction of the now unmoving serpent. "Maybe we should ask him his opinion. Or maybe he just gave it."

The priest said nothing, continuing to stare outward, his expression tight and unamused. Braxton pursed his lips, and when he spoke, his voice was filled with genuine concern.

"Eddie, there's nothing I wouldn't do for you," he said. "You know that. You're the closest thing to family I've got. And if you want me to follow you all over Africa searching for some mystical grave, fine. At least I'll have finally gotten you on a safari. But let's be honest right from square one. I don't for a second think the grave of Eve could really exist. I'm sure you knew I wouldn't. However, I am intrigued. Just the fact that old levelheaded Eddie Fitzsimmons is off the deep end on this is enough to make me very curious. And I'll admit, bizarre as this is, there may be a story here. But I'm telling you, I'll write it exactly the way I see it. There's some kind of flaw in all this. You may not see it and it may take me a while to find it, but it's there, believe me. There's something wrong with this whole business, and I think the best way I can help is to try to find out what it is."

"Yes, there's something wrong, Braxton," Eddie said tersely, his expression clouding as he looked at the snakes camouflaged amid the foliage. "There's something very wrong. With you...me...all of us. And I know you brought me in here as a joke to lighten the situation up a little, but there's no denying that what's really wrong goes back to the beginning. The guilt. The feeling of loss. The ever-present pain. The misery and senseless suffering."

The priest's eyes suddenly filled with tears and his body shook with rage as a flood of emotion swept through him.

"You want to know why I stay out in the field so long? My God, Braxton, the misery out there is so overwhelming that when I think of it, my heart feels like it's going to crack! And it's pushed me into a crisis I can't work my way through. Faith isn't enough for me anymore! I've seen too many old people, crippled with deformities from malnutrition, begging for a scrap of food. Too many babies, their bellies swollen and bloated, have died in my arms from needless starvation, while less than a mile away rich tourists slaughter animals for the sheer pleasure of killing. I don't need faith, goddammit! I need facts. I want to know why! Don't you understand? I have to know why!"

Four

FRANK GUNTHER had been sitting at the bar of the Norfolk's ground-floor lounge since midafternoon, swallowing Scotch and brooding. Now it was heading toward evening, and the lounge, located off to the left of the hotel's main foyer, was beginning to fill with predinner customers. As Frank glanced around at the people who were gathering to drink and talk in the lounge, his mood was one of bitter reflection.

The Hotel Norfolk. Meeting place for what had been some of the greatest safari gatherings on earth. Gathering ground for the great hunters. Frank turned back to his drink with disgust. Now it was filled with tourists who cared only about posing in some pictures and maybe catching a glimpse of a sleeping big cat.

A couple of years before, on New Year's Eve, some fanatic had planted a bomb that blew the hell out of one section of the hotel. To Frank, the act had been symbolic. It was like the final death stroke to what had been a dying era. The end had finally arrived. And the bottom line was that it was time to get out. Time to go somewhere that still allowed for adventure and the hunt. Like deep in the Amazon, maybe. Anything would be an improvement over the modern Africa. Man, had times changed.

When he had first come to Africa after Korea, it had been easy pickings. He was good with guns, he had a

sixth sense when it came to hunting and he had an ex-
pansive personality with a natural talent for charming
and throwing the bull. In just a few months after setting up business, he had more safaris than he could
handle. Then it had all started to go wrong.

Mau Mau. The word had spread like a savannah fire
fed by a west wind. When the leaders of the movement
spoke, the black masses listened. And then they started
killing. Everything had changed, never to be the same
again.

Suddenly Frank found himself a white man in a
country governed by blacks. There were strict laws to
protect the game from slaughter. And more and more
frequently, the people who hired Frank went out on
game runs with Nikon cameras instead of guns. In the
old days, money flowed. There was always more for the
asking. Now, in order to stay alive, instead of taking out
hunters he had to work for pansy-ass tourists like the
ones who had just hired him.

But how the hell do you start over in the Amazon
when you're headed into your late fifties and have
pissed away almost everything you ever made? Frank
drained his glass.

One big stake. That was all it would take. Somehow
he had to find a fast way to make some big money. And
there were ways. Smuggling. Dope. He'd done his share
over the years, of course, but never anything major.
Maybe it was time to take the chance. One big stake was
all he needed. The only trick was to make sure he didn't
get caught.

Kaba, the bartender, appeared in front of him, and
Frank thought the man was going to freshen his drink.
Instead, a phone was placed on top of the bar.

"For you, Frank. The girl at your office."

Frank grimaced but nodded a thank-you and picked up the receiver. "Yeah, Shirley, what have you got?"

"Frank, Mr. Bassett is here to see you. Were you supposed to take him out tomorrow?"

Frank slapped his forehead with his hand and swore into the phone. "Ohh, shit! Dog. Goddammit, I knew there was something else I had on for this week."

"I didn't have him listed, Frank. I'm sure of that."

"No, I know. He ran into me at the Tsavo Lodge last month and we set it up. Son of a bitch. I'm getting old, Shirl. I just forgot all about it."

"What do you want to do? Cancel the group you scheduled yesterday?"

"I can't do that. I'm meeting them all here in the lounge. They'll be here any minute. Besides, I've already set things up for a departure from Westwood Park. Damn. All right. Put Bassett on the phone. Might as well face the music."

Frank motioned for Kaba to refill his glass while he waited for Bassett to take the phone. In the meantime he tried to figure a way out of his oversight. He still had a fat zero for a solution, however, when Bassett's coolly controlled voice came over the phone.

"Frank?"

"Ehh, Dog. How are things?"

"You forgot, didn't you, Frank. I told you I should reconfirm the date, but you assured me it wasn't necessary."

"Okay, I owe you one, Dog."

"Does that mean when we go, you take me out free of charge?"

"Fat chance, old buddy. I don't feel that guilty."

Dog Bassett grunted into the phone. "Well, you've got to squeeze me in soon, Frank. I'm already committed."

"What have you got?"

"Rhino horns. I have several well-heeled Japanese clients who are in search of sexual bliss and would like me to furnish them with the ingredients they believe will achieve such a state."

"I don't know where you find them, Dog. I didn't think there were any Japs left who still believed that crap. How long have you got?"

"Not long. They'd like the order filled yesterday if I could do it."

Frank rubbed his face and thought for a minute. "Tell you what. I've got a group set up for Westwood tonight, going out in the morning. If they agree, why don't you come along? Discount price for my screwup."

There was silence over the phone for a moment. "Will they know the laws?"

"No problem. New York people. Green as grass. Couple of women and a little guy. It's a bullshit sightseeing tour, but at least it's not the usual group of Orientals with cameras growing out of their chests."

"How are the women?"

"Forget that. All you get is rhinos, buddy. One's a fat cow and the other is a cute red-haired Irish girl with a good chest and the nicest ass I've seen in years. I've already got her all staked out, Dog. And by the time we get back to Nairobi, I'll have checked out the old saying."

"What saying is that, Frank?"

"Red hair above, red hair below, by cracky," Frank said, with a crude laugh.

Dog didn't laugh. But then he never did laugh out loud. The most Frank could ever get out of the man was a tight, half-amused smile stretched across an otherwise hardened expression. Still, Frank enjoyed taking Dog out. Not only did he always pay well and on time, he also didn't mind short-circuiting the law when it was profitable, and the man was a true hunter.

Dog Bassett was built like a bull with no neck, and the rest of him was all muscle. No one had ever tangled with him that Frank knew of. All you had to do was look at Dog Bassett to know that if you messed with him, the odds were good you were gonna die. And no one kidded him about his name, either, although Frank had once asked him about it. The man had simply stared at Frank with that cruel expressionless look of his and answered that people had always called him Dog, and that was that. But he was more than just tough. Dog Bassett was one of the best shots Frank had ever seen, and Frank enjoyed the competition. It helped him keep sharp. Dog was one of those guys who was capable of putting a slug between the wrinkles of a gazelle's asshole in midleap without having to waste a shot, and he and Frank always had some kind of competitive bet going.

"What's the discount, Frank?"

"Twenty percent. And I'll let you have the fat one at no extra charge," Frank added, grinning into the receiver as Dog grunted in response. "It's a good deal, Dog. Better take it."

"All right. I'll tell you what. Here's the deal I'll take, Frank. You talk them into letting me tag along, and if we get the rhinos, I'll pay you full. If, on the other hand, something goes wrong and we come back with no horns, I get to take my own shot at the redhead with the nice ass.''

"Hey, Dog, have I ever failed you? You'll get your rhinos. Don't worry.''

"Is it a deal, Frank?''

Kathy Sullivan and Zelda Roote came through the lounge entrance, and Frank waved to them from the bar, flashing his best great-white-hunter smile. The heavyset older woman had changed into another loose dress that still couldn't disguise the fact that she was as wide as a half-ton truck, but the younger Irishwoman wore a new safari skirt and blouse that fit her perfectly. Frank felt a little tingle of excitement blossom inside him at the sight of her moving across the lounge.

"See you tonight, Dog. Westwood. Eight o'clock,'' Frank said into the phone, not taking his eyes off Kathy Sullivan. Then he dropped the receiver back onto its cradle, drained his glass and, belching softly, rose to greet the two women.

Five

BRAXTON PUSHED the New York Yankees baseball cap farther back on his head and sipped at the Tusker beer Frank Gunther had passed him. Although he was listening politely as Gunther walked around, covering the basics of how the camp would function, Braxton felt far from comfortable with events so far. In his opinion, Eddie had already made a very serious mistake: hiring the man with the wide grin.

Several months earlier Braxton had done a piece for the home office on the old-school white hunters who lingered on in Kenya, and his investigation had shown that along with several others, Frank Gunther was among the best of the worst. With a blatant disregard for the welfare of wildlife and the law, the man still operated according to the old rules, which meant he pretty much did whatever the hell he felt like doing. Eddie hadn't known that, of course. He had merely chosen an experienced guide from the list provided by the tourist office. And to warn him now wouldn't mean anything. The contract was signed.

Then there was Bassett, the man Gunther had affectionately introduced to them as Dog. Another beauty. Good God, the man didn't even acknowledge you when introduced. Just stared right through you with those cold eyes buried in that immobile face. Gunther hadn't really asked but rather informed them that Dog was coming along. Eddie hadn't looked happy about it, but he hadn't said no, either. Well, it was their party. If they wanted to agree to let what looked like a psychopathic escapee from a mental ward come along, it wasn't Braxton's place to protest.

Most of all, though, it was not the people in charge but the premise under which the trip was being taken that bothered him. Try as he might, Braxton found that he couldn't even begin to consider the reality of what Eddie had related to him at the museum. Yes, he had promised himself that he would make every effort to stay objective. But there was no doubt that Eddie and the two women were hooked on something, all right. Braxton could draw that conclusion with no further evidence. Like people mesmerized in a séance, they had the look of believers who had seen the table rise and had to see it again.

There was one bright spot in the whole thing, though, which Eddie had failed to mention. Braxton had found himself drawn to Kathy Sullivan the moment he saw her. It wasn't that she was overtly sensuous or anything like that. And if you had to categorize her looks, they would lean more to the cute than the pretty side. But there was something indefinable about her overall manner and appearance that made her strikingly attractive. And from the time they had been introduced at the Norfolk, Braxton had caught himself constantly taking furtive glances in her direction, as he did now while Gunther's driver, a young black named Sammy, showed the two women how to assemble the green canvas tent they would be sharing.

Across from the women, Injai was helping Eddie with his tent. Injai was another plus about the trip. The mission had assigned Injai to assist Eddie when the priest first arrived in Africa, and the man had stayed loyally with him ever since. Injai was a happy-go-lucky soul who had been a phenomenal help to Eddie and Braxton when they first came to Kenya, assisting them with language problems and providing them with an invaluable understanding of tribal customs and beliefs. A pleasure to have around, Injai seemed to be perpetually in a good mood, and though Braxton saw far less of the man now that his Peace Corps days were over, the two had gotten along well from the first and were always laughing and joking with each other whenever they got together.

The only other member of the group was a Gunther employee named Dingo, who was to be the cook and all-purpose cleanup man for the trip. Dingo didn't say much, merely giving you an openmouthed grin that revealed a row of yellowed, crooked teeth when you spoke to him.

Having finished his explanations of the basics, Frank Gunther walked over and squatted near the fire. Gesturing for the others to gather around, he unfolded a large map, placing it on the ground in front of him.

"All right, let me explain the choices of routes." His hand swept quickly over various points on the map, then came back and tapped near a large dot with the word NAIROBI printed next to it. "We're here at Westwood Campgrounds right outside the city. As you can see, there are several reserves in all directions from Nairobi. Each offers beautiful country as well as its own variety of animals. If we go north, for example, by making a wide arc left and up and back, we could cover first Lake Nakuru. Hundreds of birds nest there, and the sight of them in white masses across the clear water is magnificent. Swinging right here, we could visit the famous Thomson's Falls. Natives say the devil resides here, so you wouldn't want to miss it, I'm sure."

Gunther had meant to be amusing and was surprised by the sober response he saw on the faces of his clients. Only the new guy named Hicks smiled briefly. With a shrug, he went on.

"Farther up, Samburu Game Reserve, excellent for lion viewing. Then we would come down past Mount Kenya, by the well-known Treetops Lodge, and back into Nairobi." Gunther paused, waiting for a comment, but none came, so he continued.

"Or we could move south from here. Straight down is Amboseli, loaded with game of all kinds. On a clear day Mount Kilimanjaro's peaks can be seen easily in this reserve. Beyond that are the Tsavo Reserves with their strikingly different landscapes, and then down and to the right the coastal points of Malindi and Mombasa."

Zelda Roote moved in closer, studying the map. "Now where is the Great Rift Valley we hear so much about? Over here?"

"No, that is Masai-Mara. That is another possibility." The guide gestured with a broad motion from the top to the bottom of the map. "The Great Rift Valley is right down the center here and beyond Kenya's borders into both Ethiopia and Tanzania. Either way, north or south, I can show you many examples of the cliffs that line this great African fault. So the decision is yours." He shrugged, smiling, and lifted a thumb toward the imposing figure of Dog Bassett, who stood behind him. "Dog here is just along for the ride. Makes no difference to him. Which way would you like to go?"

No one spoke. Frank flexed, stood, and exchanged a look with Dog. The others seemed to have shifted their attention to the young woman named Kathy, who continued to stare at the map.

"Well, Mr. Hicks," Frank said, turning to Braxton, "Eddie here says you've been on safari before. Maybe you'd like to help them out and suggest a choice."

"Please, it's Braxton," the correspondent replied, coming to his feet and gesturing in Eddie's direction. "And it's not my decision."

Eddie nodded and stood also. "Yes, the decision must be ours."

"I'm sorry we seem indecisive about this," Zelda added, joining Eddie and leaving Kathy the only one still bending over the map. "But you see, Mr. Gunther, we've spent most of our time concentrating on getting here. Now that you've explained the options, perhaps we could discuss it among ourselves and then..."

It was the sound of Kathy's finger hitting the map that stopped Zelda. The hypnotist immediately turned back to Kathy as the young woman spoke loudly.

"Here!" Kathy said, tapping the map heavily over and over in the same location. The others bent down again, their eyes riveted to the spot where Kathy was pointing. "Here! We will go this way."

"Are you sure?" Zelda said, speaking quietly and studying Kathy's face rather than the map. "We could discuss it tonight and decide in the morning."

"No!" the answer came, even louder. "This is the way!"

Braxton frowned warily, his full attention on Kathy Sullivan. He had tried to catch Eddie's eye as she spoke, but like the others, the priest was concentrating totally on what the young woman said.

Weird. It was the sound of the woman's voice. And her eyes. Her eyes were strange when she looked up from the map.

Over on the log across from Braxton, Injai was no longer smiling but watching with interest. And by the side of the tent, Dingo had stopped washing the pots to stare in their direction, as did the driver Sammy from where he stood leaning against the bus.

"Amboseli. The lady's made a good choice," Frank Gunther said enthusiastically, although a bit too loudly. "Probably the widest variety of game is found there. Excellent place to begin."

"Amboseli it is, then," Zelda repeated, taking the young woman's hand and helping her to her feet. "Thank you, Kathy, for making a decision while the rest of us were hemming and hawing around."

Braxton looked closely at the woman's face as she stood. The moment had passed. Her expression appeared normal. Or maybe he had been wrong. Perhaps it was merely tricks of the firelight and the suddenness of her decision that had made him think something strange had happened. In any case, Zelda and Eddie seemed content with the choice.

"We're all agreed then," Frank Gunther said cordially. Though he spoke to everyone, the hunter's eyes were on Kathy. He allowed his gaze to drift briefly to her blouse for a moment and then grinned as his eyes met hers. "Dog and I are going to have a nightcap at the bar. It's just a short walk from here. You're welcome to join us if you like. Be a pleasure, ladies."

"No, thank you," Kathy said, her answer cool but pleasant. "If we're getting up at dawn, we'd better get some rest."

"Maybe another time, then." At the mention of the bar, Dingo was on his feet and standing next to Gunther, ready to go. Gunther's driver, however, remained by the bus, and Frank turned in his direction. "Coming, Sammy?" The young black shook his head, waving Frank off. "Suit yourself." Frank shifted his attention back to his clients as he started after Dog Bassett and Dingo, who were already moving out of the firelight toward the road. "The rest rooms are a short walk from here up the circular road. It's the stone building. Probably be best if the women went together. It's generally safe here, but you never know. Good night. Don't forget to zip up your mosquito netting."

Eddie took a couple of steps in the direction Gunther and the others disappeared, then, after a few seconds and a glance to where Sammy had already disappeared inside the bus, he moved back to the fire and sat next to Braxton.

"Don't even say it, Brax. Please. The agency told me Gunther was one of the best."

"Did they say what he was best at?" Braxton responded with a shake of his head. "I wish you had waited until you talked to me, Ed. Don't tell him where I work, whatever you do. I really worked him and several others over last year in a story I did about the fate of the white hunters of Kenya. He even called in to scream he was going to sue. I can't believe he didn't put it together when you said my name."

"Maybe he did," Zelda remarked, as she and Kathy came up to join them.

Braxton shook his head. "No, he hasn't made any connection or we'd know it. Let's hope he doesn't."

"Well, at least his friend seems nice, don't you think?"

It was Kathy who had spoken, and everyone looked at her in amazed disbelief. Then, simultaneously, they burst into laughter.

Braxton grinned over at her, and he found himself enjoying not only the joke she had made but the way her voice bubbled in quick catches of laughter and her eyes shone with reflected firelight. In fact, he was amazed at the way he was responding to this woman. His insides were bouncing around like a teenager's every time he looked at her. He adjusted the baseball cap once again and shifted his gaze away from Kathy self-consciously. What the hell was the matter with him?

"Yeah, Dog looks like he's a terrific guy," he said, following up on her humor. "Probably do anything for you."

"Or to you," Zelda put in. "Why in the world do you think Gunther brought that awful man into this?"

Braxton looked at Eddie. "Gunther knows nothing, right?" The priest shook his head. "Then it's probably a private contract between the two of them. Just making a little side money, I'd say."

"Should we allow him to come along?" Eddie asked. "I wasn't sure what the policy was."

"Looks to me like the moment has passed and he's along, I'm sorry to say, Ed. But, let's not get bent out of shape about Gunther. He may not be the world's nicest person, but he knows Africa, has done thousands of safaris and can certainly take you where you want to go. But I'm telling you right now. You might as well level with him because he's no dummy. They're probably talking about that thing that happened with the map at this very moment. You better be ready to give him some kind of explanation."

"I know. I agree," Eddie said. "I'm going to have a talk with him as soon as we move out in the morning."

"How about you, Braxton?" Kathy's voice brought his eyes to look again on her easy, straightforward smile. "I know Eddie has told you generally what we're trying to do, but I'm sure you must have questions about all this."

"Ohh, yeah, I guess there are a couple of things," Braxton said with an exaggerated nonchalance.

"Well, fire away," Kathy invited. "We'll do our best. If you're going to write about this, we should try to help you understand as much as we can right from the beginning."

Braxton nodded. "All right. Let's start with the map. What was that all about?"

Kathy glanced anxiously toward Zelda before answering. "I'm not sure. What I'm finding is that now, even without Zelda's verbal inducement, when I concentrate heavily I'm able to slip into a kind of trance. Anyway, I think that's what's happening."

"One of the first things we came to realize about this particular regression," explained Zelda, "is that while under hypnosis, though the persona that emerges cannot speak, through some sort of mental link that we don't understand, Kathy is able to interpret the feelings and desires the woman wishes to get across to us. This has been a real key to our being able to reach the point we have. For example, by using topographical artistic renderings of what this area must have looked like eons ago and then explaining them to Kathy, we are fairly certain that the place we seek is located somewhere in the Great Rift Valley."

"Which corresponds exactly with where the DNA people put our female ancestor, and where many archaeologists theorize that the forerunners of Homo sapiens must have emerged," Eddie added with a nod to the hypnotist.

"Eden?" Braxton asked, lifting an eyebrow.

"Perhaps," Zelda replied. "However, another factor that will become clear to you, Braxton, is that we can't be positive about anything. It's simply something we've learned to live with. I think I would like to verify the map decision as well as show you specifically what this is all about by actually having a session, if Kathy is agreeable." Zelda waited for Kathy's nod of approval, then asked, "Don't you think it would be the best way to proceed, Eddie?"

The priest glanced off toward the road. "Yes. Fine. Injai has been anxious to witness a session also, and there's no question but that it's the best way to get the two of them acclimated. I'm not sure it would be good if Gunther returns and interrupts us before I've had a chance to talk to him, though."

"Frank Gunther's not going to come back after one drink, Ed," said Braxton. "And his driver has already turned in. I saw him go into the bus and close the door." He glanced toward the log where the priest's devoted helper sat quietly listening. "How about it, Injai? Are you game?"

Injai flashed a smile. "Oh, yes, Buddy. Father has told me of the wonders that happen. How it is God's way of sending a special message to us. I am looking forward with great interest to seeing a session."

Braxton nodded to the hypnotist standing next to Kathy. "That makes two of us. You and Kathy go right ahead and do whatever it is you do, Zelda. You have my full attention, believe me."

Six

HYPNOTISM WAS A GREAT DEAL more than some Rasputin type swinging a pendant and whispering "Look into my eyes...." Braxton knew that. From the brief research he had once done on the subject for an article, he had learned that hypnosis was actually an induced meditative state where outside influences exercised varying amounts of control. Anyone who practiced meditation was performing a certain type of self-hypnosis.

There was no doubt that a hypnotized subject slipped into an altered state of consciousness. The thing that had always bothered Braxton about the practice was that everyone knew something happened but no one seemed to know exactly what it was. The hypnotic state was not sleep oriented, nor was it a dreaming level of consciousness. But the subject was not in a normal state of awareness, either.

However, to assume anyone in the said state could revert to a totally different human being was absurd. The explanation had to be mental gymnastics brought on by a great susceptibility to suggestion.

Of course, it was also true that Braxton had never seen anyone regressed before, and he was prejudging. So he watched Zelda intently as she proceeded to regress Kathy Sullivan. He figured her technique would tell him something about her credibility.

That was what fooled him. That was why he was even more shocked than he might have been by what he saw happen. There was virtually no technique used at all. After relaxing her subject, Zelda simply told Kathy that she would slowly count backward from ten to zero and then touch her hand. When she touched her hand, Kathy was instructed that she would instantly be there. Back to the beginning.

Later Zelda would explain that one of the unique features of the mind in hypnosis was that once it had been guided to something or somewhere, it did not again require all the preliminaries. All that was necessary was a simple instruction, and the mind would be where it was commanded to be instantaneously. However, what Zelda did that first time he watched her was so simple that Braxton could not believe the poor people sitting around the campfire with him had allowed themselves to be blinded into thinking that past lives could be brought to the surface of a hypnotized psyche.

Then Zelda touched Kathy's hand.

For several seconds, nothing happened. Everyone remained perfectly still, and as the night sounds from the surrounding darkness filled the air around them, Braxton thought he glimpsed a flash of light out of the corner of his eye. Glancing behind him, he saw that the interior light of the bus had come on and Gunther's driver, Sammy, was sitting in the driver's seat, staring out the side window in the direction of the fire. Eddie too had noticed the light, and he looked anxiously to Zelda, but the hypnotist shook her head. Too late now. They were committed.

Then Kathy moved.

There was nothing dramatic about the action. All she did was sit straighter, leaning slightly forward on the stool. But there was no question that she was no longer relaxed. Although her eyes remained closed, her body was suddenly alert. And she had changed.

Braxton stared at her, his own body leaning in toward Zelda and Kathy as he strained to determine what was different. What had she done in that shifting movement of sitting forward?

He told himself it was the atmosphere. Night sounds. Shadows thrown by the campfire. All the damned suggestibility. He looked away for a brief moment, and then back again. No, damn it. He hadn't imagined it. It was true. The person sitting on that camp stool was different in a hundred subtle ways, and they all added up to something Braxton refused to admit. All Zelda did was count backward from ten, for crying out loud. Wait. Keep watching. It couldn't be true. It was just that, under hypnosis, Kathy Sullivan was ... different.

"Where are you, Kathy?" Zelda asked quietly. The quality of the hypnotist's voice was warm, soft ... comforting.

No answer. The minute shifts in Kathy's composure continued as her body became even more alert. And stronger. That was another thing—she looked stronger. Then part of the answer came to Braxton. Suddenly he recognized what had materialized before him. The hypnotized young woman was slowly taking on the posture of a primitive. The responses she assumed were instinctive, like those of a threatened animal.

"Are you in a familiar place, Kathy?" Zelda asked casually, just as though she were asking "Pass the salt, please." "You may simply nod to answer," she continued. "Are you back in time? Back to the special place?"

Her eyes still closed, Kathy turned her head toward Zelda. But instead of nodding, as Braxton had expected, her head moved back and forth in a negative response, then remained face forward. She seemed to turn her head so that it faced directly toward the fire, as if drawn to it.

Eerie. That was the word for it. In spite of all his preset notions, Braxton had to admit he was caught up in what was taking place. It was just plan weird, damn it. The body all tense, and the head turning toward Zelda and back again the way it did.

"If the answer is no, then where are you, Kathy?" Zelda said. "Look around and tell me what you see."

Again, though the eyes remained closed, the head moved, pivoting from side to side in short, cautious turns before returning to its original position facing the fire.

"Tell me what you see!" Zelda repeated.

The word came out very softly, almost in a whisper, and Zelda repeated the question.

"I'm sorry, Kathy. I didn't hear you. Where are you?"

Zelda didn't have to ask a third time. Kathy's head turned sharply from its ramrod-straight position to the hypnotist.

"Wengahhhthaaa!"

The long unintelligible word came rolling loudly out of Kathy's throat in a powerful burst of energy.

Eddie and Zelda exchanged quick glances as Kathy's head once again turned back toward the fire. When Zelda began the session, Eddie had taken a large sketching pad from his briefcase along with several charcoal sticks and various colored markers. Now he picked up a pencil lying on the sketch pad and wrote quickly across the top of the first sheet, shooting Braxton a look as he motioned toward the words.

Braxton scanned the words quickly—"New things happening. Say nothing"—and nodded to the priest.

At Kathy's utterance, the tension level around the fire had gone up several notches. Braxton could feel it. He could also hear it in Zelda's voice. The hypnotist was trying to use a quiet tone, but Kathy's response had knocked the pass-the-salt casualness right out of it.

"I do not understand. But I know even if I am speaking to someone else, you can understand me through Kathy. Would you like to be taken deeper or regressed further?"

There was a pause, and then Kathy's head turned side to side zombie-fashion. Negative.

"All right. Fine. Who are you now? Are you still Kathy?"

And in response to Zelda's question, it happened again. Only this time, instead of only one word, a stream of sounds came rolling out of Kathy's mouth. Braxton could tell immediately they weren't just sounds, however. They had form and a rational configuration, as if the sounds were a language, a way of communicating. The truly strange part was that, though he didn't understand them, the sounds were vaguely familiar to him, and as he listened, he dug through his memory in an attempt to remember where he had heard something similar before.

Then the flow of sounds streaming from Kathy's mouth stopped. And although her head turned from Zelda, this time it did not face the fire as it had done before. And she opened her eyes.

When those eyes opened, Braxton knew Eddie wasn't kidding. Something extraordinary was taking place. For one thing, Eddie was gaping in openmouthed surprise at Kathy, and Braxton was sure he had felt the priest's body jump beside him when her eyes shot open. Zelda reacted immediately by tapping Kathy's hand in what Braxton assumed was an attempt to put her back out or under or whatever the term was. And Braxton? It wasn't fear that coursed through him when Kathy's eyes opened. It was more like a tingling nervous excitement. The eyes in that erect head had swept past the fire and were looking right at him.

As he stared unflinchingly back at them, Braxton knew he could kid himself no longer. He didn't know whose eyes he was looking into, but he did know they didn't belong to Kathy Sullivan. Rather, they were Kathy's eyes, but someone else was looking through them. Yes, that was it: *through* them.

So much for all the smug wisecracks about these people being caught up in psychic self-indulgence.

"It's all right," Zelda's voice was saying. "Relax, Kathy. Close your eyes and relax."

Braxton couldn't bring himself to turn away from the eyes to Zelda, but since the lids weren't dropping, he assumed the hypnotist's influence wasn't exactly at its peak.

"Kathy," Zelda said with more authority, "you need to relax. Close your eyes and lean back. Lean back and relax."

This time, after shifting her head to glare at Zelda, Kathy stood up.

Way to control your subject, Zelda, old girl. Braxton felt the tingle inside him grow stronger as the figure of Kathy Sullivan turned her attention back to him and, holding his gaze, crossed over to him. Zelda said nothing more, choosing instead to sit where she was and watch for the moment.

Kathy's figure stopped directly in front of Braxton. She leaned forward to study Braxton, nostrils flared, eyes examining. Then, finally, for no apparent reason, she suddenly turned, moved back to the camp stool, sat down, and closed her eyes.

Braxton blinked in rapid succession as Zelda leaned forward to speak again. This time she was cautious. And Braxton's mind was already trying to convince him that of course it was Kathy. It was merely the suggestibility, as he had originally thought. Someone looking "through" her eyes—that was ridiculous.

"That's right, Kathy," Zelda said, "just close your eyes and relax. Would you like to be brought back now? Would you like me to talk you back now?"

Again the zombie-like head turn. Negative.

Then, slowly, as if pulled from above, Kathy's right arm lifted from her side and rose into the air, where it hung limply, the hand twitching slightly.

"Now we're back on familiar ground," Eddie whispered quickly to Braxton. "She wants to draw. This may be the map confirmation we're looking for."

And though Braxton was listening to what the priest said, something else was occupying his mind. Suddenly he remembered where he had heard the sounds and intonations that had come from Kathy moments before. "Eddie, those sounds she made. I—"

"I know, Brax," Eddie nodded, cutting him off. Then the priest hurriedly gathered up the drawing materials and crossed to the women.

While Eddie went to his knees, holding the sketch pad in front of Kathy, Zelda took one of the charcoal sticks and placed it in the hypnotized woman's right hand.

Rather than gripping it correctly, Kathy closed her fingers around the object as a tiny child would. Holding it in her fist, she leaned forward, eyes opened, and began to draw.

For several minutes she remained like that, drawing in swift, crude strokes on the paper Eddie held for her. Only once did she interrupt her process to exchange the charcoal stick for a red marker, which she scribbled hurriedly with and then dropped, retrieving the charcoal stick again to continue. Finally her hand backed away and, after wavering momentarily in midair, dropped once more to her side.

With that, Kathy's eyes closed, she leaned back from her forward crouch and her entire body relaxed. Eddie had turned the sketch pad toward himself to look at it, and after a quick glance at what Kathy had drawn, Zelda removed the charcoal stick from the young woman's fingers and placed her own hand over that of her subject.

"That was fine," Zelda said softly. "Just fine. We'll talk again soon. Right now I want you to relax. Just relax. I'm going to bring you back now. And you will feel no ill effects. No ill effects at all. You will feel better than you did before. Better than you have in a long time. You will be unable to remember when you have felt so incredibly good. And you will remember what has happened while you were away, but it will not bother you. You will simply view it objectively, as you always do. And you will maintain the feeling of wellness and calmness for a long while after I bring you back.

"Now I want you to relax. Just relax. And when I count to three and tap your hand, you will be back with us, and you will be absolutely free. Take your time opening your eyes after I bring you back. Just relax and open them when you feel ready. Now relax, and one...two...three.'' On three, Zelda stopped speaking and gently patted Kathy's hand.

Several seconds after Zelda had tapped her hand, Kathy slowly came around, blinking and stretching as if waking from a sound sleep. She looked from Eddie to Zelda and, finally, smiled meekly at Braxton. Braxton smiled back and gave her a gentle thumbs-up sign that everything was fine. But when their eyes met, both knew that something had changed. Whatever had happened during the session had brought a closeness between the two of them that had not existed before.

As Eddie moved behind Kathy to give her neck a light massage, Zelda patted her subject's hand affectionately. ''You all right, Kathy?''

''Yes, fine. That one sure was different, though, wasn't it?''

Eddie nodded. ''Yes, it was.''

Braxton glanced over to the log where Injai still sat. His eyes wide with wonder, Eddie's assistant was staring mutely toward Eddie and the women. ''What do you think, Injai?''

Injai shook his head, and when he spoke, his voice was soft. ''I am not sure, Buddy. As Father warned me, there is much to try to understand.''

''To put it mildly,'' Braxton answered.

''We've never had language before,'' Eddie said. ''You and Injai have witnessed a first, Braxton.''

''Ed, I...I think I know what that language was. You do too, don't you?''

Eddie nodded. ''Yes. I wondered if you would remember.''

"Well, I don't have the slightest idea," Zelda protested. "Would one of you fill us in, please?"

"I've only heard something like it once before," Braxton replied. "At a meeting of charismatics that I attended at Eddie's invitation. It was the rising of Kathy's hand that did it for me. When that hand went up, the memory came rushing back to me."

"It's called speaking in tongues," Eddie explained. "Have you ever heard anyone speak in such a way, Kathy?"

The young woman shook her head. "I know the term, but I've never heard it."

"That's what I suspected," confirmed Eddie. "Supposedly it happens when someone is filled with the spirit of God. During prayer, their hands rise into the air and the language of tongues comes flowing out of them. Frequently it's categorized as overly emotional gibberish. However, by pursuing this, we may be on our way to filling in yet another piece of antiquity's religious puzzles."

Kathy frowned. "In what way, Eddie? And why would this suddenly begin happening now?"

The priest's eyes widened with enthusiasm, and excitement was in his voice when he replied. "The why is probably easiest to answer. My guess would be it's because we're getting closer to our goal. Now, let's consider for a moment. What if speaking in tongues is not gibberish, but rather the first language of man. The Word. The great gift of God. What if when people totally immerse themselves in prayer, they reach a trance state similar to the one that occurs during hypnosis, which in turn allows an emotional breakthrough to that first language. A language that was always there, buried deep within our genes, but can only be reached by being tapped into in a very special way. We'll have to know far more, of course, but it's definitely another avenue that must be explored. One thing is certain: as we might have expected, the deeper we get into this, rather than answers, only more and more questions emerge."

"What about the drawing?" Kathy asked. "Was it the map, or was it related to the language in some way? I've never felt such a strong need to produce before. The force moving my arm was incredible."

"That's another thing I mean by more questions," Eddie said. "Take a look at this."

The priest lifted the sketch pad in front of Kathy so that he and Zelda could study it at the same time. It only took a moment for Kathy to comprehend what she had drawn. After staring at the sheet in front of her in disbelief, she looked over at Braxton, her eyes filled with worry and uncertainty.

"Oh, my God, Braxton, I . . ."

Braxton frowned and came to his feet. What was going on? The three of them were staring at him as if he were the ghost of Christmas past. "What? Is it the map or what?"

"We've found that the best practice is not to discuss a session right away, but to give each of us time to digest what's happened before we talk," explained Eddie. "That way we can get past some of the emotional aspects and try to see what's happened more rationally. You've been hit with a lot today, Braxton. And I'm afraid this drawing is going to be the straw. I . . . I don't know what to make of it myself. Perhaps we only think the decisions are ours, and we merely follow predestined paths, after all." Eddie crossed to his friend and handed him the sketch pad. "Anyway, I'm going to leave this with you. I promise you we'll talk as much as you want tomorrow, but for now I suggest we all turn in."

Braxton looked at the priest with amused suspicion, then lowered his eyes to the pad.

Before him, produced in the same crude manner as the drawing Eddie had had with him in the museum, was a very primitive attempt to duplicate the lower section of the map Gunther had shown them earlier. However, situated near the region Kathy had pointed out was something not found on Gunther's map. It appeared to be a large, poorly defined boxlike object.

Braxton tilted the sheet toward the firelight, and then he too knew the reason for the shocked response of the others. The box shape appeared to be an opening or hole in the ground. Perhaps a grave. And inside the box were two crudely rendered figures. One, obviously meant to represent a female, had been given long hair. But more important, the hair had been shaded red. The other stick figure was obviously a male, and resting on top of his head was a crudely drawn representation of a baseball cap exactly like the New York Yankees cap Braxton was wearing.

FROM DEEP WITHIN THE SHADOWS, well out of the light given off by the overhead lamps along the main road, Frank Gunther watched the little knot of people at the campfire beyond disband and head for their tents. He swore softly.

"What the hell was all that mumbo-jumbo shit, Dog?" he whispered, leaning in toward the two men beside him. "What's going on with these people, anyway?"

Dog Bassett shrugged. "No idea, Frank. That's your problem. I'm only interested in rhinos." Dog pointed to the bus off to the right of the campfire. The interior light had just gone off. "Looks like your driver saw it too. Maybe he can tell you something."

Frank spat and shook his head. "Not that little son of a bitch. Sammy and I don't see eye-to-eye like we used to. It's like the kid doesn't know he's black anymore. I took him on because of his knowledge of English. Thought he could relate to the clients, you know. He played along at first, but it's no good. Thinks just because he's got a little education from the United States, we're on equal ground. I was going to get rid of him this trip, but I couldn't find a replacement. Dingo here can't drive worth a damn. He'd pile us into a tree inside of a mile. But we won't find out anything from Sammy, believe me. He'll keep his mouth shut just to spite me." Frank paused again to spit, then stared across at the deserted campfire. "Come on," he said, waving Dog and Dingo forward. "Let's go in. Don't worry, I'll find out what this is all about before noon tomorrow."

Dog Bassett shrugged. "I'm not worried, Frank."

Frank grunted. "Yeah, well let me tell you something, Dog. There'll be no strange shit going on while I'm running a safari unless I give it the Gunther stamp of approval."

Seven

THOUGH THE WATER HAD NOT even a hint of warmth in it, Kathy stayed inside the crude cement-block stall of the bathhouse, hoping the chill of the shower would help drive out some of the tension twisting her insides. Sporadic spurts in varying degrees of cold pounded at her neck and back, but the tension from the dream that had awakened her in the early-morning hours remained. Finally, unable to stand the chill another moment, she twisted the faucet to off, pulled back the cheap plastic curtain and, her teeth chattering, grabbed greedily at the towel on the stone bench nearby. So much for the cold-shower cure.

As always, the essence of the dream had remained in her mind with astonishing clarity even after she was fully awake. Until the end, the events had been the same, but when the terrible moment of loss came, the dream suddenly changed. This time as she watched herself move toward the mountain of flames that had consumed her mother, a hand had shot out to stop her. Turning, she had seen Braxton Hicks reaching out to her. It was so incongruous, but there he was, wearing his silly baseball cap, trying to save her—calling out her name as she fell screaming from the safety of his grasp into the searing flames before her.

She shook her head at the confusion of her thoughts and vigorously toweled the water from her body. Eddie was right. The only sure thing seemed to be that everything was getting more complicated. Why had the regression drawing suddenly included a rendering of the priest's friend? She had only just met him. Yet after the session, when their eyes met, something had been there. She had sensed it. And intuitively she knew he felt it also. A connection. An unconscious feeling of emotion had passed between them, drawing them to each other in some unspoken, instinctual way.

Though she didn't understand it, one thing was undeniable: meeting Braxton Hicks was having a strange effect on her. He was already a part of her dreams, for heaven's sake.

"About ready, Kathy?" Zelda's voice called from the adjacent stall.

"Be right there," Kathy replied, throwing down the towel and reaching for her clothes. As she did so, she caught a glimpse of her reflection in the cracked mirror that was mounted on the opposite wall. The face staring back at her was riddled with anxiety. Her stomach growled and, feeling the tension tighten into harder knots of apprehension, Kathy dressed quickly. Then, just before leaving, she scowled at her reflection with determination.

"If you think I'm going to quit, forget it," she said to the image staring back at her through the dust-covered glass. "You hear me? I don't care how weird this gets, I'm in it for the whole ride."

Feeling the tension ease ever so slightly, Kathy smiled confidently, tilted her head toward the mirror in salutation and, snatching up the towel to dry her hair, crossed through the doorway to the building's exterior.

Zelda was waiting for her when she emerged, and farther down the path, heading toward them, were Eddie and his friend. In spite of herself, Kathy felt her heart make a little skip as her eyes settled on Braxton Hicks.

It wasn't that he was particularly handsome, Kathy decided as she watched the men approach, the news correspondent waving to them with a smile. He had neither a macho nor a pretty-boy look to him. Rather, his face was expressive in a way that complemented his personality. The eyebrows helped, arching and dipping in accompaniment to the almost ever-present half-mocking smile. But most of all it was his eyes. Yes, that was it. It was the eyes that gave his face its special appeal. As he came toward them in the bright, early-morning sunlight, Kathy could see all the individual components of his personality dancing with sparkles of impish animation across the eyes of Braxton Hicks.

Yet what else had she seen in those eyes the night before, when their gazes had locked for several moments after the hypnosis session? A sadness? Pain? A brief glimpse of some inner need?

At the campsite, where he stood near the fire, Injai held a cup of coffee high in front of him and shouted toward the men. "*Jambo*, Buddy. Better be quick. Breakfast is soon ready."

"*Jambo*, Injai," Braxton replied, returning the wave. "Be right there."

Braxton noted with pleasant satisfaction that after absolutely no primping at all, Kathy Sullivan still looked terrific. She was dressed in a fresh safari shirt and shorts and was working a towel through her curly red hair. Beside her, Zelda wore a shapeless kimono, her head wrapped in a terry-cloth turban. Despite the early hour, they both looked awake and enthusiastic.

"Well, *jambo*, ladies," Braxton greeted, as he and Eddie came up next to the women. "You certainly are alert and squeaky clean this morning."

"Yes," Kathy said, shaking her hair away from her head as she towel dried it. "I think this outdoor camping really agrees with Zelda and me."

"Absolutely," Zelda put in. And, unable to resist, she pointed to where the women's camping equipment was already disassembled and stacked in a neat pile. "Our tent's down and we're ready to go."

Eddie grinned. "Oh, we noticed, Zelda."

"Where's Gunther, by the way?" Braxton asked.

"He and his friend went with Sammy to get food supplies from the market for the first part of the trip," Eddie informed him. "They pulled out just before I came to wake you, Brax. One of our big problems is solved, anyway. Mr. Gunther was waiting for me the second I stepped from my tent this morning, demanding an explanation about what we were really up to. Apparently he returned from the bar last night in time to see a large part of the session."

"I told you. Frank Gunther's nobody's fool. What did you say?"

"The truth," Eddie said. "That we were using hypnosis to glean information to help us locate the rarest of undiscovered antiquities."

"And?"

"Well he demanded I name the antiquity, of course. But, surprisingly, he didn't laugh. In fact, he promised to do all he could to help us. For a price."

"How much?"

"An additional twenty percent above total cost for any and all activities that vary from standard contractual camping safari."

"Pretty steep," remarked Braxton.

"Not really," Zelda said. "At least it's all out in the open and we know where we stand. If it becomes necessary, I'll gladly pay the price."

"And you, Braxton?" Kathy questioned. "Are you planning to stay with us now that you've had time to think it over? Or have you decided we're all out of our minds?"

Braxton looked at her with an easy smile. "I'm not sure about the sanity part, but I think I'll stick it out for the duration."

"I'm glad," Kathy said. "I was a little afraid that the strangeness of last night's session might have convinced you the experience wasn't worth writing about."

"Not a chance. First of all, I gave Eddie my word I'd see this through with him. And second, win, lose or draw, Kathy, if nothing else, last night convinced me this is definitely going to be something to write home about."

Zelda pointed in the direction of the campfire. "I think we'd better shake a leg. Injai is waving at us again."

"You ladies go have your breakfast, Zelda," Eddie said good-naturedly. "Don't worry. We'll be ready to go when the bus leaves, even if we haven't gotten our tents down and rolled up in neat little piles yet."

As it turned out, there wasn't that much of a rush. There was time not only for a hearty breakfast but for a second cup of coffee while they broke camp. When Gunther finally returned, swearing about all the time he'd wasted getting out of the jammed food market, they all helped heave the packs and equipment up to the top rack of the bus, where Sammy and Dingo stored them securely. By the time they climbed aboard the bus, the morning had become noticeably warmer, and the sun was a large, hot yellow ball climbing above the trees. With Gunther and Dog Bassett leading the way in Gunther's Jeep Cherokee, Sammy closed the bus doors and pulled out of Westwood.

Braxton extracted his Nikon from its carrying case, put the case onto the overhead rack, and slid into the seat beside Kathy several rows from the front. In the first seat, Eddie sat beside Zelda, and the two chatted with Sammy about the route they would be following. Injai was positioned directly behind the driver, staring out a side window.

Braxton tore open a package of 400 ASA color film, popped the back of the camera open, and dropped the film spool into the left-hand slot.

"Well, Kathy Sullivan," he said, slipping the edge of the film under one of the catches on the take-up reel, "we're off to see the wizard."

Kathy pulled her gaze from the buildings they were passing in the outskirts of Nairobi and looked at him.

"It's crazy, isn't it? Doing all this on blind faith. Not knowing what's going to happen or what's going to come blurting out of me."

"No argument here," Braxton said, grinning at her as he snapped the Nikon closed, then hit the shutter a couple of times to advance the film. "Craziest damned thing I've ever done—without exception."

"See," Kathy said. Her hand fluttered to her mouth, and she bit nervously at one of her fingernails. "What if I'm just loony? It could be, you know."

"I guess it could," Braxton remarked, aiming his camera toward the front of the bus and adjusting the focus. "But I don't think so. Your artwork is a little primitive, though."

"Oh, God, the painting. I was as surprised as you were, believe me. I swear to you, I had no idea that was going to happen."

Braxton lowered the camera. "I know you didn't. I watched very carefully last night, Kathy, and I know what I saw was no act. Whatever was going on, it was authentic. And that's what fascinates me." He smiled and rubbed his hand playfully across the top of his head. "On the other hand, I'm no fool either, and I did throw my baseball cap in the fire after you all went to bed last night."

"You didn't."

"No, just kidding," he said, his grin widening. "It would take more than a picture to make me part with my favorite hat. I have to be honest, though, and tell you that I may not cooperate in trying to fulfill the prophecy in your painting. I might like you, but I'm not sure I'm ready to be buried with you."

Kathy laughed softly. "I can understand how that might bother you. I know how bizarre this all must seem, and I want you to know that I appreciate your agreeing to write about this for us, and . . . I'm glad Eddie brought you along."

"So am I," Braxton said, holding Kathy's gaze for several moments until she looked out the window again.

"This land is beautiful, isn't it."

"That it is," he agreed. The last cluster of city buildings was now behind them, and open country stretched outward from both sides of the paved road ahead. "Even if we come up empty-handed, I guarantee you're going to get some peace of mind out of this. The openness here does something to a person. It snaps your perspective back into focus. Wait until you stare over the savannah or into a Kenyan night sky. That alone will help you. And you're going to see wildlife and get pictures that will be absolutely gorgeous."

"You love it here, don't you. I can see it in your face when you speak."

Braxton nodded. "I won't deny it. I don't mean to wax poetic ad nauseam, but there's something about this wilderness that eases the soul. I don't know of any other way to put it."

"Well, I hope you're right. I could use a little soul easing right now." Kathy pointed out the window to a fairly tall, strutting bird with an arc of feathered plumage extending above its head. "Oh, look. What's that bird? Do you know?"

"Secretary bird."

"Really? That's its name? Why is it called that?"

"Does all the typing for the other animals out here." Kathy laughed. "No, really. Why?"

"No idea. But you'd better get your camera ready. We're going to see a lot more animals very soon."

Kathy reached into a traveling bag next to her and took out a thirty-five-millimeter self-focusing camera. "Okay. I thought for some reason it would be a while before we saw any."

"That's one of the great things about Kenya. Right outside the capital, it's animals and wilderness everywhere. Look over there." Braxton pointed out the window to the far left. In the distance, a tall giraffe was standing among the tufts of grass, its head turned in the direction of the bus.

"Giraffe to the left!" Injai's voice boomed from the front. "I will be spotter for you, Buddy. You see it?"

Braxton waved. "Got it, Injai. Thanks. Any cheetahs yet?"

Injai laughed heartily and flashed a grin over his shoulder. "Several so far, but I want to wait to tell you. Save something for later in the trip."

"Thanks. Thoughtful of you."

As Injai laughed again, Kathy lowered her camera, the giraffe already behind the bus. "I hope I got it."

"Hard to get a bad shot here. And there'll be plenty more. It's the big cats you don't want to miss a shot of. Some are very rare. Injai has been promising to find me a mated pair of cheetahs for years now, but I've yet to see them. It's become a running joke between us."

Kathy lowered the camera, resting it on her lap. "Why does he call you Buddy?"

"When Eddie and I first came here, it was impossible for Injai to remember the name Braxton. Mental block or something, but he could never get it right, so I told him to use Buddy, because it meant friend. And it just stuck."

"Well, your name is unusual. Were you aware that it's a medical term?"

Braxton's jaw tightened and a muscle twitched sporadically. "Yes."

"I was sure someone must have told you before. Is Braxton a family name?"

"No." The news correspondent's carefree expression had become quite sober at the mention of his name, but he pushed past whatever had bothered him and went on. "Tell me about yourself. What do you do when you're not searching for lost religious antiquities?"

"I'm a nurse."

"Really? A nurse. I wouldn't have guessed that."

"Well, it's true," Kathy said with a shrug. "New York Hospital. In fact, that's where I met Zelda. We were both taking a course on massage therapy, got to know each other, and she invited me to attend one of her hypnotic regression sessions. I guess the nurse thing was inevitable. My father is a doctor—although we've never been that close. My mother died when I was born, and it's my understanding that my father pulled into himself mentally when it happened and never really came back."

"Yes, Eddie mentioned that you'd never known your mother."

"And did he tell you that one of the reasons I'm doing this is my own crazy attempt to find out more about her?" Kathy said defensively, her eyes clouding.

Braxton nodded. "Yes, he did. But he didn't use the word *crazy*. He simply explained that you were still very troubled by her death occurring at your birth; that you felt both guilt and a tremendous sense of loss."

Braxton's nonjudgmental response knocked the edge off Kathy's defensiveness and she continued with a tiny nod. "That's also why I did the regression originally. I thought maybe I could... I don't know...somehow learn something about her. Somehow ease the loss I've always felt. The guilt is part of it, I guess. But mostly it's the terrible emptiness."

Kathy Sullivan's eyes suddenly began to fill, and she shook her head, fighting back the emotion.

"Because of the way it happened, I've been cheated out of both my parents, really. Oh, Daddy has always given me the things I've needed, but there's been a distance there. Maybe even a resentment. Still, I've learned to live with that. It's not ever having known my mother that I've been unable to accept. You have no idea what it's like never to have known the woman who gave you birth."

Braxton sighed and shook his head slowly, cocking a thumb toward the front of the bus where Eddie sat talking to Sammy. "It looks like our friend Father Fitzsimmons is more aware of the ironies at work here than he's let on."

"What do you mean?"

"I mean he knows both of our backgrounds. No matter how messed up you feel you are, Kathy, there's always someone worse off. It's one of life's great truths. You asked before about the name, whether Braxton was a family name. Well, the cold fact is there is no family. The name Braxton Hicks was given to me by an O.B. nurse who took care of abandoned babies."

Kathy stared at Braxton with new awareness.

"That's right. The name is no strange coincidence. It was a gift to me from a member of your noble profession. No more than a few hours old, I was found screaming my head off in a trash can by a passing newsboy, although I assume I was born elsewhere and left among the garbage afterward."

"Oh, Braxton. How awful. I had no idea."

"Well, it's not something I tell at parties or put on my résumé. I checked on the name, of course, the first time its medical reference was pointed out to me. It's the term for the light contractions a pregnant woman has prior to giving birth. The early Braxton-Hicks contractions help strengthen the muscles of the womb in preparation for the later delivery, if I understand it correctly." Kathy nodded in agreement, and Braxton gave a short cynical laugh. "I suppose the nurse in charge may have given me the name as a joke, or maybe she liked the sound of it. Who knows. Anyway, that's my story. The closest thing to a family I have is Eddie. We may not always agree, but ever since I met him in college, he's been like a brother to me. And that's the main reason I'm here, Kathy. There isn't anything I wouldn't do for him. He's been the one stabilizing factor in my life. Now, don't you feel better? I'm the one who should be doing the regressions; at least you know who you are.''

Braxton looked away self-consciously, running his hand through his hair. "Something crazy must be going on, that's for sure. I never talk about this. Ever! And here I am spilling my guts out to someone I've known less than two days!''

When he had finished speaking, he turned back to meet her gaze, and Kathy knew then what she had felt the night before. Suddenly she understood the connection that instinctually they both had sensed, the thing that gave them a common bond. It was there in his eyes.

Like a reflection of her own pain, she saw glimpses of the same terrible, gnawing loneliness that came with her earliest childhood memories and never went away, hanging like a dark curtain of despair over her life. Unable to find the proper words to respond to what she saw in his eyes, Kathy unconsciously reached over and covered Braxton's hand with her own in a sympathetic gesture.

Except for occasional puffs of elongated cloud formations, the sky was a startlingly brilliant blue above the landscape that rolled out to the horizon. Clumps of umbrella-shaped acacia trees and low shrubs sprouted from the straw-colored plain.

"I guess none of us are as unique as we think. The magnitude of our problems just makes it seem that way," Kathy said, her face relaxing as she gazed outward. "Well, maybe you're right. Maybe all I need is a little time in the wilderness. The sky is clear, that's for sure. You can see for what must be miles. And the color of the land is, I don't know, sharper somehow.''

"No pollution," Braxton replied.

Kathy smiled and leaned her head back against the seat, closing her eyes. "If only this were a pleasant sight-seeing trip. But who knows, Braxton Hicks... maybe we'll both gain something valuable from it all.''

Braxton said nothing but instead gazed down to Kathy's hand, still covering his own, and then back to the soft lines of her face, aware and at the same time amazed at how strongly he had come to feel about the woman beside him in such a short time.

Suddenly, out of nowhere, an old Simon and Garfunkel tune that had once been a favorite of his came flooding into his mind. The voices sang in quiet unison: "'Kathy, I'm lost,' I said tho' I knew she was sleeping...."

Then Art Garfunkel's vibrant tenor voice soared: "I'm empty and aching and I don't know whyy... yy...yyyy...."

Eight

EVEN THOUGH IT WAS LATE AFTERNOON, the remnants of midday heat refused to dissipate, and Frank Gunther was in a foul mood. He hated days like this. Ordinarily by this time it was cooler. But today was one of those days when the swelter would not leave, the only breeze coming from the heavy air that rushed through the side windows as the Cherokee ground its way through the sparse bush country in the general direction of the Amboseli Game Reserve.

Stationing Dingo on the roof rack of the Jeep as lookout, Frank had left the main road around noon in hopes of spotting a lone rhino early in the trip. That way he could get Dog off his back and concentrate on the new developments—figure out how he was going to make them work to his advantage. Although the more he thought about it, the more he realized that Dog Bassett, dealer in African rarities both inside and outside the law, might be just the person to have as a partner if these people were really onto something.

Glancing in the rearview mirror, Frank reassured himself that Sammy was keeping the bus right behind them. Then he shifted uncomfortably, hating the feeling of his khaki shirt clinging to his back, and pushed off the top of the cooler that sat between Dog and himself. He pulled a Tusker beer from what was already more water than ice and, turning, held it up as he spoke to the man next to him.

"Another beer, Dog? It's mighty hot. Going to be a while before we stop to set up camp. And we're sure as hell not going to see any rhino out wandering around in this heat. Those big suckers stay put when it's like this."

"Sounds good," Dog said, accepting the bottle.

Frank nodded and snapped off the cap of the bottle with an opener he extracted from his vest pocket. Then he smacked the roof of the Cherokee a couple of times and shouted, "Wake up, you lazy asshole!"

Dingo lowered his head into the window from above, and Frank shoved another open bottle of beer at the grinning face peering in sideways at them.

"Here, and keep your eyes open."

"No *kifaru*, Bwana. Hot!" Dingo answered, gratefully accepting the beer with an ever-wider grin.

"You keep your eyes open anyway, you hear me?"

Dingo nodded obediently and disappeared from view.

Frank took a long pull on his own beer, grimaced, then belched. He glanced over at Bassett. "Actually, they misnamed this here *bee-ah*, Dog. It may be called Tusker, but it tastes like it comes from the other end of the elephant—especially when it begins to get warm." Dog gave Frank a look. "A little humor, Dog. I meant it tastes like elephant piss."

Dog appeared bored. "I got it, Frank."

Gunther scanned the bush ahead of them as he drained his beer. Then he spoke again, deciding to test the partnership waters. "So what do you think about what I told you this morning, Dog. Think these people are on the level? Could they really have some kind of inside track on finding this grave?"

Dog's expression remained unchanged as he looked over at Frank, but his eyes narrowed when he spoke.

"I've been thinking about it, Frank. Let me ask you this: If the grave was real, and if it was found, what do you think a discovery like that would be worth?"

Frank smiled broadly. Aha! The subject had caught Dog Bassett's interest. "You're a man after my own heart, Dog. My thoughts exactly. And I would say the contents of such a discovery could bring in one hell of a payoff. The right person would pay a small fortune for the remains of the first human being or whatever else there might be at such a place, don't you think? Could be mighty profitable even split two ways."

"If it's real."

"Only way to find out is to stick with it until the end of the trip. Interested?"

Dog stared ahead. "Maybe. Maybe, Frank. We'll see how it goes."

"Kifaru...mbele...kushoto!" Dingo shouted from the roof, and Frank sat forward, pointing out the windshield while automatically slowing the vehicle.

"I'll be damned. Looks like it's your lucky day, Dog," Frank said, hardly believing his own luck as he cut the engine. Behind them, Sammy came to a stop and killed the bus motor also, following his employer's lead. "Out in front of us and off to the right. See it?"

Dog nodded, and finally Frank saw the stoic face break into a smile. The rhino was a beauty. Meanwhile, Sammy had slipped out of the bus and quietly crept up to the driver's side of the Cherokee.

"Okay, Sammy," Frank said, reaching behind him to pull a .458 Winchester magnum from its padded rack. He handed the weapon to Dog and lifted a smaller .300 gauge off the upper rack for himself. "Get your ass back there and tell them to be quiet and sit tight. They're about to have the rare opportunity of seeing two real hunters in actions."

Sammy gave Gunther a look, pointing out over the hood of the Jeep. Of course Frank knew what the look was for. The rhinoceros was a female. He had seen it just before Dingo shouted, and he had also seen the small baby, now shielded by the huge body of its mother, who had shifted protectively at the sound of the distant motor. Hiding the baby behind her, she raised her head in curiosity and stared in their direction with her short vision.

Frank chose to ignore Sammy's look. Screw it. A rhino was a rhino, and this one had the horns; big ones, just like Dog wanted. Besides, there simply weren't that many of the big bastards around nowadays. The baby probably explained why she was out. She had to find food, heat or no heat.

There was no way Sammy was going to keep the clients in the bus, however. They were already streaming out the door and, in imitation of Sammy's movements, creeping to the back of the Cherokee.

Dog came around beside Frank, gesturing at the oncoming clients. "You sure it's all right to fire in front of them, Frank? I don't care how green they are, everybody knows you don't shoot rhinos."

"So we tell them some bullshit story about it being a killer," Frank hissed irritably. "You want this bastard or not, Dog?"

Dog Bassett shrugged, but before he could reply, Eddie and the others were clustering around them.

"You're not going to shoot that rhino, are you?" Braxton asked, reaching them first.

"Got to," Frank replied. "It's the rogue we've been alerted about. Park officials sent out a notice that it's turned killer. We've been instructed to shoot it on sight."

Kathy was shaking her head. "I saw a baby out there. I know I did."

"You hear that," said Braxton. "Come on, Gunther. That's no rogue. She's got a baby."

"Killers have babies too, Hicks," Frank said, turning to face Braxton. "Don't call me a liar, mister. Got that? And don't tell me my job. Now get back and keep quiet." He turned back to Dog. "You want it, go ahead, Dog. I'll back you up."

Exasperated, Braxton turned to the smaller man behind him. "Eddie?"

"Do you know what he says to be a lie, Braxton?"

"Well, no, not for sure, but . . ."

"I'll take it," Dog answered Frank, deciding not to wait for Eddie to make a decision.

As Frank nodded and placed the barrel of his weapon over the Cherokee's hood, Dog Bassett moved to the other side, leaned against the Jeep's back end, and brought up the Winchester.

Zelda Roote's thick hands clenched in tight fists on her hips and she took a step forward.

"Mr. Gunther, I want you to stop this right now," she demanded loudly, her plump face reddening with anger. "I am not going to stand here and let you shoot that rhinoceros."

Gunther glanced at the hypnotist with amused amazement. "I'm not going to shoot it, lady. Dog is. And frankly, I don't think there's a whole hell of a lot you can do about it."

"All right now, just a minute," Eddie protested, moving past Zelda toward Gunther.

But Dog Bassett was neither listening nor waiting. He tightened the stock against his shoulder, leaned forward, and was sighting in for the kill when a loud, distant, piercing cry sounded. It was a chant-shout of alarm that shattered the late-afternoon silence.

The rhino bolted immediately, but as if to make sure, the screeching cry sounded a second and then a third time as the great female thundered away, her little baby now visible and scurrying frantically on its short, squat legs after its mother.

"Look!" Kathy shouted to Zelda, pointing at the tiny scampering rhino. "I told you there was a baby."

Dingo had jumped to his feet on the roof of the Cherokee and was staring into the distance, but Frank Gunther knew what had made the sound, and he swore softly to himself, smacking the hood beneath him with his fist.

"Twamba...Bwana," Dingo was saying, "Twamba *hapa*!"

"Yeah, I know, Dingo," Frank growled as Dog came up beside him. "I didn't think that was the cry of a goddamned bull elephant. Is he coming this way?"

"Ndiyo," Dingo said excitedly. "Yes, Twamba is coming. Still far away, but coming fast."

"On foot and alone?"

Dingo looked down and shook his head, giving Frank an openmouthed smile that revealed his crooked teeth. "Twiga with him. Twiga follow him like always. Twiga very big now. High off ground. No longer baby."

Frank spit forcefully into the dirt. "All right. Watch him. Let me know if he does anything funny before he gets here."

"Who the hell is Twamba, Frank?" demanded Dog, his face flushed with anger as he stared after the prize rhinoceros thundering away in the distance.

"Just a native, Dog," Frank replied with forced casualness. "Nothing to get excited about."

"Very tall," Injai said, staring out over the savannah. "That can be seen, even from a distance. He appears to be a giant. Yet look how he moves with such grace and speed toward us. And he's followed by a giraffe. See it. The giraffe moves right with the giant."

Eddie exchanged a look with Braxton and took another step in Gunther's direction. "I've heard of Twamba but never seen him. Why did Twamba shout, Mr. Gunther? Could it be that Braxton was right, and Twamba correctly frightened away the game?"

"No, Eddie, Hicks wasn't right," snarled Frank. "Twamba is a meddling black, that's all, who just allowed a killer rhino to escape so that it could gore a few more innocent people." Refusing to look out, as the others did, to where the tall native was approaching, Gunther took the Winchester from Dog and handed it to Sammy, who reached into the Cherokee and replaced the weapon on its padded rack. "Still coming, Dingo?"

Dingo nodded down at them. "Right to us. Twamba wants to see you for sure, Bwana."

Frank leaned against the Jeep's hood, still holding the lighter-gauge weapon loosely in his hand, and gave Sammy a mocking look. "Hear that? You're about to get a close-up view, just like you've always wanted."

"Who is this Twamba?" Zelda asked.

"Why don't you tell them about Twamba, Sammy," Frank said, still eyeing his driver. "He's your goddamned hero." The young driver had been staring into the distance, and though he turned now to his employer, he said nothing. Frank's voice took on a harsh edge. "Go on, damn it. The lady asked about Twamba. Tell her."

Sammy's eyes shifted nervously, and he took a hesitant step forward. He knew Frank Gunther was in an ugly mood. He had seen it before. The casualness was only a temporary calm. The explosion always came. He fidgeted, unsure how he should comply with the request, and when he spoke his voice was tentative.

"Twamba is Masai," Sammy began, unable to keep the admiration he felt for the man from coloring his words. "A Masai warrior. But more than just a warrior, he is a great healer and knows much of medicine, herbs and the ways of the spirits."

"That is how I've heard of him," Eddie added. "Several times they told me Twamba had been to a village to help the sick before we arrived with food and medical supplies. Natives believe he's something of a miracle worker."

Frank grunted and spat again, but Sammy had committed himself and pushed on. "He is also, unlike most of us who have taken on the ways of a white civilization, at one with nature. Like the animals, Twamba is a part of the land, living free. And a symbol to all black men of their heritage and their lost way of life."

Frank's thumb casually flicked on and off the safety of the weapon he held loosely in his right hand. "He's also a black who should mind his own business," he remarked.

"Twamba is concerned for the animals," Sammy said quickly. "His ways are not our ways."

"Why does the giraffe follow him?" Injai asked, enthralled by that phenomenon.

Again Sammy's voice filled with admiration. "No one knows the certain facts, but they tell of Twamba finding the giraffe as a newborn. The baby's tiny legs were caught under its dead mother who had been shot for sport and left to the vultures. Finding it barely alive, Twamba splinted the baby giraffe's legs and, using his special knowledge of herbs, nursed the newborn back to health. Now it will not leave him."

Twamba was much closer now. He held his spear and shield waist high as he came, and had slowed his smooth running to a steady, confident walk. The giraffe followed a few steps behind, its towering head and long neck weaving back and forth behind the slender Masai warrior.

"But it looks like a mature animal," Zelda observed. "Would even a cared-for giraffe when full grown stay with a man as this one does?"

"No, Twiga is not easily tamed from its instincts of the wild," Sammy said, smiling. "But he who comes is no ordinary man. He is Twamba!"

Frank tensed, and his voice cracked as he pushed himself from the Jeep into a standing position. "Horseshit, Sammy. Twamba's no different from any other black. Don't be an idiot. I thought you had an education. Go start the bus, and be ready to move." He flashed his clients a white-hunter smile. "All aboard, folks. We're moving out."

"You won't stay to talk to Twamba, then?" Eddie asked.

"Waste of my time." Frank smiled. "I might teach him a little lesson, though, about interfering with a white hunter." He shifted the weapon in his hand and spoke softly over his shoulder, his attention now on the approaching Masai. "I thought I'd shoot me a giraffe.

There are so many around these days, they're getting to be a nuisance."

Sammy had paused on his way back to the bus when Gunther spoke, and his mouth opened in shock. "No. You cannot. Speak to him. Warn him. But do not do this."

"I told you to get into the goddamn bus, Sammy," Frank said, his thumb pushing off the safety as his finger curled around the trigger on the weapon. "Now do it. Stay down up there, Dingo. Masai spears never miss, and he may throw."

"All right, hold it, Gunther," Braxton intervened. "That's enough. Your driver's right. You can't just shoot the man's giraffe."

With professional speed, Frank Gunther extracted the pistol from its holster at his side with his free hand and passed it to Dog Bassett. He glared at Braxton. "I told you, Hicks. Don't give me orders. Dog, this son of a bitch or anybody else tries to interfere, you shoot them. Got it?"

"You're the boss," Dog answered, accepting the pistol and turning his cold, expressionless face toward Braxton and the others.

"This is incredible," Zelda sputtered in protest. "You can't simply—"

"Wrong, lady," Gunther interrupted with a cruel smile. "I can do whatever I want. This is my playground, not yours. Here we play by my rules. And no black interferes with my hunting. Ever!"

Frank Gunther had been holding the boot of the Winchester's polished walnut stock against the hood, and as those behind him watched in disbelief, he expertly swung the butt to his right shoulder in one swift movement. Grasping the barrel with his left hand, he trained the sights upward toward the head of the animal, leading it slightly to compensate for the sway caused by the giraffe's leggy movement.

In the end it wasn't Braxton or an outraged Zelda or any of the other members of the safari who interfered as Gunther brought the sights across his target. It was his own driver, Sammy.

He gave no thought to the consequences involved, and he probably wouldn't have been able to stop himself if he'd wanted to. Sammy simply was not capable of standing by while Frank Gunther shot Twamba's giraffe. At the exact moment his employer's finger tightened on the trigger of his weapon, Sammy yelled.

"Twamba," the driver screamed in Swahili. "*Hatari!* Danger. Stop, Twamba. *Simama!*"

Against an expert shot like Gunther, a hastily shouted warning wasn't much of a deterrent, but the timing helped, and it proved to be enough. The approaching Masai reacted to Sammy's yell by halting a fraction of a second before Frank squeezed off his shot. Twamba's sudden stop momentarily confused the animal following him, and the giraffe sidestepped awkwardly as the rifle Frank held cracked loudly. The express head from an exploded cartridge hissed past the high, double-horned head, missing its mark by a fraction of an inch.

Dog instinctively shifted the pistol in Sammy's direction but did not fire, unsure of whether Gunther's instructions applied to his own driver.

"You little bastard," Frank snarled over his shoulder, and then he dropped to one knee, snapping back the bolt of the rifle and shoving another shell into the chamber.

Twamba had reacted to the sound of the shot with astonishing speed, and Injai shouted with excitement as he and the others stared in amazement at the Masai's agility.

"Look, he's on the giraffe's back," cried Injai. "It is beyond belief, but he rides a wild giraffe."

Even Sammy could not believe his eyes, but it was true. At the sound of the shot, the giraffe had veered sideways, and with dazzling speed, Twamba had grasped the neck of the towering animal, swung his body onto the sloping back, wrapped his long legs around the thick shoulders and, in a strange half-seated but stable fashion, was riding the giraffe as it thundered away from them.

Frank Gunther was not impressed, however, and steadied himself as he drew a bead on the departing animal, moving the barrel far ahead and to the left, waiting for the giraffe to come into the sights of the scope mounted on the top of his weapon.

"Keep watching, boy," Frank said, "he'll soon be riding thin air, 'cause that giraffe is about to become dead meat!"

But Sammy had committed himself now. He had gone over the line and there was no turning back. He had taken Gunther's verbal abuse too long, and now it was over. The man who had chipped away at his pride would insult him no more. His warning to Twamba had ended it. Oblivious to Dog Bassett's pistol and everything else around him, and feeling a surge of pleasure as the weight of restraint lifted from him, Sammy lunged toward his employer.

"I said no!" the young black screamed.

Despite its noble intent, Sammy's lunge was pathetically inadequate against a man like Gunther. Most of the time Frank was lax, his movements lethargic. Excitement and crisis, however, transformed him into a trained hunter who functioned with a speed and skill that were both deadly and dangerous.

Seeing Sammy coming at him from the side, Frank dropped his bead on the giraffe and heaved himself into a turn, arcing his weapon in a savage swing at his attacker as he spat the curse "Goddamn little asshole" through his clenched teeth. Sammy ducked his head to avoid the Winchester's swing, but Frank compensated for the dodge, and the steel barrel connected with a slapping crack, smashing into Sammy's skull.

The pain came in searing waves that coursed through his head, but with a cry of rage, Sammy dove at Gunther again. All reason was lost, and he became frantic in his pursuit. Clutching wildly, he grasped Frank's bush jacket, but as he attempted to take advantage of the chance hold, Frank brought the rifle barrel down again on his attacker's head, and this time Sammy stopped. A weak whimper broke from his lips, and his body collapsed in a loose heap on the ground.

Not even pausing, Frank spun himself back to his original position, fell to one knee and brought the gun up to eye level. He squinted into the scope, but the target was now a distant moving image, all but gone.

Slowly he stood, staring motionless across the sun-drenched savannah. Shadows matted the sweeping plains as the late-afternoon sun dropped behind intermittent clumps of acacia trees. A herd of wildebeests accompanied by several zebras grazed as they moved across the vista, migrating through the region, and a light wind was now stirring the air, easing the stifling heat. Sweat glistened on Frank's face, and he seemed not to see the scene before him or notice the shifting breeze.

His expression glazed with hatred, he glanced behind him to where the others stared in silence, still held at bay by Dog's threatening pistol. Then he spun around again, bringing his foot back and delivering a savage kick into the midsection of Sammy's inert form.

"Stupid asshole," Frank shouted. Then he kicked again, harder.

As Kathy screamed for Gunther to stop and Zelda gasped in horror, Braxton was in motion, with Eddie and Injai right behind him. Together they grabbed at Gunther's arms, pulling him away from Sammy's body.

"All right, that's enough," Eddie ordered, as Frank wrestled in their grasp. "Shoot us if you want, but you're not hurting this man anymore."

"Get your goddamn hands off me!" Gunther growled, breaking away from them with a sudden, powerful twist. As Eddie bent down to examine Sammy, Frank aimed his weapon at Braxton and Injai and backed toward his Jeep. "Dingo, get down here and drive the bus. Sammy's fired!"

While Zelda and Kathy rushed to help Eddie with the injured Sammy, Dingo scrambled down from the Cherokee and ran back to the bus. Keeping his eye on Braxton, who glared hatefully back at him, Frank took the pistol from Dog Bassett and handed him the Winchester. "Get in and put this on the rack for me, will you, Dog?"

Dog Bassett walked around the Jeep, and Frank slid the pistol back into its holster. Though he addressed the women, his eyes stayed on Braxton. "We're leaving, ladies. I suggest you all climb back into the bus right now."

"You can't just leave this man here," Kathy protested. "He's hurt."

"You watch me," Frank answered, pulling open the driver's door and sliding into the Jeep. "Now, are you people coming or not?"

After exchanging a look with Eddie, Zelda rose to her feet and stood defiantly beside Braxton. "We're not leaving without this man, Mr. Gunther."

"Suit yourself," Frank said, turning to shout behind him. "Dingo, throw their luggage off the top of the bus. They're staying. And don't forget the shit inside. I don't want to be accused of stealing!"

Zelda's mouth dropped open in disbelief. "You wouldn't dare! You can't just leave us here. We have a contract."

"You made the choice, lady," Gunther snarled. "I'm not asking you twice."

"Leave us here and you'll lose your license, Gunther," Braxton said. "I give you my word. I'll make sure of it."

Frank barked with laughter as they watched Dingo scramble to the top of the bus and begin dropping pieces of luggage to the ground. "For what? Disciplining an employee? Not a chance. If you people decide not to get back on the bus, I can't force you—although I will tell you there's a lodge about a mile to the west of here. You'll find the dirt road to it right over that ridge. I suggest you head there before too long. It'll soon be feeding time for the game around here, and they'll attack anything as long as it's meat."

"You are a despicable man, Mr. Gunther," Zelda said, spinning around in anger and crossing back to where Eddie knelt, cradling Sammy's head in his hands while Kathy examined the young African's injuries.

"Nobody's perfect," Frank said, grinning back at her. Behind them, Dingo emerged from inside the bus and added several smaller bags to the pile of luggage on the ground. "That it, Dingo?"

"*Ndiyo*, Bwana!"

Frank slammed the door of the Jeep and leaned out the window as Dingo started the bus. "You folks have a nice safari, now."

Braxton took a step toward the Cherokee. "I mean it, Gunther. Your days as a guide are numbered. Eddie didn't mention that I work for a paper in the States that has already done an exposé on you and several other guides. By the time I get finished with you this time, you'll never take out a safari again."

The smile left Gunther's face and he leaned farther out the window. "So you were the one who wrote that shit! I'll be damned. I knew there was something I didn't like about you, Hicks. Now I've got another reason to hate your ass. Let me tell you something. Next time we see each other, you better forget the threats and head the other way, because you ever touch me again, mister, and I'll kill you. I don't give a shit who you think you are or who you work for."

Not waiting for a reply, Frank Gunther shifted the Jeep into gear. Then, with a skidding of tires, the hunter drove away, followed by Dingo in the bus. And Braxton, Eddie, Injai and the two women caring for Sammy were left to stare in silence after the departing vehicles, which became smaller and smaller until finally disappearing over the distant horizon.

Nine

"HOW IS HE?" Eddie asked, watching intently while Kathy examined Sammy's skull.

"Hurt, but I don't think it's critical," she said, continuing to press her hand against the unconscious man's head wound. "This gash looks worse than it really is. I was able to stop the bleeding by applying pressure. We'll know for sure when he comes to."

"So what do you think, Ed?" Braxton knelt down beside the others. "Think we're off to a good start?"

Eddie shook his head tiredly, but it was Zelda who answered.

"Well, I for one am just as glad Gunther's gone," the hypnotist stated with a huff. "I don't think I've ever encountered such a disgusting human being. We're better off without him."

Eddie nodded. "I agree about Gunther, but I don't know about being better off, Zelda." He glanced out over the savannah, where the huge orange ball of the sun was slowly sinking behind the horizon. "What do we do now? Think he was telling the truth about the lodge, Braxton?"

"I hope so," the correspondent replied with concern, "because I know he wasn't lying about the animals starting to prowl during the hours before dusk. We've got to do something, and before long, too."

"I could try to reach this lodge before dark, Father," Injai said, coming to stand behind the priest. "There must be those there who could help."

"Thank you," Eddie said, looking up at Injai gratefully from where he knelt, "but you don't even know the way for certain. We must wait and see if this man regains consciousness."

Suddenly Zelda gasped in alarm. Frowning, Braxton turned to see a towering giant standing directly behind them.

Braxton knew from his appearance that the native was a Masai. Still, he was the tallest man Braxton had ever seen, although the towering giraffe that stood a few feet behind the man dwarfed even the giant in comparison.

A dust-stained red ocher robe covered the man's midsection and was draped over one shoulder. Thick strands of beaded jewelry hung from elongated earlobes and wound around the man's neck, and on his head gleamed many tight braids of hair now soaked with sweat. In his left hand he held a large painted shield that was almost half the length of his body and was shaped in a narrow oval, and in his right hand was a long, wicked-looking, ornately decorated spear. A tiny bell dangled from the Masai's pierced left earlobe, and it jingled as the man took a step toward them.

"I believe Twamba has decided to pay us a return visit," Braxton whispered hurriedly, smiling up at the sober-faced warrior. "You don't think he believes we were the ones who shot at him, do you?"

"Let's hope not," Eddie replied softly. He too was smiling as he came slowly to his feet. "*Jambo*, Twamba."

Now that he had adjusted to the tall man's presence, Braxton could see that Twamba was much older than his lean, muscled body made him appear. It showed around his eyes and in the lines that creased the leathery skin of his face. This was no young warrior fresh from his initiation rite of single-handedly killing his first lion. The Masai staring at them was a man of experience and knowledge.

Ignoring Eddie's greeting, the warrior moved past the priest and Braxton and stared down at the injured driver. Muttering an unintelligible command and motioning for the women to step back, Twamba placed his weapons on the ground and knelt beside Sammy.

With a delicate touch, the Masai moved his hands over the driver's head, examining the wound and the area around it. He glanced up at Kathy and nodded at her with a grunt of approval. Then he moved his hands to the back of the driver's neck near the top of the spine. Slowly he massaged the area, applying a gentle pressure to specific places with his thumbs, and after a moment, with a groan of pain, Sammy opened his eyes.

"Usismame," Twamba uttered softly in Swahili as the driver's eyes darted around wildly and his body jerked in fright. "Do not move."

Then Sammy saw for the first time who it was that knelt next to him. The fright left his eyes and a weak smile formed on his lips.

"Twamba," he muttered in a choked whisper of relief.

The Masai lifted his head to speak to Kathy, and the tiny bell hanging from his earlobe tinkled lightly. *"Maji."*

"He wants some water," Braxton interpreted, crossing to where the luggage had been dropped and bringing back a thermos while the Masai moved his hands over the young driver's chest, neck and shoulders.

"Wapi panauma?" Twamba said, and when he spoke Braxton could see the wide spaces in his bottom gum where the lower incisors had been pulled, as was done to all Masai children.

"He's asking where it hurts," Braxton translated for the women, handing Twamba a thermos cup filled with water.

Sammy was fully conscious now, and with an agonizing effort he pulled himself up on one elbow and looked at those around him. "The answer is everywhere." He winced in pain, bringing his hand to his head wound. "Where is Gunther?"

"Gone," Eddie responded, kneeling next to Twamba.

Sammy frowned in surprise. "He left you?"

"Certainly looks that way," Braxton said, pointing over to the piles of luggage.

"I am sorry," Sammy said. "It is my fault." The driver attempted to stand up but, wincing in pain, found he could only make it to a sitting position.

"Nonsense," said Zelda. "One of us probably would have tried to stop him if you hadn't. It was a courageous thing you did."

"Is the pain bad?" Kathy asked.

"I have felt better," Sammy told her.

Twamba had removed a pouch from his belt while they were talking, and after loosening the string tie, he tapped a powdery substance into the water cup Braxton had given him. He stirred the contents with his long, slender index finger, then offered the cup to Sammy, touching his finger to his own mouth.

Sammy accepted the potion, grimacing at the minute brown fragments that floated in a circular motion on the top of what was now gray water. Twamba nodded and tapped his mouth again, and the driver reluctantly brought the cup to his lips, pouring the liquid down his throat, not stopping until the container was empty.

With a smile, he handed the cup back to the Masai. *"Asante sana."*

"Vizuri," Twamba answered. The Masai tucked his pouch back into his belt, handed the cup to Braxton, and, retrieving his weapons, rose to his feet.

Once again the young driver attempted to stand, but Eddie shook his head. "Relax. You're in no shape to move yet."

"No, we cannot stay here," Sammy insisted, as Braxton and Eddie reluctantly helped him get up. "It will be dark soon."

"Gunther said there was a lodge near here," said Braxton. "Is that true?"

Sammy nodded. "Yes. It is not far. I will take you there. From it, I will call for help. Do you wish to continue with the safari?"

It was Zelda who answered, after exchanging a look with the others. "Well, yes...I suppose. Of course, we'll have to return to Nairobi and make some new arrangements. Do you think we can take the business about Gunther to the authorities?"

"It would do you little good," Sammy told her. "Gunther pays much to important people in the authorities so that he will be left alone." Sammy paused a moment, then seemed to reach a decision. He shook his head firmly and straightened his shoulders, stepping from the men's grasp to stand unaided. "It was my fault this happened. You should not have to return to Nairobi. I will take you where you wish to go. I know of a bus, and I have relatives who will assist me.''

"No, Sammy," Eddie objected. "Don't be ridiculous. That isn't necessary. Believe me. You heard Zelda. This is no one's fault.''

"Is it that you do not wish to have me guide you? That you do not have faith in my abilities?''

"Well, of course not," Eddie began. "It isn't that. But you're injured, and..."

Sammy shook his head to cut Eddie off, then placed his hand over the wound and displayed his open palm. "No. It is not serious. You see. The bleeding has now completely stopped. I have had many worse wounds. I will be well very soon. Already I am feeling better.''

Several sharp commands filled the air, and Sammy gestured at Twamba, who stood next to his towering giraffe, waving with his spear for them to follow him. Shrugging off his pain as best he could, Sammy crossed to the mounds of luggage and picked up a bag, motioning for the others to follow.

"Twamba says we must go. He will be certain we reach the lodge safely. Come. It is feeding time for the animals and dangerous to be unprotected on the open savannah.''

"All right, but give me that," Eddie said, hurrying over and relieving the driver of the bag he held. "You shouldn't be carrying anything yet. I don't care how much better you're feeling." The priest handed the bag to Injai, who took it along with two others on the ground near where he stood.

Weaving slightly, Sammy nodded with a weak smile as the others began gathering up the remaining luggage. "You are right. But the strength will return soon. I know. Twamba's medicine has great power." The young driver looked from Eddie to Zelda, then to Braxton, who stood next to Kathy. "And we are agreed?"

"Well, all right," Zelda said. "I have no objection if the others don't to having you take us under your wing—as long as you think you're up to it. It would save us a lot of time and effort. Eddie?"

The priest shrugged. "Fine. Injai here could even drive for us if you'd like. He's excellent behind the wheel."

"Then we are agreed," said Sammy. "It is my duty for the distress I have caused you. But more than that, it would be my honor. I must be open and speak with truth to you. I listened with personal interest to what was said at your meeting last evening, and I heard when Gunther spoke to Dog Bassett about your goal of finding the ancient grave. What you seek is of great fascination to me. If there is such a place, it would be the black man's first people also, would it not?"

Eddie nodded in agreement. "Absolutely."

"Good," Sammy said. "I would very much like to be a part of such a discovery. So, it is settled. When we reach the lodge, I will call for new supplies and a vehicle, and then I will help to guide you to the place of mystery you seek."

GUNTHER WATCHED THE BUS behind him swerve violently as Dingo tried to keep the vehicle under control. The hunter swore loudly. "The stupid bastard's going to roll the bus if he doesn't watch it. I knew he couldn't drive. Goddamn that Sammy. Cocky little asshole, but he knew how to handle anything on wheels."

"So, what now, Frank?" Dog said evenly. "You going after the Masai?"

"Fat chance. Twamba is long gone by now, Dog. Count on it."

Dog shrugged. "So it's cool off and then circle back and pick up the clients?"

"No, Dog, I don't think so," Gunther said, a slyness creeping into his expression. "The fact is, I think my driver may have done us a big favor with his little rebellion. Gave us an opportunity to drop back fifteen and survey the situation."

"Meaning?"

"Well, let's think for a minute. What's going to happen with them? First of all, I know I didn't kill Sammy. He was still breathing, so he'll come around. And I told them about the lodge, so they'll get there without too much trouble. Now, what do you think they'll do? Quit? Go home?" Frank shook his head in answer to his own question. "Not a chance. They'll either keep going by themselves or find someone else to guide them. My guess is Sammy might even do it. If I didn't knock his brains out, that is. The bastard always wanted my job anyway, claiming it should be a black man who showed people his country and all that shit."

"What's the point, Frank?"

"The point is, Dog, that if these people really can find the grave of the first woman, we've suddenly found ourselves in a wonderful position. We're no longer leading but following. And with very little effort on our part we could just keep right on following until the time was right, and then it would be like taking candy from a baby. Very profitable candy, I might add. Now I don't know about you, but I've reached the point where I could use some substantial cash. And it appears fate has just tossed a rare opportunity in my lap, which I'd be a fool not to take advantage of. So my proposal is this: If there turns out to be a grave, we go partners right down the middle."

"How would you go about making sure we end up with what's in it?"

"You leave that to me. But understand, once we start, it's total commitment. I make sure we end up with what's in the grave, and you make sure we get rid of it for a huge profit—although I may need your help to acquire the prize. Deal?"

Dog's expressionless face studied Frank for several seconds. "Would you really have asked me to shoot one of those people, Frank?"

"If I had, would you have done it?" Frank asked in reply.

The man next to him grunted. "Hard to say until it actually happens. Okay, Frank, let's follow them and see what turns up—providing you'll still get me my rhino."

"Dog," Frank said with a grin, "I'm going to find you a rhino with the biggest goddamn horn in Kenya."

"Then we've got a deal, Frank." Dog hit the container between them with his hand. "You got anymore elephant piss in here?"

"Sure do," Frank answered with a loud laugh. He flipped the top off the container and extracted two Tusker beers. After snapping the caps off them, he handed one to the man beside him and lifted the other in a toast: "Dog, my man, here's to the beginning of a wonderful and lucrative partnership."

Ten

IT HAD TAKEN A NIGHT and most of the next morning after they reached the small Amboseli lodge, but finally the response to Sammy's phone calls arrived in the form of a rusted-out touring bus that came lumbering into the lodge's parking area. An uncle of Sammy's named Chegee had brought the vehicle to them, and the old gray-haired member of the Kikuyu tribe also agreed to help his nephew and serve as the trip's cook.

As he had predicted, Sammy seemed to recover with miraculous speed from his injuries, and Kathy said she would love to know what the Masai had given the driver. In fact, the group could not have been happier with Sammy. The young black, with his concern for their welfare and open sincerity, was like a saint, compared to Frank Gunther.

Twamba had not accompanied them to the lodge. He had stayed right with them even after they found the road Gunther had mentioned, leading the way with his ever-present giraffe and watching alertly over them. But once the lodge came into view, the tall Masai warrior exchanged words with Sammy for several minutes, then raised his spear and, with a wave, disappeared from view.

Though the accommodations had proved to be expensive, the members of the group enjoyed their night's stay at the lodge. The food was excellent, and they spent the time chatting, playing cards and simply relaxing. Consequently, when the bus pulled out the following morning, with Injai grinning from ear to ear in the driver's seat, everyone was feeling good-humored, the incident with Frank Gunther now nothing more than an unpleasant memory.

As they settled in for the ride, Chegee positioned himself behind Injai. Eddie and Zelda were seated right at the front, close to Sammy, who stood in the well of the doorway. And back toward the middle of the bus, as had been the case for most of the previous two days, Braxton sat next to Kathy, the two of them watching the scenery roll by, talking and laughing softly together.

The bus hadn't been on the road long when Eddie came strolling down the aisle, followed by Zelda and Sammy.

"Sammy has some questions," Eddie said, dropping into the seat in front of Braxton and Kathy. "I thought this was a good time for us to talk. Perhaps you'd like to start off by asking Zelda about the hypnosis, Sammy."

The young man nodded. "While attending school in America, I learned many things. I know about the practice of hypnosis. It is used to help people remember things. Is that not correct?"

"That's one of the uses," Zelda answered pleasantly, sitting down next to Eddie. "Recently it's been discovered that hypnosis can also be used to take people back into events that have occurred in the past. We've always known that certain traits like hair color or general body build are inherited. Now scientists are discovering that much more than we ever imagined is also inherited. Through hypnosis, we're learning what some of these things are."

"And that is how you gained the information Gunther spoke of?"

"Yes, we stumbled onto it by accident. I was regressing Kathy, taking her further and further into the past through hypnosis, when the information about the first humans suddenly started surfacing. Naturally we continued to explore it. And once we discovered that Kathy could give us facts through drawings, the information came pouring out of her."

Sammy's eyes suddenly lit up in understanding. "Drawing! That is what you were doing the first night at the Westwood campsite."

"Exactly," said Zelda. "Once Kathy is regressed, the communication comes to us through automatic drawings."

"And it is with these drawings you hope to make the archaeological find?"

"Yes," Eddie put in. "Along with Kathy's help. Although no English is spoken during regression, after the sessions Kathy has an uncanny ability to understand what has taken place, and so far she's been able to help interpret not only the drawings but also the wants and desires of the personality that emerges during hypnosis."

Sammy suddenly frowned. "I do not understand. Are you saying it is someone else who is communicating to you during the hypnosis?"

"Well, here's where things get a little sticky, Sammy," Braxton said, with his easy smile. "I'm still having trouble with that one myself. Better skip over that area for the time being until you've seen a session."

Sammy looked at the people seated before him and nodded, his expression sincere and serious. "Twamba, the one who returned to help me, is a great wise man and understands many things that others do not see. Things that are of the spirit world. I too have always wanted to understand such things but have been blind to them. I know many would not believe what you have told me. But I also know that the way to become truly wise is to keep the mind open to all possibilities. I am trying to learn to do this. And I would very much like to see the hypnosis you speak of practiced."

"Don't worry, Sammy, you will," Kathy said. "So far we only have a general idea of the location we're seeking. We'll have to have more sessions as we go in order to be positive."

"In fact, we'll need to have a session tonight," Zelda added. "You're welcome to join us."

"I will look forward to it," Sammy answered. Then with a pleasant nod he turned and moved back up the aisle to the front of the bus.

By noon, even with the windows open, the heat inside the small bus was becoming oppressive, and Sammy signaled to Injai that it was time to pull over. The driver swung the vehicle alongside a wooded area and cut the motor. Sammy pulled the doors open and turned to speak to the people behind him, who were standing and stretching their travel-weary muscles.

"We stop here for the day and set up camp. Movement in the midday heat is not wise." While Sammy spoke, Injai and Chegee climbed out of the bus and began unlashing the overhead equipment. "Assemble the tents by the shaded areas near the trees in a semicircle facing the open," Sammy instructed. "Chegee will build a fire in a central place in front of them. This will prevent any curious animals from wandering into camp during the night."

Zelda looked up from stuffing her camera back into her travel bag. "You don't mean they actually come into camp, do you?"

"It is not unusual for that to happen. Remember, this is their home, not ours. Chegee and Injai will hand the equipment down to you. As soon as we are set up, we will have a light lunch."

"We're with you, Sammy," Eddie said, edging by the guide to the bus doorway. "Come on, ladies, let's set up the camp. That is, if you're not too tired."

"We're right behind you, Ed," Zelda answered, following quickly after the priest. "Let's not forget who had their tents down and packed that first morning, please."

"Watch your step, Father!" Injai shouted from above as Eddie emerged through the doorway.

Eddie glanced down just in time to avoid dropping his foot into what appeared to be several softball-size brownish mounds. "Ahh, close one. Thanks for the warning, Injai."

Braxton stuck his head out a side window near the front of the bus. "There's a picture for you, Zelda. Some animal droppings, huh?"

"Very impressive," Zelda agreed as she stepped carefully down from the bus, withdrawing her camera from the bag on her shoulder.

"Zelda," Kathy said, following her, "you're not really going to take a picture of that."

"Absolutely. These are the kinds of things you don't hear about. People won't believe it. Look at the size." With an amused glance at the young woman next to her, Zelda brought the camera to her eye, the mechanism whirred, and a square frame slid out of the compartment. In spite of themselves, the others gathered around to watch the picture develop.

"Not bad," Zelda said, pursing her lips in approval as the images materialized.

"Crisp and clear," Braxton agreed.

Zelda smiled smugly at him. "You didn't think I'd do it, did you?"

"Of course I did, Zelda. I hope you'll make copies for all of us. I don't think I have a picture like that from any of the other safaris I've been on."

"My pleasure. What is the animal, do you suppose?"

Braxton studied the ground for a moment. "Oh, that I can tell you. Lion, no question. Can you imagine the size of it? Must have been a male."

Injai's laughter sounded above them. He said something in Swahili, ending with the word *simba*, and Chegee cackled loudly in amusement as they carried equipment from the bus.

"Braxton jokes with you, Zelda," Sammy said, handing down a tent roll from the overhead rack to Eddie. "It is elephant dung. They must have passed through here early this morning from the looks of it. There's probably more, so keep your eyes open."

"Damn right," Braxton said. He took the tent bundle from Eddie and handed it to Kathy. "Here you are. I know you ladies will want to start immediately." Kathy smiled as she accepted the tent from him. "If you thought New York was bad, Zelda, wait till you've been here a while. You're right. This is the part of safari life they don't tell you about. The big evening campfire activity is scraping out the ridges on the soles of your shoes."

"Say, Sammy," Eddie said, taking another tent roll. "I do have a serious question for you about a somewhat pressing matter."

"I think I have the same question," Zelda added. "And I'll need an answer before we set this tent up. *Kipo wapi choo.* Is that right?"

"Perfect," Braxton told her. "You've been doing your homework with your Bartlett's pocket traveler, eh, Zelda? I'm afraid you're in for a disappointment, though. See the tall grass over there beyond what will be our campsite. I'd say that's the best choice."

"If we're talking about the bathroom," Kathy said, setting down her bundle, "I could use one too."

"Actually, we're talking about no bathroom, Kathy," Braxton informed her.

Sammy climbed down from the roof rack and pointed off to the left. "Braxton is correct. Use that spot far into the weeds there. Injai will pull the bus across the area to block the view. And the women should go together each time, just in case..."

"In case what?" Zelda asked, her eyebrows raised.

Now that the equipment was unloaded, Injai started the bus, backed it up a few feet, then pulled it in front of the area Sammy had indicated.

Eddie pointed toward the ground and spoke with mock seriousness. "In case whatever left this is still out there, I suppose, Zelda. And don't take too long if you want to stay in first place on tent assembly."

"I won't stay too long in those weeds, believe me, Ed," Zelda answered. She rummaged through her handbag a moment and retrieved a roll of white toilet paper. "Come on, Kathy."

Kathy looked at the paper roll. "We just leave it out there?"

"Unless you want to bring it back with you." Braxton grinned. "But watch out for snakes," he added as the two women turned to go. "Better check before you squat."

"Who invited this man to join us?" Zelda called over her shoulder.

Braxton laughed as he pulled the tie string on a tent, rolling it out in front of him. "Give me a hand here, Ed. We'll help you erect yours first."

The priest shook his head. "In a minute. I wasn't kidding. I'll go over here in the woods since the ladies are gone." He paused and grinned. "Are there really snakes, do you think?"

"Would I lie to you?" Braxton slipped the two sections of the center tent pole together as the priest hurried away.

Eddie disappeared into the woods and Braxton jokingly started to shout something after him, when suddenly, from beyond the bus, a woman's scream was heard.

"That's Zelda's voice!" Braxton shouted. He had already allowed the canvas he was holding to slump limply to the ground and now started running toward the screams.

The heavyset hypnotist came puffing around the back of the bus, one hand desperately clasping her billowy trousers together at the waist while the other swatted frantically at her thighs.

"Get them off me!" she pleaded, colliding with Sammy. "Oh, God, get them off me!"

"What?" the guide asked, standing awkwardly next to her, unsure how to help her.

Then Braxton arrived, grabbing her shoulders protectively as he spoke.

"What is it, Zelda? What's wrong?"

"Bugs!" Zelda screeched, cringing in his arms. "They're crawling inside my slacks...on my legs." She continued to beat at the outside of her pants while Kathy raced up to them from behind the bus.

"I think it's ticks," Kathy said, thrusting the roll of tissue into Sammy's grasp. "Look. She put this down for a minute. Isn't that one on the side?"

Injai, who along with Chegee had joined them, leaned forward to look over Sammy's shoulder.

"Oh, yes," he said with loud enthusiasm. "Teeks for sure. That is teek. Always bad this season of year. Hot and damp. Multiply very fast."

"Ticks!" Zelda yelled. "Ticks! Oh my God! Ticks in my pants!"

Sammy flicked the tiny hard-shelled insect away from the toilet paper with his index finger. "No, you have knocked them away by running. See, they brush right off. You are fine now, I'm sure, Zelda."

Eddie, who had dashed out of the woods, came panting up to the group. "What is it? What's happened?"

"Zelda has ticks in her pants," Braxton answered matter-of-factly.

The hypnotist pulled away from him angrily. "I'm warning you, Braxton. No jokes. I'm in no mood." She shuddered. "I'm sorry I panicked, Sammy, but...ticks. Oh, I hate those disgusting bloodsucking things. I think I would have preferred snakes."

"I understand," the guide said sympathetically. "But they are more of an irritant than a danger. You simply must be sure to check for them frequently. Otherwise one might become embedded in the skin, which could be serious. I'm afraid they are just a part of tent camping."

Zelda straightened and cleared her throat. "I see. Another cute item no one tells you about. All right. It took me by surprise, that's all. I'll deal with it."

"Sure you will," Kathy said. "I'm not very crazy about them myself." She pointed toward the one tent already assembled by Chegee and Injai. "May we use that tent a moment?"

"Of course," Sammy agreed.

Kathy took the older woman's hand. "This way, Zelda. Let's check. Make sure there aren't any more. We'll both feel better."

"Fine." Zelda hitched up her slacks with both hands. "I could use a place to fix my pants anyway. I can't believe this."

"Want us to do your tent?" Braxton called after them.

"Don't you dare touch my tent," Zelda ordered, stopping. "Either of you. I'll put up my own damned tent!"

"All right... all right," Braxton said, exchanging a grin with Eddie as he raised his hands defensively. "Only trying to help."

"You may change now too if you wish," Sammy added. "It is too hot for a game run, so we will be going for a swim after lunch."

"Looks like it's not my day," the plump hypnotist muttered to Kathy, her composure slipping a little more. "If there's anything I can think of that I hate more than bugs, it's being seen in a bathing suit."

Eleven

IT WAS A SPRING-FED POOL that Sammy took them to after the noon meal, and the setting was serenely picturesque, making the heat less noticeable. A scene out of Eden, thought Braxton; however, under the circumstances he decided not to mention the comparison as he stood on the edge of the sparkling pond.

The moss-rimmed, rocky border merged into sections of thick, short grass, a rich, deep green patchwork crisscrossed by thin, spiraling streams of water that overflowed from the pool. The lush green contrasted sharply with the brownish blanket of savannah grass beyond. Small Thompson's gazelles flicked their stubby brown and white tails to and fro as they nibbled at the more tender tufts of foliage, all the while keeping a safe distance from the gathering of people near the natural pool.

"The temperature is cooled by a spring that flows in from beneath the layers of rock," Sammy informed them. "You'll find the water very refreshing. It is also the last chance to bathe for several days, so take advantage of it." He pointed to the small, shallow puddles of clear water that formed along the network of streams. "Dirty laundry can be washed there. I am going to a nearby lodge to check reports on animal locations so that we may take a game run later this afternoon." Sammy climbed through the bus doorway to join Chegee, then turned for a final word to the group. "We won't be long. Swim and enjoy yourselves."

Eddie waved as the bus pulled away, then started to unbutton his shirt. "Well, a swim sounds like a great idea. I, for one, have had it with the heat. I can't wait to get in that water. Who's with me? Injai?"

"Perhaps later, Father," Inajai said, hoisting a cloth bundle he had brought off the bus. "Sammy gave me a job to do—wash laundry. You go ahead."

"I intend to do just that," Eddie said, dropping his pants so that he stood poised near the water's edge in floral bathing trunks.

"Okay, Ed!" Braxton shouted with a whistle. "If the mission people could only see you now."

"You said I needed to get away and relax, Braxton. And that's exactly what I'm attempting to do." With a smile to the others, who were removing their own clothes, the priest bent his pale knobby knees once, tilted sideways, and flipped his skinny frame into the pool, knifing his way through the sparkling water. It was a smooth dive with barely a splash, and seconds later Eddie's head cleared the surface and a whoop of pleasure pierced the still air.

"Fantastic!" the priest shouted. "Absolutely terrific. What's keeping you?"

"Is it cold?" Kathy asked. She was wearing a pale green one-piece suit, and Braxton couldn't help noticing how magnificently it showed off her trim figure. After folding her clothes in a neat pile, she bent down to test the water, dipping her hand over the edge.

Braxton tossed his pants in the air. "I hope so," he shouted, and tightening the drawstring on his suit, he ran to the edge and leaped high into the air, landing legs bent, butt first with a shattering splash near the pond's center. Kathy shrieked, dodging the sprays that threatened to douse her, and Eddie trod backward in rapid retreat while Braxton resurfaced, shaking the water from his eyes.

"I knew it," Eddie roared. "No class. What kind of a dive was that?"

"Eddie, my friend," Braxton said with a grin of satisfaction, "I can't tell you how good it makes me feel to see you take that dive and be paddling around out here with me like a couple of kids. Come on, admit it. It feels good to let go and not give a damn once in a while, doesn't it?"

"Not bad," Eddie said with a laugh, kicking up a spray of water into Braxton's face that made him gasp in alarm. "Not bad at all."

Braxton wiped the water from his face with a sputtering laugh, then turned back toward shore. "Come on, Kathy. It's great."

Holding the mossy edge, Kathy eased herself over the rocks with a squeal of shock at the coolness of the water, then swam gracefully toward the center. "Oh, it is nice."

Eddie suddenly frowned. "Wait a minute. What's this?" He was looking at Zelda, who stood by the pond watching them, still fully clothed in her kimono. "Get your clothes off, Zelda."

"Whoa... wait a minute, Ed!" Braxton bellowed, swimming toward Kathy. "Let's not get carried away with this loosening-up thing."

"She knows what I mean," Eddie went on, ignoring Braxton's gibe. "Well, aren't you coming in?"

"No, I don't feel like swimming right now." Zelda sat down and dangled her feet in the water. Still frowning,

Eddie dog-paddled his way over to her. "This is fine for me right here," she insisted.

Grabbing a jutting rock slab, the priest hoisted himself onto the ledge beside her. "Now, Zelda, that is ridiculous and you know it."

"What is?" She moved away slightly in annoyance. "You're dripping on me, you know."

"Good. Maybe it will get you in the water."

"Ed, I don't feel like swimming."

"I don't believe it," Eddie said, coming to his feet. He reached down and took Zelda's hand. "Stand up a minute."

"Would you please stop being ridiculous." The hypnotist resisted momentarily, but Eddie persisted, so she struggled to her feet. As soon as she was up she pulled away from his grasp and brought her hands to her hips. "There, are you satisfied?"

"No, not quite." Eddie stepped back from her and placed his own hands on his hips, mirroring her posture. "I want you to look at my body."

"What! Eddie, what is the matter with you?"

"Nothing—and that's precisely my point," he said, holding his chin high, oblivious to the water dripping from his short, skinny frame. "First of all, I'm a priest standing here in front of other people practically naked. Not the easiest thing in the world for me to do, I assure you. Secondly, this is not the most virile body in the world, but just because I don't have a perfect shape doesn't mean I'm not going to enjoy myself. And it shouldn't mean that to you, either. It's damned hot, Zelda, and that water feels terrific. Now, are you going to go swimming with the rest of us or not?"

Zelda stared at the shorter man beside her, then, shaking her head, she began to undo her kimono. "Oh, for heaven's sake. If you're going to make such a big deal out of it . . ."

"I am," Eddie beamed, extending his hand to her. With forced casualness Zelda allowed the shapeless cloth to drop from her plump form and was left standing there awkwardly in a large one-piece bathing suit. Never taking his eyes from her face, Eddie grasped her hand and pulled her gently to the rock's edge. "Shall we make a double jump?"

"I'll follow you," Zelda responded with a determined smile, hands on her hips. "Lead the way, Father."

Eddie threw his head back in laughter, and Zelda, no longer able to resist, joined in his merriment. Giggling in carefree abandon, the two of them plunged into the water, while Braxton and Kathy cheered and applauded enthusiastically.

They swam in the cool water until both body and spirit felt refreshed, then the four climbed from the pool and spread out along the grassy edge to soak in the sun's soothing rays. As the afternoon wore on, they laughed and talked quietly about those insignificant things that are so much fun to kick around when relaxation is the main order of business. No one brought up hypnosis or regression, or the real reason they were out in the middle of the savannah. There was among them an unspoken need to enjoy the peace in which they found themselves for just a little longer before coming to grips with any kind of reality. For a while, at least, it was almost as if everything were right with the world.

Injai was the one who broke the spell. He had finished his laundry duties, and the damp garments and linens were spread neatly across the rocks to dry in the sun. When he called to them, he was only doing the job he loved—spotting game. Looking up they saw a large gathering of baboons making its way forward far out across the savannah. The sight was too much for Eddie, and he jumped to his feet, his period of relaxation at an end.

"What is it, Injai?" he called, stepping into his trousers. "Baboons?"

"Yes, Father," Injai answered, strolling over to the four of them. "Many in this troop. See the big one in front. He is leading them to a new home."

"Let's have a closer look," the priest said, buttoning his trousers. "Who's with me? Zelda?"

"Why not," the hypnotist answered gamely, as Eddie extended his hand and helped her to her feet. She had put her kimono back on immediately after climbing out of the water, and now she brushed the grass off the back where she had been sitting and grabbed her camera bag.

Eddie looked down at Braxton and Kathy, who, still in their bathing suits, were lying face to the sun in the grass nearby. "How about you two?"

Kathy shook her head, not even opening her eyes. "Not me. This is wonderful. I'll stay with the sun."

"Say *jambo* to them for me too," Braxton said with a wave.

"I had better accompany you, Father," Injai said. "We will approach quietly. Try to get close for pictures. But if the big one turns, do as I say. Baboons can be vicious, and if he turns, the troop will also."

"Give a holler if any cheetahs come loping by, Injai," Braxton added.

The older man grinned. "Oh, I yell to you fast for sure, Buddy, do not worry."

Eddie motioned forward enthusiastically. "Well, let's go. Lead on, Injai."

"Don't get burned, you two," Zelda warned with a smile, slipping her camera strap over her neck as she started off after Injai.

Braxton yawned lazily and sat up, shading his eyes with his hand as he watched the trio moving cautiously toward the migrating simians. "I can't get over the change in Ed. See how happy and enthusiastic he is. I knew it would be good for him to just get away for a while."

"I can't believe he got Zelda to go swimming," Kathy said, her eyes still closed. "She swore to me there was no way she was going to be seen in a bathing suit."

"Well, he may be relaxed, but once a priest, always a priest," Braxton responded. "It's a part of his nature. Eddie just can't help helping people to help themselves."

"I know. He's a wonderful person. I wish I'd gotten better acquainted with him when we were younger. He would have been a wonderful friend. He's the main reason I'm still semi-sane after this whole hypnosis thing."

Braxton nodded, still watching their friends approach the moving baboons. "Eddie Fitzsimmons is the most selfless person I've ever known, Kathy. He's what more priests should be and aren't. In fact, he carries it to the extreme and doesn't take care of himself to the point where it's hurt his health. That's why I worry about him. It's in literature somewhere."

"What is?"

"That the truly good can't survive in the midst of a wicked world. They merely help, setting an example for the rest of us, and then are taken. This whole grave thing may have thrown him into what he considers to be his own mental crisis, but I think in the end it's going to be beneficial. This is the first time I've ever known him to do something for himself. It's got to be good for him."

As he spoke, Braxton leaned back on one elbow, his head resting against his hand. He looked down at Kathy without speaking for several moments. He hadn't meant to stare, but he found he couldn't help himself. The woman lying next to him had him hooked, and there wasn't a damned thing he could do about it.

For years he had consciously avoided letting himself get too involved with a woman, determined not to become committed to someone until he had finally come to grips with his own unknown past. And that, of course, had yet to happen. The fact that he was still roaming around in a foreign country like some adventure-hungry kid who refused to grow up, attested to that.

He stared back out toward the horizon in an attempt to concentrate on the baboons, but it didn't work. It wasn't passing simians that filled his thoughts but the way Kathy Sullivan looked as she lay there beside him, her legs pulled up so that her feet toed flatly at the grass, her arms folded casually across her waist, her skin now rosy from exposure to the sun. Unable to stop himself, he glanced back down at her. Her eyes were open, gazing up at him.

"You stopped talking," she said quietly. "Concern about Eddie?"

Braxton smiled whimsically. "The truth is I was thinking about how good you look in that bathing suit, Kathy Sullivan. Which immediately pushed all thoughts of my friend Eddie into the background, I might add."

"I know," Kathy said, propping herself up on an elbow as she turned to face him. "It was a far-from-priestly look that I saw in your eyes."

Braxton sat up, wrapping his arms around his knees. When he spoke, the playfulness in his voice had been replaced by a heartfelt sincerity.

"Kathy, I came on this trip as a favor to my friend. To help him if I could. Not to—"

"Can I tell you something?" Kathy said, interrupting him as she brought herself up to her knees and leaned back on her heels.

Braxton gave her a smile. "Is it that you think I look good in a bathing suit too?"

Kathy chuckled softly, and then her expression became quietly serious. "Yes, I guess partly. But it's more than that. I felt it that first night after the session when I glanced over at you. You felt it too, didn't you? And it's more than just your figure being included in the drawing. Something happened between us during the hypnosis. There was a recognition of some kind."

Braxton held her eyes and took her hand in his. "Kathy, I am desperately attempting to sort out what's real and not real in this whole business, and I'm not having a lot of luck. The only thing I know for sure is that I am drawn to you. Even though I'm trying to stay objective, and in spite of the fact that I've known you for less than a week, I love to talk to you, and I've already revealed some of the deep dark secrets of my past to you. And when I looked down at you just now lying there in the grass, my insides turned into Jell-O instant pudding."

Kathy smiled and leaned over, giving Braxton a soft kiss. She lingered for the briefest instant, then broke away as desire threatened to surface. "What a romantic way you have of putting things."

"Well, I'm a writer, you know. It comes naturally. But I mean it about talking to you. I want to learn more about you. About the only thing I really know is that you're a nurse."

"Okay. Fire away. What would you like to know?"

Braxton shrugged. "I guess I'm still not sure I understand completely what a girl like you is doing in a place like this."

It was Kathy's turn to look away, and she stared across the savannah to where the tiny figures of Eddie and Zelda could be seen following Injai toward the baboons. She appeared to consider Braxton's question for a moment, then answered in a voice no louder than a whisper.

"I'm searching," she said quietly, her voice catching. "That's the only way I can explain it. To you and to myself. There's nothing extraordinary about my life so far. I guess I've just sort of let events carry me. The nursing thing seemed like a natural thing to do. But nothing's ever been that important to me or really taken hold of me in life—unless it was trying to look after my father. But even that has always been on a superficial level. There has never been a way to reach him; to break the shell he built around himself. I tried so hard for so many years without success that I guess I've given up. I've come to accept the fact that I'm not the woman he loves. I . . . I'm the one who is responsible for him losing the one he loved."

"Kathy, I didn't mean to bring up . . ."

"No," Kathy said, inhaling deeply and shaking her head as if to sweep the emotion from her. "I denied the truth for too many years. Now I simply live with it—

although I can see that the reality of the distance be-tween my father and myself has forced me to finally stop floating and grab for something.''

She swept her hand dramatically before her. "And this is it, Braxton. This trip. I guess that's really the an-swer to your question. The truth is that if I can't reach my father, then I have to try to go in the other direc-tion...and somehow find out more about the woman I never knew. I thought that maybe through hypnosis I could, I don't know, go back to the birth and try to make some kind of connection. Don't you see? I don't have any choice. I have to connect with *someone*.''

She had been determined that she would not let the private agony that surged beneath her words surface. Though she allowed the release of tears to come in pri-vate, she had resolved to remain composed with oth-ers, especially with this man whom she had known for such a short time.

But she couldn't. As she spoke, she met Braxton's eyes, and the dam simply broke. Suddenly she was sob-bing. Crying her eyes out like a stupid idiot. And he was holding her, and she no longer cared that she was crying.

"I'm messed up, Braxton Hicks," she said, once the outburst of tears had subsided to gentle sobs. "I mean I'm really messed up. And I'm scared about what's happening inside me. About what happens when Zelda takes me back in time. I try to be brave, but the truth is I don't know what the hell I'm doing here, and I'm really frightened about everything that's happening.''

"I'd say that's pretty understandable," Braxton re-sponded softly as she wiped with embarrassment at her eyes. "And as I told Eddie, I'm here to help in any way I can. I mean that, Kathy." He took her hand in his. "If you need to talk, I'm here. I'm not a priest. And I'm not Zelda, who's guiding you through all this. I'm just an innocent bystander who's willing to listen. Sometimes that's the best thing there is, you know."

The sound of a motor approaching in the distance caught their attention, and after glancing in the direction of the noise, Kathy removed her hand from Braxton's and brushed his cheek affectionately.

"Okay, I'll remember that. Just don't be surprised if I take you up on it every now and then. For now it looks like you have a reprieve from having to lend me your shoulder to cry on. I think Sammy's back."

The approaching vehicle was now coming into view, and Braxton frowned. "That's not Sammy. Too small. Looks like a Jeep." He helped Kathy to her feet. "Better put some clothes on. I think we have company."

Kathy nodded and slipped on her blouse as Braxton picked up his khaki shorts and climbed into them. Then she pulled her own shorts over her suit as they both watched the oncoming car. It was close enough now for Braxton to see that he'd been right about the vehicle. The car came to a stop, and Kathy grabbed involuntarily at Braxton's hand again. Now that it was close, there was no doubt as to the identity of the vehicle. The Jeep that had halted in front of them belonged to Mr. Frank Gunther.

Twelve

THERE WERE THREE MEN in the automobile. Dingo was perched behind the wheel, smiling through the dusty windshield at Kathy and Braxton with a wide, crooked-toothed grin. In the back seat, his face as expressionless as ever, was Dog Bassett, and beside the driver, wearing a broad-brimmed safari hat, sat Gunther.

"Braxton," Kathy said with a quiet gasp.

"I see him," Braxton replied, his tone hushed. "Just stay nice and calm until we find out what he wants." Shifting his gaze slightly, Braxton could see Injai pointing in their direction and heading back with Zelda and Eddie toward the pond. They were still pretty far away, however.

The right front door of the Cherokee opened, and with an audible heave, Gunther pushed himself through the opening.

"*Jambo*. Hot, ain't it," the hunter said, shoving the door closed and crossing toward them. He smiled broadly, but Braxton felt no reassurance. It was a practiced smile, stretched across a jaded face and unable to mask an underlying cruelty in his expression. The man's attention moved from Braxton to Kathy, where it held in undisguised appraisal. A lecher's eyes searching out an opening in the top folds of her blouse.

"Yes," Braxton replied, returning what he hoped was an equally insincere smile of his own. "We just finished a swim in an attempt to cool off."

"That right?" Gunther lifted his arm and pulled off his hat, wiping his shirt sleeve across his forehead in the process. Then he lowered his arm, resting the hat on the butt of a short pistol sticking out of the holster around his waist. Braxton felt his insides tighten a little as his eyes settled on the gun.

"What do you want, Mr. Gunther?" Kathy said, refusing to be intimidated by his blatant gawking.

"Well, I wanted to check and make sure nothing had happened to you people. I've been feeling guilty about leaving in such a fit of temper the other day."

"As you can see, we're fine."

"Oh, yes, I can see that, all right. Looks like you and Hicks are getting along real well. You're also both a damn sight braver than I am, I can tell you that."

"What's that supposed to mean?" Braxton asked.

"Parasites," the hunter said, glancing sideways.

Braxton and Kathy looked also. Another vehicle was approaching off to their left, and this one was no Jeep. It slowed as it came up beside the trio of people making their way to the pond, stopped long enough for them to climb aboard, then began moving toward them again. Braxton felt his tension rise a notch. Sammy was back.

"Parasites?" he repeated.

Gunther kept his eye on the approaching bus, giving Braxton minimal attention. "These still-water ponds are full of them, Hicks."

"Sammy says this pond is spring fed from underneath," Kathy said. "So it couldn't be stagnant. I'm sure he wouldn't suggest we swim in it if it were."

Gunther snorted. "Sammy! What makes you think Sammy has the first clue about what the hell he's doing? It looks damned still to me. But you want to believe Sammy, you suit yourself." The bus came to a stop near the Cherokee, but Gunther ignored it. He leered at Kathy. "I'd just hate to think of those slimy things crawling around inside a body as pretty as yours."

The bus doors snapped open with a metallic clang, and Gunther turned slowly in the direction of the sound. Injai flew through the opening, rushing past them without a word to where the laundry lay randomly spread out on the rocks. He began snatching it up hurriedly, speed his major concern.

Sammy appeared in the doorway, but stopped short of stepping out completely. His jaw muscle was twitching badly and he was shaking visibly, holding on to the metal jamb for support. An instant judgment told Braxton it was fear that had a grip on their guide, but when Sammy spoke, he realized he was wrong. It wasn't fear but rage. And Sammy's hold on the door frame was a desperate attempt to control that rage.

"Get in, please," he managed to say coldly to Braxton and Kathy.

"Well . . ." Gunther said loudly, his posture straightening as he stared at Sammy. "Well . . . well, well. I'll be goddamned. Look who's here! Now this is a surprise. Hey, Dingo! Stick your ugly head out the window and see who's got a safari of his own going."

Dingo pushed the upper part of his body through the open window on the driver's side of the Cherokee, stretching his neck for a look at Sammy. Then, seeing the group's new guide, he ducked back into the car, clutching the steering wheel as if he were afraid someone were going to take it away from him. The man in front of Braxton laughed loudly, and pushed his safari hat back on his head.

"Ya know, the fact is I miss you behind the wheel, Sammy. Dingo never could drive worth a shit. Always popping the clutch, jerking the wheel around like an asshole." The two seemed oblivious to those around them now, the big man swearing freely while Sammy stared unblinkingly back at him. "Yeah, poor Dingo's scared shitless I'll get rid of him. But I'll keep him. You know why?"

Sammy remained silent when Gunther paused. Injai brushed hurriedly past the guide, throwing the laundry to Chegee in the first row of the bus, then dropping into the driver's seat. Eddie was sitting across from the seat filled with laundry, his expression one of apprehension. Braxton could see Zelda peering anxiously at the scene through a closed window near the rear of the bus. Gunther shifted his weight and spoke with barely suppressed anger.

"I'll tell you why, Sammy. Because he's loyal, goddammit!" Then his voice softened again, and the practiced smile returned. "How's your head, anyway, Sammy? I was hoping I'd knocked some sense into you, but it looks like I was wrong. Just made you cocky enough to think you could lead my clients on your own safari. Which means you're still as big an asshole as you ever were. Ain't that right, boy? Huh?"

Several things happened at once. Injai hit the ignition, and after a whirring grind, the motor of the bus started with a cough. Sammy stepped down onto the ground, a strangulated sound issuing from his throat. Gunther's body suddenly became taut, and his hand dropped to his hip, where it rested on the curved butt of the pistol. Eddie was out of his seat, moving toward the doorway, but it was Braxton who stepped between the men, even as Kathy tugged to pull him back.

"Come on, you little son of a bitch," Gunther bellowed, his anger no longer subdued. "You need another lesson? I'll give it to you. And this time I'll finish the job. I'll teach you to steal my clients. And I'm only going to tell you once, Hicks—get the hell out of my way."

Braxton ignored Gunther's threat and moved to face Sammy, his mind screaming at him in amazement that he was turning his back on a vicious man with a gun. Peripherally he could see the figure of Dog Bassett emerge from the Cherokee, but his focus was on Sammy. He spoke evenly to the guide, all the while watching Eddie, hoping the priest would tip him off if he was in real trouble.

"Didn't you say we were leaving, Sammy?" Braxton looked at Kathy. "Go ahead, Kathy. Get on the bus." She nodded, then hurried by the three men. Grasping Eddie's hand, she stepped up through the doorway. Sammy didn't move. Braxton was standing so close to him he could feel the younger man's body shaking in tight spasms. "I think we're all ready now," Braxton said.

Eddie stepped out of the bus, and with the assurance only a priest could have, he placed his arm across the guide's shoulders. "Come on, Sammy, let's go," he said calmly, and without a word, the guide turned and climbed into the bus. Wasting no time, Braxton hustled into the bus right after them. However, once through the doorway he turned back around, unable to resist. Gunther was again relaxed, slouching with ease.

"We'll be going now, Gunther," Braxton said. "Thanks for looking us up, but we're fine. I don't think you have to check on us again."

The white hunter's eyes narrowed cruelly, and his lips curled into a dry smile. "Oh, I wouldn't feel right if I didn't," he said. "We'll see you again. Count on it. This business isn't finished. You hear me, Sammy?"

Sammy didn't even acknowledge the man by turning in the direction of his voice. Injai snapped the doors closed, shoving the long-handled floor shift into first gear. The rear wheels spit dirt as the bus drove away.

Frank Gunther stood motionless, watching the bus drive off into the distance. Dog Bassett came to stand beside him, following the direction of his gaze.

"Well, you sure let them know we're around, Frank," Dog said evenly.

Gunther jerked his head in agreement. "Yup. Good for them. Make them nervous. Keep them off balance, looking over their shoulders. People are never easier to take advantage of than when they think they're prepared. Now, I'm going for a quick swim. How about it, Dog? You want to take a dip?"

Bassett's eyes widened. "What about the parasites?"

Gunther laughed. "Don't believe everything you hear, Dog. Take a quick dip. It'll do you good."

"But shouldn't we follow after them? They may try to get away from us now that you've alerted them to—"

"Eh, Dog. Don't insult me, huh! You think I'm not smart enough to follow an asshole like Sammy? I'm not going to lose them, all right?"

"All right, Frank. A swim does sound good."

"Now you're talking," Gunther said, unhitching the holster at his waist. He started to unfasten the buttons on his shirt, glancing off in the direction the bus had disappeared. "That Kathy sure is one damn good-looking Irishwoman, isn't she? I think it may be about time to figure out a way to get the young woman into our camp for some private conversation. What'd you think, Dog?"

"Whatever you say, Frank," Bassett answered non-committally, stepping out of his pants.

Gunther laughed crudely, stripping off his shirt. "You don't fool me for a minute, Dog. You'd go for that just as fast as I would." Dropping his pants, he turned and bellowed in the direction of the Jeep. "Dingo, get your ass out here with some cold Tuskers!"

Thirteen

THE PASSENGERS SAT in silence while the bus bumped and jounced across the rough grassland. Finally, after the pond—and Gunther—had disappeared from view, Eddie got out of his seat and made his way down the aisle to where Braxton sat.

"I thought you did a fine job out there, Braxton," he said. "It could have been a very bad situation."

Braxton shrugged. "No, you were the one who saved it, Ed. If you hadn't intervened in such an authoritative way, I'm afraid Frank Gunther would still be kicking Sammy and me into ground chuck."

"But why do you suppose he chose to drive up like that?" Zelda asked.

"Well, you can be sure it wasn't because he was concerned about us, the way he let on," Kathy observed wryly.

"How about it, Sammy?" Eddie said, turning toward the front, where their guide had taken his usual position in the well of the doorway. "What do you think? Could it have been because he's angry that you elected to guide us?"

Sammy had been staring out the front windshield, giving Injai directions, and when he turned to face the others, his face was furrowed in thought.

"No. There will be many opportunities in the future for him to confront me. I believe Gunther's main interest lies with you."

"Why?" Zelda questioned.

Sammy took several steps down the aisle toward his passengers. "This grave that you seek. Could not the things it contains be of value to others?"

"If we're right in our assumptions, I would say priceless," Eddie replied.

"Then it would be worth much money."

The priest nodded. "To the right person, it certainly could be."

"I believe that is the answer," Sammy said with conviction. "I also saw that Dog Bassett is still with him. Bassett is a man who deals in the trading and sale of things that are not always within the law. He has many connections on the coast at Mombasa and would be the perfect person to trade items of great value illegally for Gunther."

Kathy leaned forward, placing her hands on the seat in front of her. "What are you saying, Sammy? That Gunther is following us, and if we find something, he'll try to take it from us? Do you really think he'd do such a thing?"

Sammy spoke with sincere concern. "I am not trying to worry you, Kathy, but I know this man. There is little he would not do for money. Especially if he thought it would be quick and easy."

"But surely he wouldn't just attack us, Sammy," Zelda said, somewhat aghast. "I mean, really..."

"This is not America, Zelda," Sammy told her. "The savannah is a wild and often desolate place. Anything can happen to people, and then be covered by the creatures who roam here without a trace to tell what really happened. Sudden death here is not shocking. It is simply a part of our life. People like Gunther can and often do use that to their advantage."

Kathy sat back in her seat again with a discouraged sigh. "Swell. As if things weren't difficult enough, now we have Frank Gunther to worry about."

Braxton looked from her back to the guide. "What do you suggest, Sammy?"

The guide frowned, pausing momentarily before he spoke. "What do you know about the actual location of the grave? It would not take us that long to reach the spot you chose on the map if we traveled through the heat of the day. Could you find the grave quickly once we arrived there?"

It was Zelda who answered. "Nothing is certain. We're assuming the information will get much more specific, but we don't know that it will. I've been very careful to simply let things evolve naturally during the hypnosis sessions rather than push for facts. However, I could begin playing a much more dominant role in our next session, I suppose. What do you think, Kathy? Is it time to try to get some specific information?"

Kathy's mouth formed a nervous smile as the others looked at her. "Yes, I guess so, Zelda. That's why we're here, isn't it? I know your concern is for me, but I'll do my best not to let anything throw me. When we get back to camp, let's go for it. If whoever or whatever it is that communicates through me really wants to find the grave of Eve, it looks like it's time for her to tell us exactly where it is."

There were nods of agreement all around, but no one spoke, and a sober silence settled over the interior of the bus as the vehicle made its way to the place where they had camped. Even Braxton couldn't think of any clever remark to lighten the mood. And though he gave both Eddie and Kathy confident smiles of encouragement when they caught his eye, an uneasiness had settled over him that he could not quite identify. He had been certain that by this time he would have understood what was actually happening with this regression business, but the truth was, nothing had become clear. To make matters worse, he was becoming emotionally attached to Kathy Sullivan faster than he would have believed possible. All of which he found very unsettling.

From the front of the bus, Injai suddenly broke the silence, speaking quickly in Swahili and ending with the word *simba*. Sammy crossed to the driver's seat and stared off to the left, where Injai pointed. The young guide grinned broadly and motioned to the others for silence. On Sammy's signal Injai nodded, and in one motion he turned off the motor without braking and slowly rotated the steering wheel to the left so the bus coasted in a silent arc, then stopped.

With his finger to his lips, Sammy motioned everyone to the left side of the bus, whispering as he moved down the aisle.

"Have your cameras ready. With luck, you'll now see why we do game runs in late afternoon. Look closely at the tall weeds in the long narrow patch of grass off to the side there."

Braxton saw them first, probably because he knew what to look for. Then, with the help of Sammy and his silent gestures, everyone focused in on the reason for the stop.

Almost completely submerged in the tall grass were two female lions, their heads, bellies and flanks hugging the ground. Beyond them in the more open vegetation, a group of delicate miniature antelopes grazed, their movements alert but unsuspecting. Cameras came up and shutters whirred and clicked as the two lean beasts, like giant house cats, stalked their prey, only the rippling muscles of their shoulders tensing and releasing as they slid forward on the ground.

"Watch beyond the Grant's gazelles," Sammy whispered, pointing to the high grass on the other side of the grazing herd. "Luck is with us. We are in the perfect spot."

Then it happened. Sammy had been right. Without warning, out of the tall grass the guide had indicated leaped a third lion.

Amid a flash of skittering hooves, the gazelles scattered with great leaps, their late-afternoon meal forgotten. As several veered in the direction of the unmoving bus, the trap became apparent to the enthralled spectators. At some unseen signal, the two lions in the foreground came to life, their powerful bodies lunging at the fleet, slender animals.

And then, shoulder through torso extended to its full length, covering ground at a dazzling speed, the smaller of the first two lions connected. Its claw caught the soft shoulder of a gazelle in midhop, pulling it to the ground. Almost simultaneously, the other beasts were there, but it was the first who sank her wide jaws into the slender neck, ensuring the kill.

Still holding the neck locked in its jaws, the lion shook the limp body back and forth until finally, assured the animal was dead, it released its grip. Nosing the tiny body over, the lion sank its fangs into the soft belly, tearing and pulling at the thin underskin to reach the warm flesh beneath as the other lions joined her.

"Oh, how horrible," Kathy said, lowering her camera and looking away.

Sammy glanced at her, then turned back to the scene of the kill. "No, Kathy. Only feeding time. Here it is a way of existence. Life and death are part of that same existence."

Braxton observed the guide perceptively. Sammy had changed since the incident at the pond with Gunther. The confrontation with his former employer had affected him noticeably, and there was a harshness in his features now.

"We give these acts a morality," Sammy continued, "but it is our concept, not theirs. It is something I noticed while in America. People attach their own morality to the actions of animals. There is no morality on the savannah. Here it is either kill or be killed as all attempt to survive."

IT WAS NOT UNTIL LATER, before the evening meal, that Braxton learned just how worried Sammy was about their own survival. He was returning from a rest-room stop in the weeds when he noticed Sammy crouched near a small compartment attached to the underside of the bus. Casually he strolled over to speak to him before going around to the opposite side of the vehicle where everyone was gathered around the campfire.

At the sound of Braxton's approach, Sammy shoved the item he had been examining back into the open slot of the compartment and slammed the rectangular metal door shut. Braxton hadn't intended to snoop, but even in the dim light he couldn't miss seeing what Sammy had returned to the container. There was only one thing that had a wooden stock and a thin, round metal barrel. Sammy rose to his feet as Braxton came up beside him.

"Sorry," Braxton said. "Didn't mean to startle you, Sammy."

"It is all right," Sammy replied. "I was inspecting some things."

"So I saw." Braxton figured he might as well not lie. "I didn't realize you had weapons on the bus."

Sammy shrugged. "It is best to have them for an emergency."

"Makes sense." Braxton paused a beat. "Were you checking the gun because you think it might be needed?"

"I am checking them because it is best to be prepared," Sammy answered evasively, kneeling and pulling the door of the undershelf open again.

Braxton squatted down beside him. "You have more than one in there?"

"Yes. Several. Certain situations could call for weapons of different calibers. One would not stop a raging bull elephant with the same weapon needed to halt an attacking leopard. And, since you ask, there is reason to be cautious . . . other than Gunther, that is. I did not wish to alarm the others, but I learned at the lodge today that the pride of lions in this region has grown dangerously large. They are even considering issuing permits for restricted hunting of the animals to eliminate possible danger to campers and the people in this district."

"How large is dangerous?"

"Twenty . . . perhaps thirty strong. It happens occasionally. Cubs do not leave. An aggressive male keeps many females with him. Those we saw today were undoubtedly part of it, out hunting on their own."

"How worried are you?"

Sammy pulled one of several weapons from its slotted space within the opening, snapped open the bolt and peered into the barrel. "I am not. Just being careful. I have agreed to guide you. It is my responsibility to protect you."

Braxton watched as the guide slid the bolt of the weapon back in place, returned the gun to its slot, and withdrew another for inspection.

"I had a .22 as a kid, but nothing of this caliber. How hard is it to shoot one of these?"

Sammy looked from the rifle up into Braxton's face. "To shoot is easy. It is the killing that is difficult."

"Sammy, I know I interfered between you and Gunther at the pond. I want you to understand, I was only trying to help."

"You should not become involved," Sammy answered, returning to his weapons inspection and taking a holstered pistol from the compartment. "It is my problem. I was wrong to let him anger me today. I should not let my own hatred come in the way of my job as your guide. But the man has hurt me greatly. It is hard for me to see past that."

"Understandable," Braxton agreed. "The man damn near killed you. And you're certain he's going to continue to follow us?"

Sammy spoke evenly. "Yes. Just as I am certain it is not over between us. He stated it today. It is only a matter of time. Please understand. I am grateful that you wanted to help me today. But when the time comes, you must not become involved, Braxton. It is not only the beating. Gunther has shamed me many times. With me it is a matter of honor. Gunther believes he can do as he pleases with people. Sooner or later someone must show him that he cannot."

After a moment the young guide looked down at his hands again. He stared at the pistol he held, then shoved it back into its holster with a hard determination.

"I have no experience to support these thoughts," he said quietly, "but I imagine that when using one of these, it is hardest of all to kill another man."

Fourteen

IT WAS ONE of those perfect African nights—clear, with a light breeze that made it just cool enough. After the evening meal, at his friend's urgings, Eddie had followed Braxton up the ladder to the bus's roof. Coffee cups in hand, the two of them were sprawled out on the roof rack, staring up into the twinkling black panorama of the Kenyan sky.

"Dwarfs the imagination, doesn't it," Eddie observed as he gazed upward. "Well worth taking a few moments to simply enjoy. I agree with you there, Braxton. Look at that moon. I swear I can see most of the craters."

"I'm telling you, Ed. Listen to me. You know how many nights you've been out in the open and never taken the time to enjoy it."

"I know...I know. This trip has been very good for me as far as that's concerned."

"And the soul? How's that doin', my friend? Things seem any clearer, or is there still a mass of religious confusion swirling around inside?"

The priest shook his head as he continued to look up at the star-studded sky. "Only the heavens are clear—not the way that leads to them. That remains in the darkness for me, I'm afraid. But I am attempting to relax a little. And moments like this do help. For that I'm very grateful, Braxton."

"Listen, Ed," Braxton said, lowering his voice so that the others clustered around the fire could not hear. "I know you're probably wondering about what's developing between Kathy and me. I want you to know that—"

Eddie raised his hand in protest. "Stop right there. First of all, I don't have to wonder. I can see what's happening. The two of you aren't exactly glaring at each other when you're together, which is most of the time."

"All right, but I don't want you to think that because Kathy's an attractive woman, I'm just..."

"Braxton, the truth is, I've never seen you act this way about any woman."

"You think I don't know that? I can't believe it. I don't know what's going on. I mean this whole situation isn't even sane to begin with, and I'm sitting around giggling with the woman like some kind of lovesick teenager."

Eddie shrugged. "So, enjoy it. You're both adults. And my impression of Kathy is that she can take care of herself. She may seem vulnerable as far as the business of the trip is concerned, but I'm sure she's told better men than you where to get off."

Braxton could just make out Eddie's face in the darkness, and he saw that his friend was smiling. "You're enjoying this, aren't you?"

"What? Seeing you off balance for once because you've allowed your defenses down to the point where you might actually become involved with someone? You bet I am! You've always had this stupid thing about your past—that because you don't know who you are, you're like a leper or something. Well, the fact is that's ridiculous, Braxton. Who cares about your past? So what if your father was a killer, or a millionaire's son or even a bum. The only thing that matters is what you are now. And you know it! It's about time you stopped being such an ass about the whole thing. As you so frequently enjoy telling me, relax. Go with it. It will do you good.''

Braxton looked at his old friend incredulously. "My God, what have I created by telling you to relax a little. You've never talked to me like this before, Ed.''

"Well, I've meant to for some time now. How much longer do you intend to go on avoiding some kind of commitment? Until you're an old man, alone in a room somewhere with nothing but pee stains on your underwear?''

Braxton laughed softly. "Graphic image. Okay. I get the message. I'm not sure how I feel, Ed, but I will promise you that I won't run from it without giving it a chance. But answer me this.''

"Yes?''

"Do you really think my father could have been a killer?''

"No, of course not. I didn't..." Seeing Braxton's grin, Eddie suddenly realized his friend was leading him on, and he stopped. They were both quiet a moment, but then the priest spoke again, this time in a much more sober tone. "Although, in truth, all our forefathers have been killers at one time or another, all the way back to Cain, haven't they?" He was staring up into the heavens again. "I guess that's the catch of real commitment—even commitment to one's God. Along with the joy of devotion comes the pain of doubt.''

"Eddie, even if there is a grave, do you really think you'll find an answer buried in some hole in the ground?''

The priest shook his head. "Of course not. I'm not naive. But I'm hoping it can help me to better understand what's buried inside here," he said, patting his heart lightly.

Though the night air had been filled with the sounds of the animals who came to life on the savannah when darkness fell, none of the cries had been distinct enough to draw particular attention. However, as Eddie finished speaking, a distant savage roar cut loudly through the darkness, and Zelda jumped up from her camp stool near the fire.

"What was that?"

"Simba," Injai answered. "Lions are roaming."

Braxton called down softly from the roof of the bus. "Just the sweet sounds of the jungle night, Zelda. They'll put you right to sleep."

"Hardly, Braxton," Zelda retorted, staring out into the darkness beyond the perimeter of the camp. "That one sounded very awake and alert to me. Wasn't it awfully close?"

"No," Sammy said, stepping from the interior of the bus and walking over to the fire. "Far off. On clear nights the lion's cry carries over great distances. Sometimes miles. And I have learned there are many in Amboseli at present, so we will be hearing many other times from them."

"Well, it certainly is a gorgeous night," Eddie said, following Braxton down the ladder on the outside of the bus and joining the others around the fire.

"Enjoy it now," Sammy said good-naturedly, the sparkling night sky seeming to have improved his earlier dark mood. "The sudden coolness could mean rain. It may cloud over soon."

"Isn't this the dry season?" Eddie asked.

"Yes, but it is not that unusual to have a sudden storm. This has been a strange season. There have been several such storms lately. It will pass quickly if it comes."

"No cheetahs today, but good lion viewing, eh, Buddy?" Injai called from the side of the bus where he worked at the evening dishes.

"Top-notch, Injai, but I'm still waiting for the cheetah payoff, my friend."

"Oh, look," Kathy said, pointing upward and bringing everyone's attention once again to the sky. A brilliant oval flare of white light blazed across the heavens, pulling a dazzling tail in its wake. "Isn't that beautiful."

"That's some shooting star," Zelda said in amazement. "You grow them big here, Sammy."

The guide shook his head. "It is too big for a star. Perhaps a comet. If so, others out here seeing it in the night sky will not share your appreciation of its beauty. They will be hurrying to their prayer huts in fear that Enkai, the black god, is red with anger."

"Bad omen?" said Kathy.

"Yes. The Masai, who out of all Africans remain most true to our heritage of living with nature on the savannah, fear the appearance of a comet in the sky. They believe great trouble will follow. It is said a comet was seen just before the Europeans first invaded these lands."

Another roar sounded from far away and, jumping slightly, Kathy edged a little closer to Braxton. "Well, I still say it was beautiful."

A voice spoke Sammy's name, and the guide walked over to meet Chegee, who emerged around the front of the bus. The older man appeared agitated and delivered several rapid sentences in Swahili to which Sammy nodded solemnly.

"Anything wrong, Sammy?" Braxton asked, stepping over to join them.

"Perhaps," the young guide said. "Earlier, thinking I saw lights through the trees behind our tents, I sent Chegee to check. He tells me my concerns were correct. There is an open area on the other side of this woods, and a camp has been set up there. I will go see who camps near us."

Sammy's words snapped everyone out of their stargazing reverie, and they gathered in concern about the guide.

"You don't think it could be Gunther, do you?" Zelda wondered, apprehension filling her voice.

"You may have noticed we have not seen that many other people," Sammy replied. "I have purposely chosen a route away from the main areas of travel. Not many guides know this place. I will see who has chosen it."

"I'd like to accompany you," Eddie said. "We should know who it is also."

"I'll go with you, Ed," Braxton joined in.

"We must go quietly," Sammy said, glancing at Eddie and Braxton. Then he nodded reluctantly. "All right. Do exactly as I say. And move in absolute silence." The guide turned to Chegee and issued a command. The gray-haired man hurried to the bus, reemerging with a gleaming wide-bladed machete, which he offered handle first to his nephew.

"You're coming up with one hell of an arsenal out of that bus, Sammy," Braxton said, eyeing the long blade. "How many more weapons do you have hidden away?"

"This is not a weapon," Sammy said slyly, taking the machete. "Slasher is used for clearing—shrubs and thick weeds."

Eddie inspected the ivory handle that butted against the blade. "What did you call it?"

"Slasher," Sammy answered. He swept his arm back and forth to illustrate. "See . . . it is used to slash weeds away."

"Aptly named," Braxton said, watching Sammy. "Is it necessary? We're only going to look."

Sammy shoved the blade through a loop in his belt, where it hung at his waist like a broad sword. "It is dark. We may need to clear our way through the woods. And I am using caution. As you warned Zelda and the others before, Braxton, one must watch for . . . snake in the grass. Is that the phrase?"

Braxton arched an eyebrow. "That's the phrase."

Sammy nodded and motioned for Chegee to position himself at the front of the bus. "Injai will stay by the fire with Kathy and Zelda. Chegee will watch for any danger until we return." The women nodded and Sammy looked at the men next to him. "Stay close to me."

"Be right back," Braxton said, glancing first at Zelda, then meeting Kathy's eyes. "Keep the coffee perking."

"Oh, we'll be right here, don't worry," Kathy said.

"Be careful, please," Zelda added, eyeing the black night beyond the edge of the camp with concern.

"Come," Sammy ordered, and the three walked over to the trees behind the tents, then disappeared into the darkness.

Because of the clear sky overhead it was easier to see than Braxton had imagined it would be, and he and

Eddie were able to follow Sammy with ease as they moved stealthily through the trees. Soon, after raising his hand for caution, the guide halted their progress and pointed ahead to a glimmer of firelight that could be seen coming from a clearing near the perimeter of the trees.

It was not a big camp—three tents at most, a larger one between two smaller ones. Two men could be seen, though not clearly, sitting on small fold-out canvas camp stools next to the fire.

Braxton brought his face close to Sammy's and spoke in a low whisper. "Is it Gunther?"

The young guide's jaw muscle jumped spasmodically, and he pointed to the center tent, where someone was lifting the flap. The man who emerged wore a wide-brimmed safari hat, and from his carriage there was no doubt as to his identity.

Sammy's right hand went to the ivory handle at his waist as he watched Gunther stroll to the fire. Now that their eyes had adjusted to the lighted area beyond the darkness, it was easier to make out the faces. Braxton recognized the man who stood when the hunter approached the fire as the driver Gunther called Dingo. And when the man who remained seated turned around, the fire highlighted the expressionless face and burly shape of Dog Bassett.

"Can we get closer?" Eddie whispered to the guide.

"Yes, I also want to know more about this. Use caution and stay low. Remember the example the lions gave this afternoon."

With agonizing slowness the three worked their way forward in half-crouched positions. Suddenly loud screeching and a frantic rustling high in the trees directly ahead of them broke the stillness. In panic they dropped to the ground, hugging the thick vegetation for security. At the clearing beyond, Dog Bassett rose to his feet, and all three men looked outward. More screeching sounded, and Dog Bassett could be heard speaking to the hunter next to him.

"Nyami!" Gunther replied in Swahili, then translated. "Baboons. It's just a troop of baboons getting antsy in the trees over there." He picked up a stick of firewood and indicated for Bassett to follow him. "Come on, Dog. We better scare them off. Once they start that shit, it can go on all night."

Braxton shifted, digging and flattening his body and head to the ground. Gunther was coming right at them. Feeling movement next to him, Braxton turned to see Sammy ease the machete from his belt loop and bring it up to his face. Near him, Eddie shook his head, his expression objecting vehemently to the guide's actions.

Braxton experienced the same sensation he had earlier in the day when he had turned his back on an angry Gunther. Only the feeling was stronger now, and he knew its identity. Fear was clamping its icy grip onto his senses. His lower spine began to ache, and he realized he must have twisted his back in his frantic effort to hide. Great. No more cute conjecture. This was reality. And the reality was that the whole situation was crazy. The hypnotic regression. Chasing after some mythical grave. Confronting a man like Gunther. All of it. What the hell did they think they were doing? Then an even more pressing reality pushed his thoughts aside, and Braxton caught his breath as Frank Gunther and Dog Bassett stopped not more than ten feet in front of them.

"Go on, you hairy bastards," Gunther yelled, waving the stick he held through the branches above him. *"Go somewhere else to fight over who gets it tonight!"* The stick sliced noisily through the leaves, followed by

further screeching and heavy movement as the troop scattered to a more distant location before settling into relative quiet. Gunther grunted in satisfaction. "See, Dog, you just gotta show them who's boss."

"Yeah, I see, Frank," Bassett answered quietly.

"Let's wait a second to make sure they've quieted down so we don't have to come out again." Gunther shoved his hands into his pockets as he glanced around. "Hell of a nice night."

Braxton felt the dull ache in his back transform itself into a stabbing pain, but his fright was easing. If they hadn't been discovered yet, they probably wouldn't be. All they had to do was not budge until Gunther left, which was wishful thinking, he realized, as the hunter's hand came out of his pocket and unzipped his fly. The action was followed by the sound of a heavy stream of urine hitting the ground.

"Too much beer," Gunther muttered, belching loudly. "Drinking's a nasty habit, Dog. Not to mention the fact that you got to take a leak every five minutes. I'd quit if it weren't so damned enjoyable. Feel free, by the way. We probably won't be coming out here again."

"I'm fine, thanks," Bassett answered.

"S'matter?" Frank said, eyeing him. "You embarrassed to whip out your schlong in front of me, Dog?"

Bassett gave Gunther a tired look. "I don't have to piss, Frank. So tell me. What do you plan to do? Just stay with them for the next few days until we see what's what?"

Gunther zipped up his pants. "You got it. Now that we've shown ourselves they ought to get their asses in gear and move out. We just keep on their tail for a while without bothering them. Let them feel confident again.

Then when they get where they're going, we'll be right behind. Come on, we better get back and turn in. They'll probably break camp early if I know that little bastard Sammy, and I want us to be up and ready to follow them from a discreet distance. And listen, you want to watch yourself if you come out here later to piss, Dog. There are a lot of honeybadgers in the area."

"Honeybadgers?" Bassett said, giving Gunther a curious look.

"Oh, yeah. They may be wide, heavy, low-slung bastards with their weasel-shaped heads, and I know they look slow, but they're fast as hell, have razor-sharp teeth and are vicious to boot. That's why you gotta watch out for them. See, they can't go for the throat. Not tall enough."

"I don't see your point, Frank."

"If one comes at you while you're out here pissing, you will. Since they can't reach the throat, they go for the balls." Dog Bassett's eyelids slowly closed, then opened again as Gunther roared with laughter, slapping the man next to him on the back as they walked toward their camp. "Course I've never had such an experience, but that's what they tell me, Dog."

Hardly allowing himself to breathe, Braxton watched until Gunther and Bassett were once again in conversation with Dingo at the fire. Then Sammy nudged him gently, and with a finger to his lips, the guide indicated for them to rise. He didn't have to tell them to move cautiously, and making their way in silence, the trio slipped back from the edge of the clearing. Once they were far enough into the trees, Sammy signaled them again, and they moved with greater speed back to their own camp.

With a wave to Chegee, they came around the bus, and the women and Injai rose quickly to meet them as they approached the fire. Kathy, noticing the way Braxton was walking, was the first to speak.

"Braxton, what's wrong? Did something happen?"

Braxton arched his back to ease the pain and moved toward a stool. "I think I twisted my spine the wrong way."

"You tripped in the darkness, Buddy?" Injai asked.

"No, diving for cover." Braxton sat down carefully and massaged the aching area. "I really thought we were in for it."

"I worried for a moment myself," Sammy agreed soberly.

Eddie stopped beside the guide and looked at him with concern. "You weren't actually considering using that machete, were you?"

Sammy met the priest's eyes. "The choice did not become necessary."

"Will you tell us what happened?" Zelda asked anxiously.

"Nothing happened, thank God," Eddie responded. "But we did get some answers."

"Well . . ."

"What do you want?" Braxton said. "The good news or the bad news."

Zelda gave a short sigh of exasperation, her hands coming to her hips. "Braxton, please."

"Okay. It's Gunther. He's parked on the other side of these woods, and he knows we're camped here."

"I'm not trying to be funny," Zelda said, "but what's the good news?"

"They don't plan to do anything but follow us until we reach our destination. Isn't that right, Ed... Sammy?"

The priest exchanged a look with Sammy and nodded.

"Then what?" Zelda continued.

"We don't know," Eddie answered. "But at least we know Gunther doesn't intend to bother us for a while."

Braxton rose to his feet again, his hand pressing against his lower back. "Look. I want to say something before this goes any further. I don't know about you, Ed, and I can't speak for Sammy here, but I was scared shitless playing Natty Bumppo in the woods out there. We have to do some serious talking. This is no game. If Gunther had stumbled onto us out there, it could have gone very badly."

"What are you suggesting?" Zelda asked, her voice taking on an edge of defensiveness. "That we quit? After all we've put into this, and now that we're so close, we simply pack up and go home?"

"Zelda, listen to me," Braxton went on, a little too loudly. "Someone could have gotten hurt tonight. Maybe even killed. I don't mind looking for a grave, but I'd prefer that it doesn't end up being my own."

"There is more at stake here than you worrying about yourself, Braxton," the hypnotist replied, her own volume increasing.

"Oh, yes, I know all about what's at stake, Zelda. But my personal opinion is that your little glory trip to make sure you end up in the hypnotists' hall of fame with Mesmer and Rasputin isn't quite worth getting people killed."

Zelda's face reddened and she visibly bristled. "Well, it looks like we're finally getting your honest opinion about all of this, Mr. Hicks."

"I never said I bought it, did I?"

"No, I guess you didn't. I merely assumed that since you were along, you supported what we are trying to do. I suppose I was wrong to make such an assumption."

Braxton exhaled with exasperation. "Zelda, listen. I'm not saying—"

"No," the hypnotist countered angrily. "Let me tell you something, Braxton. I am not some kind of quack. And this is not just some kind of game I'm playing. I don't gamble with people's lives. I believe in what I'm doing with all my heart. Do you understand? If I didn't, I wouldn't be here."

Kathy had moved between Braxton and Zelda as they argued, and she raised her hand tentatively, interrupting. "Braxton, please, I know you're concerned about the danger, but arguing isn't going to solve anything." Not waiting for a reply from either of the two people next to her, Kathy turned her attention to the priest, who stood across from them. "Eddie, what do you think?"

"I think we should have a hypnosis session," he said as the others turned to him. "We know the Gunther situation. Maybe Zelda can steer the regression to get some specific answers that will really help us regarding the grave. Then, with the total picture of where we stand, we'll talk as Braxton suggests."

DOG BASSETT STOOD next to Gunther at the campfire, looking out toward the woods. "You sure they're gone, Frank?"

"Couldn't be surer, Dog," Frank answered. "They moved out right after you and I walked away from them."

Bassett nodded his head with approval. "You're all right, Frank. I have to give you that."

Though pleased with the compliment, Frank shrugged. "Thank the baboons, Dog. Camp near them and they'll tip you off every time. And you deserve some credit too. That was an Academy Award performance out there. My guess is they bought it hook, line and sinker."

"Then we're ready?"

Gunther shook his head. "Almost. We'll wait a few hours to be sure they're down. I'll break camp in the meantime, so we can move out immediately. Then we go in and get her."

"There's something I don't understand, Frank. If you were planning to take the woman all along, why did you show yourself to them?"

Gunther's expression hardened. "I don't like people who turn on me, Dog. I want that little bastard Sammy to know I nailed him. The way I've got it worked out, there'll be no proof, but he'll know. And there won't be a goddamned thing he can do about it...even if he makes it back. Last chance to back out, Dog. Once we grab her, that's it."

"How do you plan to take her without her making any noise?"

"Well, I'm counting on your muscles to hold her for me, Dog, while I give her a few knockout drops with a hypo kit I have. Use it mostly on animals, but it'll work, don't worry."

"Suppose after we have her, she won't tell us where to find the grave? What then?"

"Oh, she'll tell us, Dog. Don't be concerned about that." Gunther flashed a smile. "I can be a very persuasive man."

"And you're sure they won't try to follow us?"

Gunther grunted and glanced behind him. "Dingo, you got that meat cut up yet?"

From where he was working, the driver flashed the men a crooked-toothed grin and held up a huge piece of raw flesh dripping with blood. "Soon, Bwana. Plenty meat here. Feed us for many days."

Gunther smiled. "Feeding us is not quite what I have in mind, Dingo."

Through the cool night air, a loud, elongated roar sounded, followed by another and then yet another. Dog turned his head to listen. "That lion sounds closer than before."

Gunther nodded. "Yeah. Much nearer. And not one lion. Many lions. Nothing draws a pride of lions like fresh, raw meat, Dog. Nobody's going to follow after us immediately, believe me. What's with all the questions, anyway? You chickening out on this or what?"

Bassett looked directly at Gunther, but the eyes were cold, devoid of emotion. "I just like to be sure, Frank. That's all."

Gunther nodded and began taking down the tents behind them. Actually, he was feeling very good that he had included Dog in this little enterprise. Dog was a man he could depend on. Frank had little doubt that in a clutch, Dog Bassett could be one mean son of a bitch. Frank was sticking his neck out on this one, and he knew it. He had to make it work. And he would, too.

Still, he was glad Dog was there as a backup, because no matter how good things looked, something could always go wrong.

Fifteen

"WHERE ARE YOU?" Zelda said softly, touching Kathy's hand with a light tap of the index finger.

They were seated close to the campfire. The night had darkened now, clouds covering the sky as Sammy had predicted. Of the Africans, however, only Sammy was among the close observers. The other two had chosen to position themselves by the bus several feet away. But though they sat in the shadows, they watched: old Chegee, his eyes wide with wonder, and Injai, desperately trying to concentrate on the proceedings so that he could understand this strange thing that the priest he so admired and his friend Buddy had gotten involved in.

Across from the hypnotist and Kathy, Eddie was kneeling on the ground, the sketch pad and drawing utensils ready in front of him; Braxton, his back still throbbing, sat on a camp stool next to the priest; and nearby was Sammy, taking it all in.

A lion roared somewhere out on the savannah, and others answered, their cries carrying in the night air. Braxton shot a quick glance beyond the tent into the darkness, then back, giving Eddie a tight smile. Kathy's eyes were closed, and her body swayed on the camp stool where she sat, but she had yet to respond after the relaxation and regression phase.

A spent ember crumbled the fire, and the wood shifted, causing sparks to leap into the air. Warmed timber near the hot core ignited, and tall flames shot up from the glowing center. A huge leafless tree with broad branches stood behind the tents where the woods began, and its twisted boughs were highlighted by the new brightness, causing wavering shadows to crisscross in eerie reddish-orange patterns on the cluster of people below.

Kathy's head came up from its relaxed position, her eyes still closed, her expression searching and troubled. Zelda touched the young woman's hand and spoke again.

"It's all right. Everything is fine. Where are you?"

No response.

"All right. I'm speaking to Kathy now. Kathy, I know you hear me. We're going to do something different this time. I'm going to give you control. Do you understand? When I touch your hand, Kathy, you will be able to speak, even though you can only observe what has been and are not truly there. It is the same as in your recurring dream, Kathy. You can see through the eyes of the one from the past. And you are going to help us understand. I want you to tell us what you see. When I tap your hand, it will give you control. Answer yes if you understand."

Zelda's index finger tapped lightly against the back of her subject's hand, and Kathy's voice came in a soft whisper, her lips barely moving. "Yes-s-s."

Zelda glanced across to the others with an emphatic nod, then continued, her voice comforting but in command. "Very good, Kathy. Now listen to me. It is the other who is there. Not you. Nothing you see can touch you. It is not real. It happened long ago. But through the other, you can see and help us understand. Look around you. You will see what is there."

Kathy's head turned, as if surveying, and Braxton could barely make out the rapid movement of her eyes as the curved bulges shifted erratically beneath the closed lids.

"That's right," Zelda continued. She tapped her subject's hand again. "Tell me, Kathy. What do you see?"

Without warning, Kathy's head flew back, weaved from side to side, then centered again, the words emerging in a hissed whisper, as if coming from somewhere far away.

"Dark ... It is ... dark."

Zelda and Eddie exchanged a glance, and the hypnotist spoke again, her voice strong and in command. "Yes, I know it is dark, but that won't prevent you from seeing. You will be able to see. Do you understand? I'm going to tap your hand, and when I do, you will see what is in the darkness." Kathy nodded, and Zelda's finger struck her hand. "You can see the darkness open now. Look! Look around you. What do you see?" Kathy's head rolled from side to side. Zelda tapped again. "What do you see?" Again the head roll, but no response. "All right, let's try a different approach. There must be a reason why you are in this place. Can you tell us why? Why have you come to this place of darkness?"

The reaction to Zelda's question was immediate. Suddenly Kathy's head tilted backward with a snap that jarred her whole being, and then she was sobbing, her body shaking as the emotion broke from her. But Zelda was ready, never losing control; she took Kathy's hand in her own, comforting, soothing.

Braxton felt himself leaning forward, wanting to reach out to Kathy, but Eddie had grabbed his arm.

Shaking his head, the priest nodded toward Zelda, who was talking the grief-stricken woman beside her back to calmness.

"It's all right. I want you to move away from there. Now. Right now. Move away. It's all right. You're fine. You do not have to answer that question. You are not involved now, only watching. Do you understand? Relax now. Just relax. You will see, but without emotion...only see as an observer...to learn and understand. Do you hear me, Kathy?" The sobs subsiding, Kathy nodded slowly. "Fine. We need to know what you see, but if you want to stop, we will. Do you want to stop now?"

There was a pause, then a look of determined anger surfaced on Kathy's face momentarily, and she shook her head.

"Very good. When I tap your hand, you will see and know, but not feel emotions. You are only observing. It cannot hurt you. It may have hurt you before, but now you will only see it. Understand?" Again the determined nod, followed by Zelda's quick tap. "Fine. Now, in the light that has replaced the darkness, what do you see?"

As had happened before, Kathy seemed stumped, her responses stopping momentarily and her head rolling from side to side. Then her expression changed dramatically. Confusion gave way to relaxation, and just as quickly that too was transformed into wonder. Yes, Braxton was sure that was the right term. A childlike wonder shone from Kathy's face.

"Light," she said softly. "A warm, beautiful light."

"Very good. And is this light at the place we seek?"

Kathy's brow furrowed and her head tilted questioningly.

"Is this the special place we seek, Kathy? Look deeper. Through the light. What do you see through the light?"

Again the head tilt, but no response.

"All right. Give me feelings, emotions. What does this place make you feel?"

A smile. Innocence replacing wonder. "Warm. It is warm."

"I see," Zelda continued. "Very good. Look around, Kathy. You need to know this place. To remember it. Do we know this place?" No response. "All right, then you must tell us more of it so that we can understand. Is there a word we have that could help us understand this place you see? A word we use that could help us identify this place?"

A frown, and Kathy's head went back. Braxton suddenly realized he was holding his breath, and he exhaled slowly. In spite of all his skepticism, he had to admit he was caught up in the believability of the moment.

"What is the word that will help us know this place?" Zelda prodded gently. "We must understand to find it."

And then it came. Kathy's head rose to its normal position and the word floated out softly between her lips. "Womb..." she whispered.

Even Zelda hesitated briefly as they all reacted to the word Kathy had uttered. Everyone had been sure the answer would be Eden or something similar, but this term brought forth a myriad of new questions and possibilities. Next to him, Braxton could see that Eddie's face was alive with excited animation, and using his hand, the priest signaled Zelda with an enthusiastic rolling motion. Zelda turned back to her subject.

"Do you mean womb as found in a woman?"

"No..." Kathy answered, the warm smile remaining. "It is only a word. It is only like a...womb."

"Of course, I see. All right, Kathy. Very good. Now I want you to see beyond where you are. Do you understand? We must know what is beyond this place. When I tap your hand you will see clearly through this womb and tell me what you see."

A tap, and Kathy's head rolled from side to side until finally centering again. Suddenly her radiant expression changed. No outbreak of sobbing came from Kathy this time. Still, there was no mistaking the emotion. Sorrow crowded her face, etching its way in deep furrows around the eyes and mouth. It was a quiet, deeper registering of the emotion, the kind brought on by complete loss.

"What do you see?" Zelda asked again.

Tears emerged from behind Kathy's closed eyelids and slid slowly down her cheeks. Her answer came in a voice that no longer belonged to a mature woman but rather, to a small child. And though it had the form of words, the words were unintelligible. The answer came in long, tormented cries of mourning in the language Eddie had identified as tongues.

"No, we cannot understand. It must be English. Kathy must answer. Kathy, tell me in English. What do you see?"

The flow of sound caught momentarily, broken into spurts of gibberish. Then Kathy gave a howl of anguish, and as tears streamed down her cheeks, a guttural reply poured out of her in the voice of a tiny infant.

"Maaaaaaa! Maaaaaaaaaaaaa!" the tight little voice cried forlornly. "Maaamaaa!"

Kathy's head snapped back with a force that jarred her entire body. Back and forth, again and again, her head rolled from side to side as half-garbled sounds broke from her throat.

"For God's sake, Eddie, that's enough!" Braxton whispered, leaning close to the priest. But Eddie remained motionless, his eyes on Zelda as the hypnotist shot a warning glance toward Braxton that left little doubt he should stay out of it. Then she pulled Kathy to her, grasping her hand, tapping it forcefully and speaking with a strong, commanding presence.

"Move away. Move away! It's all right, Kathy. I understand. Move away. It is too painful. It's not important. We do not need to know. It's all right. It's all right. Move away and feel no emotion."

The sounds slowly eased and finally stopped. Kathy's mouth closed, her head came forward and suddenly her eyes shot open.

The three observers started slightly when Kathy's eyes opened. Stretching out her hand in warning, Zelda signaled them to remain still and she pushed on quickly. Immediately they realized that the hypnotist was right. Kathy's eyes were open but unfocused. It was not the firelit campsite her eyes viewed, but something beyond the vision of the rest of them.

"It's all right, Kathy," Zelda said, tapping the young woman's hand once more. "Do you wish to stop now?"

There was no response as Kathy's eyes stared straight ahead into the leaping flames of the campfire.

"I think we should stop for now, Kathy. Close your eyes, and when I tap your hand, I want you to relax."

Again, there was no response. However, before Zelda touched her, Kathy's hand and arm began to rise slowly into the air.

Eddie gathered up the drawing materials and was instantly across the space that separated him from Zelda and Kathy, holding the sketch pad up in readiness. Zelda took a charcoal stick from the priest and handed it to her subject.

"Of course, I understand," she said as Kathy's hand grasped the drawing tool in a tight fist. "Kathy can only see. You need to show us. Good. Very good. Show us the place of light Kathy spoke of. Show us so that we can take you there."

As he listened, Braxton realized that, without missing a beat, Zelda was no longer speaking to Kathy but to the persona, the Eve of the regression. Along with the others, he watched in rapt attention as the hand moved to draw on the pad Eddie held before it.

But this time the drawing never came. Suddenly Kathy's hands went up, guarding her face against whatever she saw emerging from the mists of her hypnotic trance. She hurled the drawing tool toward the fire and her arms struck out erratically as wild, frightened monosyllables tore from her throat.

Zelda caught her subject's hands in her own, and clasping them still, she drew Kathy to her.

"All right," the hypnotist said, her voice soft and soothing. "You have helped us enough. It is time to stop now. I'm going to bring you back. Do you understand? I want you to move away from what you see. Move further and further away from it now. When I tap your hand, watch what you see recede in front of you until it is smaller. Smaller and smaller still. And smaller. That's it. See it grow smaller and more harmless until it is a speck far away from you. And when I tap your hand again, the speck will disappear. Be gone. Ready? Now."

At Zelda's tap, Kathy's body started in one tiny spasm, and then she seemed to relax.

Zelda continued, "Yes, it's gone now. Before you there is only blue. You are surrounded by the serene, calming blue atmosphere. Relaxed. Calm. And I'm going to count from ten backward now, and when I reach zero, I will tap your hand a final time, and you will be back. And you will remember what you have experienced, but you will feel refreshed and calm. You will feel totally calm and refreshed and at peace. Take a deep breath now as we begin to return. Ten . . ."

While Zelda talked Kathy back through the numbers with calm reassurance, Braxton felt the stabbing pain in his lower spine hammering for recognition, and he stood in an attempt to ease the ache. The session had distracted him for a while, but now the pain refused to be ignored. He arched his back gently, hoping for relief, and as he did so, he looked over at Sammy. The guide had not moved. He was staring at Zelda and Kathy with wide-eyed astonishment. Next to him, Eddie was placing the drawing materials back into their case. Finishing her reverse count, Zelda gently tapped the back of her subject's hand, and Kathy opened her eyes.

"Okay?" the hypnotist asked quietly.

"Yes," Kathy said, looking around with a small smile to the others. "Fine. We . . . we didn't learn much, did we?"

Zelda patted her hand. "Enough. Each time, no matter what happens, we learn a little more."

"Can you tell us what happened at the end that stopped the drawing?" Eddie asked, crossing over to them.

Kathy frowned. "Well, like all the other times, the real information is still blocked from me. Although when Zelda told me to see, I could distinguish vague changes in light. It . . . it was almost as if I was reacting to what I was unable to really see personally. But at the end I think it was fire."

Eddie frowned. "Fire? You were looking in the direction of the campfire. Is that what you mean?"

"No, I mean a huge wall of fire. Like a blazing, impenetrable wall. But I can't be sure. I'm sorry, Ed. I tried, but I couldn't get very much."

"It's all right, Kathy," Zelda said. "You did fine. Do you know what you said when I asked you to see beyond the place you called a womb?"

Kathy bit at her lip, then nodded. "Yes. There was no mistaking that. But, again, it was more like an involuntary reaction. I . . . I saw nothing. So I can't be sure of anything." Kathy shook her head and sighed. "When will it ever start becoming clearer?"

Eddie gave her a sympathetic look. "When we finally get there, I imagine," he said.

Braxton shifted impatiently. "So, is it time to talk?"

"Yes," Eddie answered. "I suppose we can't afford to wait until we've had time to think about the session as we usually do. You look terrible, Brax, standing all hunched over like that. You really did hurt your back, didn't you."

Braxton straightened and grimaced. "Swell timing, huh."

"I'll try to massage the ache out of it, if you like, Brax," Kathy said, walking over to him. "Where is it, the lower spine?"

"Yes, but I'm okay. What about you? Don't you need to rest or something after all that?"

She smiled and shook her head. "No, thanks to Zelda, I always feel fine afterward. Now tell me where it aches. Here?"

"Mm-hmm." Braxton reached behind him to guide Kathy's hand to the sensitive area. "All across the lower—right here. Ahh. Easy...easy. Yes, that's the place. But it can wait, really. I'll live. Let's finish this discussion." Braxton smiled toward the black man standing near them. "How 'bout it, Sammy? Any thoughts to share?"

"It is strange and mystifying to me," the guide replied, his eyes darting from Braxton to Kathy to Zelda.

"It is to all of us, believe me, Sammy," Eddie told him.

"All right, first of all, Zelda," interjected Braxton, "I want to apologize for being so flippant before. I was out of line and I'm sorry. I know you're sincere in all this. And I can also see you are extremely competent."

Zelda waved Braxton off. "There's no need to apologize, Braxton. You've had to accept a great deal in a very short time."

"Okay, fine. Maybe I need more time to grasp it all, or maybe the pains coursing out of my sacroiliac are distorting my judgment, but the way I see it, we're not a whole lot closer to knowing the exact location of our goal than we were before. Why don't we let Sammy show us some of Kenya's finer sights, which would take Gunther on a merry goose chase, and then go back to Nairobi."

Kathy's hands stopped massaging and she stepped forward, beside him. "And what? Go home, Braxton?"

"Kathy, listen to me. That was not an easy thing you just went through. What if it gets worse? What if next time, the regression suddenly becomes too much, too overpowering for you. Then what?"

Kathy met Braxton's gaze, and she placed her hand lightly on his arm. "I appreciate your concern, but I have faith in Zelda."

"As do I," Eddie added. "She is always on top of things and I trust her abilities completely."

"Braxton, though it appears to be disturbing to the onlooker, an open emotional response is not all that dangerous," explained Zelda. "Inner feelings are bound to surface when the person being hypnotized relinquishes control. That's merely part of what hypnosis is all about."

Braxton shook his head in irritation. "All right. You people want to go on toying with someone's head, fine. But, damn it, what about Gunther? The results of our sneaking around in the woods tonight could have been disastrous."

"But they weren't, Braxton," said Eddie. "And we did learn valuable information."

"Eddie, Sammy here didn't pull out his slasher with the intent of hacking down shrubs. What's the matter with you?"

"Nothing," the priest answered sternly. "In spite of the possible danger, I firmly believe we're doing the right thing."

Braxton eyed his friend carefully. "What are you telling me, Ed? You think we're moving under some kind of great God-given protection or something?"

"I believe we're supposed to reach our goal, yes, Braxton."

"Ed, you saw what Gunther did to Sammy. You think he wouldn't do the same thing to any one of us to get what he wants?"

The priest rubbed his hands over his face and then, completely unconscious of his actions, folded his hands together as he might in prayer. "Braxton, I'm willing to go on talking, of course. But if you're asking me what I think we should do, I vote to continue."

Braxton threw his hands into the air and then winced in pain immediately after doing so. "Okay, fine. I'm outvoted. Fine. So, we go on. But tell me this. Where? Huh? Where do we go from here?"

There was an awkward silence, then Sammy cleared his throat, drawing the attention of the group to him.

"May I speak?"

"Of course, Sammy," Eddie answered.

The young guide nodded. "I have involved myself in this, and I can see the sincerity of your purpose. But much puzzles me. I need help to understand. And I see that perhaps you might want help also. There is one who has already come to our aid that we could call upon for such help. One of nature's chosen, he is schooled in not only the art of healing but also the magic of that which is unseen. He has a knowledge of things that are beyond others. I would like to bring him here. It is possible he could tell you much of what puzzles you."

"You mean the Masai called Twamba?" Zelda said. "You want to get Twamba to help us?"

"Yes. Do not overlook our ways and our knowledge, Zelda. This is Africa, and there are many things that can be learned from the Africans who are of this land. It is possible Twamba could tell you much of what puzzles you. He is also at one with the land. There is no area he would not know of. If you continue, it is he, not I who should lead you."

"Yes, but why would he help us?"

"He will listen and help if he can. Many have gone to Twamba with problems about the spirit messages from the unseen world, and he is known to have aided with answers of great clarity." Sammy smiled knowingly. "He also spoke to me of an interest in Gunther, for Twamba wages a continual battle against the white hunter's senseless slaughter of animals. Twamba is a great warrior and could also provide protection if needed."

"Sounds like we can't afford not to get in touch with the man," Zelda said. "Any objections, Braxton?"

Braxton shrugged and smiled. "Hey, if we're going on, why not? The more the merrier."

"How will you reach him?" Eddie asked.

"He is a Masai, and his people are near here. If you agree, I will go now. Should it be the correct time for him, he and I will return together. This will take until late into the night, but tomorrow morning we could all talk further."

"Fine," Eddie said. He reached forward, took the guide's hand and grasped it firmly. "And, Sammy, thank you for trying to find ways to help us. You're right. Perhaps the answer is to turn to the people who belong to this land. Having you offer to lead us has been the best thing that has happened to us so far, I know that."

Sammy smiled shyly. "I will take the bus. Injai and Chegee can remain here to help, should you need anything. I do not feel there is a danger tonight, but if you prefer, I will also leave weapons."

Eddie shook his head. "Not necessary."

"Until I return, then," Sammy said, turning to go.

Injai, who had sat quietly at his place beside the bus, stood and accompanied Sammy to the doorway. He exchanged a few words with the guide, then stepped away, and the bus pulled out of view into the darkness.

As he walked back into the firelight, Injai made no attempt to conceal the fact that he held the ivory-handled slasher in his hand.

"Why the machete, Injai?" Eddie asked, with a frown of disapproval.

"In case of a stray animal, Father," Injai said with a shrug, not meeting the priest's eyes as he looked from the machete to those around him. Chegee said something to him then, and the older man disappeared behind the tents.

"You're not frightened by all this, are you, Injai?" Braxton said teasingly. "I was counting on you to help me maintain my nerve."

"Oh, no, Buddy, I am not afraid," Injai answered, flashing his familiar good-natured grin. "Not as long as I have this slasher near me."

Braxton laughed loudly, ending with a grunt of pain as his backache flared.

"Braxton," Kathy said, "you'd better let me have a look at your back."

"Okay, nurse—" Braxton nodded "—maybe you're right, if you're not too tired."

"No, but you'll have to stretch out somewhere."

Braxton gestured toward his tent. "Fine, step into my office."

"What do you think, Eddie? Can we trust the two of them in a tent alone together," Zelda said jokingly.

"I don't know—does seem chancy," the priest agreed with a grin. "He's not that injured."

Braxton looked at his friend in surprise. "Hey, Ed. Cut it out. I'm in pain."

"I think I can handle him," Kathy said good-naturedly, lifting the front flap of Braxton's tent. "Come on, injured one, inside with you."

The two disappeared into the tent, and as they watched them go, Zelda and Eddie exchanged a knowing look. Just then Chegee appeared out of the darkness and stopped to speak quickly to Injai at the fire.

"Anything wrong, Injai?"

The driver shook his head. "No, Father. Chegee checked the outer edge of camp. No problems. Do not worry, and sleep well. Chegee will be standing guard. Good night."

The priest yawned. "Well, Zelda. I'm going to bed. I suggest you do the same. I don't think we need wait up for Brax and Kathy to reappear."

Zelda glanced toward the tent. "I agree. Do you think we could end up having any problems as far as the two of them are concerned?"

Eddie kicked a fallen log back onto the fire. "Zelda, I've always made it a practice not to give advice about blossoming relationships because the plain truth is my opinion and advice will mean nothing. People in love hear only themselves. I do know Braxton's feelings for Kathy are honestly straightforward. He told me as much so I wouldn't be concerned. Is what's happening between the two of them right? I don't know. But I do know there isn't a thing we could do about it anyway."

"I suppose you have a point. Who knows, maybe it's all more complex than we even imagine. There was the picture of the two of them that came out of the earlier session, after all."

Eddie nodded. "I haven't forgotten, believe me—as I'm positive neither of them has, either. Although I'm sure Braxton doesn't hold much stock in that. You aren't upset because of his spouting off, are you? I've known him a long time, Zelda. He's only trying to help."

"I know," Zelda said, shaking her head. "He's simply stating what he believes is best, like the rest of us. I wish I knew what to do now, Eddie. I honestly thought this last session would give us some final answers."

"Yes, so did I," the priest agreed. "Instead, we must continue to plod blindly along. Did you see her expression change during the session when you asked her about the place of darkness. I've never seen such deep sorrow come into a person's face like that. I could only think of Milton."

"Milton?"

"Yes. *Paradise Lost.* There was such a look of loss on her face. Strange, I've been supposing all along that such a discovery will somehow make it easier for me to accept the condition of things. Give me a better understanding. Show me there is hope. Tonight, seeing the sorrow on Kathy's face during the session made me realize the opposite could be true. The discovery could also destroy all hope."

"You don't really believe that," Zelda said softly.

The priest sighed deeply, looking from the fire to the cloud-covered sky above them. "No, I suppose not. It's partially on the belief that there is hope that I decided to do this. There must be hope to use as a defense against all the misery in the world, mustn't there? Without it, there is nothing left but despair."

Sixteen

IN THE DULL LIGHT that filtered through the tent walls, Braxton found his sleeping bag and, with considerable moaning, eased himself into a sitting position on top.

"Should I take all my clothes off or anything?" he asked innocently as Kathy knelt beside him.

"Just your shirt should be sufficient," she responded with a smile. "Here, let me help you."

Braxton unbuttoned the front of his shirt. "Can you believe it? How the hell could I screw up my back in the middle of all this?"

"All right, just relax. Maybe I can fix it. I'm sure I can at least ease the pain." Kathy helped him pull first one sleeve, then the other from his arms. She placed the shirt near them and gently guided Braxton into a prone position. "Over on your stomach. Let's find the problem spot. That's it. Now relax. I won't hurt you."

"I trust you," Braxton said, exhaling deeply as Kathy's hands rippled over the muscles of his back with a firm, soft motion. "No, farther down. Ahh. That's it. Right there."

"It sure is," Kathy remarked, working her way knowledgeably over the lower right part of his back. "The muscles are all knotted up. Don't tense when you react. Try to reverse it and let go."

Braxton, his head turned sideways and resting on his left cheek, closed his eyes and did as he was instructed.

He felt her hands kneading his skin in strong, circular motions. Almost immediately he experienced sensations of relief in the area, and he exhaled again, willing himself to let go.

"That's better," Kathy said, widening her movement.

"You've got good hands, lady. Should I not talk?"

"No, it's all right." Kathy reversed direction as she reworked the tender spot. "Just don't tense up."

"I won't. It feels better already. Listen, I'm sorry if I sounded negative out there. But you were very upset during that session. I'm not sure it's such a great idea to keep doing the hypnosis if you have to go through that again. I mean, I don't care how good Zelda is, it can't help but have an effect on you."

Kathy's hands paused a beat. "Oh, it affects me," she said, as her hands once again continued their strong, sure massage. "I could never put into words the grief that filled me when Zelda commanded me to look through the light. And even though I couldn't see, I know what I felt, and I know what word formed in response to those feelings."

Braxton rolled onto his side, raising himself on one elbow. "Kathy, there could be many explanations for why you said that. Couldn't there?"

"No," she responded firmly. "I know there is a reason. That's why I won't quit. Not until I see for myself what caused me to feel such pain and... sorrow. If it is in any way tied in with my own mother and her dying during my birth, I...I have to know." Suddenly her eyes clouded, and she shook her head against the tears that threatened to surface. "Damn. I'm not going to start crying like an idiot again."

Braxton pushed himself into a sitting position and took Kathy's hand in his own. "Why not? You want to cry, go ahead. You helped me with my pain, didn't you?"

Kathy tried to smile as he spoke, but unable to help herself, she went into his arms. She did keep herself from sobbing uncontrollably this time, but silent tears streamed down her face nevertheless. For several long minutes she remained like that, crying quietly against Braxton. And Braxton Hicks, this man she had known for only a few days, held her tightly to him, rocking her gently and whispering her name as if it were the most natural thing in the world.

At last she pulled back slightly and attempted a smile, appreciation and warmth shining through her tear-filled hazel eyes. "See, I have everything under control now."

Braxton smiled with gentle concern as he pushed a fiery strand of hair back from her face. "Yes, I see that."

Kathy shook her head. "I can't believe this. Every time I talk to you I start bawling."

"Maybe it's because you know it's all right. I'm flattered you feel that comfortable around me."

"Well, anyway, thank you. I guess that session was a little harder on me than I thought." Leaning forward, she ran her free hand lightly across Braxton's lower spine. "How do you feel? Did my leaning on you destroy your back all over again?"

"No, it's really improved, honestly," Braxton answered, holding her gaze. "Having you lean on me only made me feel better."

Kathy sniffed loudly and wiped at her face with the back of her hand. "I must look terrific."

"Yes, you do, as a matter of fact," Braxton said, tracing the outline of Kathy's face with his index finger. "Terrific."

"I . . . should get back."

"Maybe you'd better stay."

"Braxton . . ."

"I'm not sure I'm all right. I might have a relapse. I think maybe you'd better check me out some more. What do you think?" He took Kathy's hands, slowly pulling her close to him again. And as he did so, his expression changed. The teasing humor was replaced by vulnerability. "I don't want you to leave, Kathy," he said softly. "I don't know how it happened so fast, or why, but I know I can't control it and I don't really care. Because the honest truth is, I'm not sure I ever want you to leave."

As Braxton drew her to him, Kathy felt a totally new emotion waking up inside her. And she knew that he was right. Whatever might happen, she neither wanted to nor could hold back.

He brought his head down to hers slowly, meeting her lips lightly, then more firmly, but with a tenderness that surprised her in such a strong, vibrant man.

She looked up at him and saw the source of that tenderness. Once again it was in his eyes—undisguised and unmistakable. He really did care.

He started to speak, but she touched his lips with her finger and shook her head, smiling.

"Yes, I know," she said lightly, "you don't have to say it. Jell-O instant pudding."

Then she was in his arms once more, crushing herself to him. And as she held him, a surging release of anxiety swept through her. She felt the wetness on her cheeks and knew she was crying again, but that didn't seem to matter as Braxton held her even more closely to him.

"It's going to be okay, Kathy," he said in soothing whispers as he softly kissed her eyelids, her cheeks and then her mouth. "I promise you that. Everything is going to be okay."

And then a feeling of urgency swept over them, and Kathy moved against Braxton, her mouth opening to his, her arms wrapping around his neck, as emotions sought to express themselves in the heat of desire. As his mouth covered hers with increasing passion, Kathy found herself helping Braxton's gentle hands remove her clothing, and she kissed him again hungrily as his hand brushed softly against her naked breast, causing new flames to ignite deep within her.

Still clad in panties, but unable to wait any longer, she pulled back the sleeping-bag cover and slid in beside Braxton, loving the touch of his skin meeting hers. She lost herself in the delicious warmth that blossomed over and over as Braxton's fleeting hands touched, explored, excited and then moved on. A fierce need swelled within her. More than mere sensuality, it was a need to drive all disturbing emotions from her; to lose herself in passion, where, for that briefest of times, everything else could be forgotten.

The heat of urgency pushed her to him, and she moved against his maleness, her own hands seeking, caressing him with tantalizing strokes, loving the gentle yet arousing way he stroked her in return.

And then his hands hooked the edge of her panties, and she helped him slide them down her legs and off. He had sat up to remove them, and now he took her in his arms, his mouth opening to meet hers and his hands returning to caress her thigh and the now-naked flesh.

Her breath caught, and she heard a small moan escape her throat as together they sank back down into the sleeping bag. And she responded with her own caresses, her hand seeking his throbbing hardness, wanting him to love her.

Then without warning the vision came to her, and her eyes snapped open to stare at the dark canvas near where they lay. Shadows shifted like the billowing flames of a wall of fire, a fire that threatened to envelop her, swallowing her in a blazing agony. Unable to drive the fearful image from her mind, she felt her body stiffen.

"Kathy?" Braxton said, lifting his head and looking down at her.

Kathy sat up, oblivious of her nakedness. Without answering, she crawled out of the sleeping bag and pushed back the flap at the entrance of the tent, forcing herself to look out into the darkness beyond . . . to see the terrible, consuming flames that had leaped from a dream to reality.

But there was nothing. Only blackness beyond the campfire's glow, and rumblings of an approaching storm overhead.

"What is it?" Braxton said, moving behind her, slipping his arms around her.

"I suddenly saw the flames . . . of the regression, and I felt a terrible wave of dread."

He rubbed her shoulders. "Is it gone now? Are you okay?"

She turned and kissed his lips softly. "Yes. I'm sorry. I know it was stupid, but it was something I suddenly couldn't control. I had to see outside the tent . . . to be sure."

"It's not stupid. Whether the vision exists or not, the feelings are real, and you have to respond to that."

"Are you always so understanding?" she said gratefully, snuggling against his chest. "That was pretty rotten timing...."

"Oh, we're far from finished," Braxton told her, smiling. He reached up to close the flap, but she placed her hand on his arm.

"No, leave it partly open. Please. I...I need it that way."

"Okay," he said, glancing up as a flash of lightning lit up the sky. "Looks like Sammy was right. It's going to rain."

"Braxton," Kathy said, touching his face in tender exploration as she looked into his eyes. "You're right about all this affecting me. I...I'm holding on as tightly as I can, but then it comes at me out of nowhere, like just now, and I'm suddenly overwhelmed with fright. Frightened because I'm so lost in all this I...I'm no longer sure what's real or imagined anymore. I know there couldn't be a worse time to become involved in a relationship, and yet I want to. But it also frightens me. Is this real, Braxton? What's happening between us?"

"It certainly feels real to me," he answered, taking her hand and kissing her fingers lightly.

"All right, but if later you discover it isn't, don't tell me until this is over. I...I've had to be alone for so long, I couldn't stand to be alone again...right now."

And through her own fears, Kathy watched an unguarded pain seep into Braxton's eyes, and she knew he understood, because he shared her pain.

"Hush," Braxton said softly, his own emotion filtering through his voice. "Don't say any more, Kathy. Dear...dear, Kathy. Neither of us is alone anymore."

They lowered themselves back down to the sleeping bag, and he covered her body with his. "I'm here, and I'm going to stay with you. You're not alone. I've fallen head over heels in love with you, Kathy. Do you hear me?"

"Yes, I hear you—oh, yes, Braxton, I hear you," her mind shouted. But she could not answer, so strong was the emotion within her. And so she responded with a renewed passion that caught them both up in a flood of desire.

Lions roared beyond the dark perimeter of the camp, but lost in their loving, they were both oblivious to the sounds. And as the release of so very, very much shuddered through her, Kathy felt the birth of unqualified joy sprout deep inside her.

And while lightning split the sky above them and the first drops of rain tapped against the canvas that surrounded them, they rose to meet each other, to ease their sense of loss. Over and over, they came together, straining body against body through the act of love, until finally, in that one shattering moment, reality dissolved and all loneliness vanished when, in a flood of ecstasy, they became as one.

IT WAS RAINING much harder now, but neither Braxton nor Kathy seemed to notice or care. Braxton had closed the flap against the rain, and they lay nestled inside the folds of the sleeping bag, warmed by the afterglow of love. Kathy snuggled closer against Braxton's chest, kissing his neck lightly and running her hand over his spine, massaging the area that had given him pain.

"How's your back? Any better?"

"Mmm," Braxton answered, trailing his own hand along her back until he brought it to rest on her buttocks. "Much better. I think this method is even more effective than the massage."

Kathy smiled. "Maybe, but you'd better let me work over that back again before we fall asleep, just to be sure."

Braxton stretched, then winced. "Maybe you're right. You don't mind?"

"Not at all." Kathy pulled the cover of the sleeping bag back and sat up. "Come on, roll over."

There was very little light now. If she had thought about it, Kathy would have realized that the rain had dampened the campfire, and for some reason Chegee had not rekindled it. But she could sense Braxton's eyes moving over her nakedness, and the state of the campfire never entered her mind.

"Too skinny or too fat?" she asked, loving his eyes caressing her, feeling the edge of desire stir in her once more.

Braxton placed his hands on her waist and eased them up her body, cupping her breasts. "You are just right."

She clasped his hands in hers and brought them to her lips, kissing them. "You're in pretty good shape yourself, Braxton Hicks, with or without a bathing suit. But you'd better turn over or the massage will lose in favor of method two."

"Tempting," Braxton said, rolling onto his stomach, "but it might cripple me for life."

Kathy leaned down, methodically working her palms over his back. "Relax now. Let go. Let yourself drift away. I want you to drift into sleep."

"I'm relaxed, but I don't think I'm going to fall asleep with you all naked and tempting next to me," he grunted beneath her skilled hands.

"Just stop talking and relax," she replied as she eased the remaining tension out of his tender back muscles.

"Okay, nurse." Braxton exhaled heavily. He felt a shiver of pleasure as Kathy's lips kissed his back softly. Then her sure hands moved over his body, forcing the tension out of his legs, his buttocks, up his back and out of his shoulders. He realized she was humming a soft melody as she worked, and he smiled in pleasure.

Braxton could not remember when he had been so content, and he suddenly wanted to tell Kathy all over again how strongly she had affected him. And he would. When she finished the massage, he would pull her to him and tell her how he felt.

But waves of relaxation overcame him before he had a chance, and Braxton drifted from consciousness thinking about the fact that, as always, good old Eddie Fitzsimmons had been right: for the first time in his life, he had dropped his guard and gone with his feelings. And the result so far was unqualified happiness.

KATHY COULD TELL by the slow rise and fall of his back beneath her hands that Braxton had fallen asleep. She ran her fingers with a professional touch over his lower back muscles. He would be much better by morning. She had been able to work most of the tension out.

Not wanting to move quite yet, she sat there, looking down at the outline of his naked form in the darkness in an attempt to take in the reality of what they had just shared. Wondering at the fact that this man, with his impish, delightful humor coupled with his sensitive understanding, could have come into her life. Especially at such a time, when her entire direction was so bizarre and uncertain.

Maybe it was a sign. Perhaps it was all for a purpose and would turn out all right, as Eddie seemed to believe. And perhaps this search really would help her to clear up her own feelings about the mother she had never known.

She shook her head as thoughts of her mother and the emotions she had felt during the regression crowded into her mind. No, she would not deal with all that now. They could discuss it together tomorrow after Sammy returned with Twamba. Now was a time for the two of them, and a time to savor the happiness Braxton had given her. All she wanted to do now was crawl into the sleeping bag and drift to sleep, feeling Braxton against her.

She frowned with irritation, suddenly realizing she had to pee, and would have to do so before she could go to sleep. She shivered. It was much cooler now that the rain had come. Or maybe she just felt it because she was sitting there naked. She smiled and ran her hand lovingly over the man beside her. Let it be cold. She liked being naked with this man.

But now she became aware of something else. It was darker. There was no firelight outside, and she wondered why. Chegee was on guard, and even with the rain, he should have tended the campfire. Now that she was concentrating she could hear the night sounds, and the roar of lions seemed closer and more threatening. Damn. She really didn't want to go outside, but she'd never make it till morning.

"Okay, nature calls," she muttered, reaching over Braxton for a blanket that lay next to the side wall of the tent. She'd cover herself from the rain, slip right outside the tent for a second, then snuggle back in beside Braxton.

A shadow fell across the outside of the tent and Kathy froze, her breath catching. Or maybe it wasn't a shadow. She couldn't be sure, for it was gone now.

No, enough of this. The way to conquer fear was to confront it. There was nothing out there. Hadn't she almost ruined their lovemaking by foolishly having to look outside? She snatched up the blanket and wrapped it around her.

"Be right back, my love," she whispered. Then, pulling the top of the sleeping bag across his body and kissing him on the cheek, she covered her head with the blanket, pushed back the flap and slipped outside.

FRANK GUNTHER was cursing his luck and starting to get a little worried, although he'd never let Dog know that. Taking out the guard had been simple. A hard gun butt at the back of the skull. But he'd known that would be easy. Any day he couldn't outmaneuver a black would be some day. And the raw meat had been hung all over the camp, with enough blood dripping from it to draw a pride of hungry lions like flies to shit.

What bothered Gunther was that he had already silently sliced open the backs of three tents and hadn't found her. There was something else too: no Sammy. He had been half hoping for an encounter with the little son of a bitch, and now he couldn't even find him. Or the reporter, Hicks. Plus, the bus was gone. Too many unknowns. He didn't like it.

But, okay, to hell with Sammy. One tent left, and the girl had better be in it or they were screwed. Followed by the muscular hulk of Dog Bassett, he crossed toward the rear of the final tent.

It was a sixth sense that warned him. He'd always had it. During the war it had saved him more than once.

And as he approached the rear of the tent, he knew someone had moved inside it. Instantly he backed off toward the trees, Dog moving right with him. Frank signaled to his companion that they would wait for a moment in the rain-filled darkness. Another lesson from battle. Never rush or panic. Extreme caution, especially at night, brings victory. Anyway, it would as long as that goddamn bus didn't suddenly come rolling into camp.

Seconds ticked by, and then the rustle of movement told Frank he'd been right. A blanketed figure emerged from the tent nearest them, moved around the front and stopped, crouching near the side wall.

Gunther cracked a dry smile. By God, maybe the odds were with him after all. The small size and graceful movements just weren't masculine. There were only two women in the camp, and he'd already seen the fat one asleep in the second tent he'd sliced open. That meant the jackpot was right in front of them. Nice of her to step out to greet them. Made everything neat and easy, not to mention the fact that it also saved him from having to hurt anyone else unnecessarily. He could leave that to the lions. He signaled Dog. Okay, stoneface. Let's go get her.

A hypodermic materialized in Gunther's right hand, and with a curt nod, Dog Bassett stepped from the darkness of the tree cover. The plan was moron simple. Since Dog was stronger, he would grab her while Frank gave her the needle, and then away they'd go. Piece of cake.

Frank was surprised at Dog's speed. Light and fast as a cat, Bassett crossed and *bam!* he had her. Of course Frank, who was pretty damn good himself, was right beside him. Dog had her on the ground, his legs wrapped around the center of her body, holding her down, while his left hand covered her mouth. The blanket had fallen from her, and Frank, his eyes accustomed to night vision, didn't miss the fact that she was naked as a newborn babe, though built a damn sight better than one.

Dog held the woman with methodical sureness and nodded to Gunther. As Frank moved forward and she caught sight of his face, the woman's body flexed and squirmed in desperation. But Bassett was strong, and her frantic movements never fazed him. Frank jammed the needle into her white butt, drove the plunger home, and she went limp.

Without any hesitation, Dog scooped the body up, blanket and all, and moved out toward the trees, the way they'd come. Frank wiped the rain from his face, the sound of lions catching his attention. Experience told him how close the big cats were. He glanced quickly around.

A campsite with no fire. In the old days, the human smell might have kept the lions away. Not anymore. Too many tourists had seen to that. And Frank had heard about the unusual size of the pride roaming this region. With that many, they were always hungry. The fresh meat hanging around the camp like Christmas-tree ornaments would clinch it. In a very short time, lions were going to be all over the camp, tearing up everything in sight.

All these thoughts came to him as he hurried after the fast-disappearing Dog Bassett. Frank increased his speed, stepping over the unmoving form of the gray-haired black who had been standing guard. As he ran, he could just barely make out the loosely swinging arms and bobbing head of the unconscious girl who hung limply over the broad shoulders of the man in front of him. Incredible. Dog hadn't even seemed to notice the woman was naked. Well, by God, Frank had noticed. It would be a cold day in hell when he missed something like that.

Seventeen

IT WAS A SOUND. A sound that filled his head with a long, unending roar, dragging him out of the heaviness of sleep to consciousness.

Braxton's eyes shot open.

Darkness. He tore the sleeping bag away from him and sat up. He shook his head and focused his attention. He was in the tent. It was night. Outside, heavy rain hammered at the top and sides of the canvas.

But there was more.

The roar that had jarred him awake had not stopped. It was real. Savage and deafeningly real—and right outside his tent. The roar of carnivores.

And there were screams!

"Kathy," Braxton muttered, feeling a dreadful swell of nausea within him. "Oh, my God. Where is Kathy?"

Frantic, Braxton jammed his feet into his pants and fastened them at the waist. For a moment he stopped and stared without understanding at the pile of Kathy's clothing lying nearby. Her clothes were still there. Where was she? He scooped up the flashlight at the top of his sleeping bag and stumbled toward the tent entrance. As he did so, two strong beams of light shone through the canvas wall and a new sound reached his ears: the blaring of a horn.

"The bus," Braxton said aloud, pulling the tent flap open. "Sammy!"

Sticking his head out into the rain, he couldn't at first comprehend what he saw. The scene was fragmented, filled with the chaos of undefined movement. Bodies in random motion, jerking across the beams of light, then into the darkness again. But they were animal shapes. Lions. It seemed there were lions everywhere, though it was hard to see because the bus lights kept shifting as the vehicle barreled into camp, smacking with heavy thuds against the sinewy bodies that darted into its path.

The lights shifted again and the horn blared, and Braxton strained to see order in the confusion. He wiped at the rain that pelted his face. He *had* to see, damn it! Comprehend the action and sound. He swept his eyes over the camp, desperately trying to make sense of what was going on. And where was Kathy?

The beams of the headlights hit on a spot at the opposite side of the camp, and the bus screeched to a halt. Several lions looked up from where they were feeding, staring into the blinding light. As they did so, another lion lunged forward, snapping at the meat, but a huge male snarled loudly, striking out with his paw, and the intruder quickly retreated.

As his eyes focused on the scene, Braxton's breath caught in his throat. The carcass the lions were feeding on was no dead animal but a man. It was Sammy's old gray-haired uncle, Chegee...or rather, what was left of him. A female lion clamped the arm of the man tightly in her jaw and shook it, causing the other, loose limbs to slap at the muddy, rain-soaked ground. The male returned to its feeding, sinking its teeth into the body's soft midsection, tearing at the flesh. A loud clang sounded as the bus door was flung open, and the male looked up again, a strand of skin catching in its long, jagged front teeth. From the lion's stained jaws dripped a dark liquid that Braxton knew was not part of the rain.

He pointed his flashlight at the bus in time to see Sammy's short figure charge through the open bus doorway, a long-barreled gun in his hands. Sammy jammed the butt of the weapon against his shoulder and, pointing the barrel into the air, fired. A loud, cracking explosion broke through the air, flames leaping from the end of the gun into the blackness of the storm-filled night, and the lions around the dead man scattered. Sammy pumped his hand up and down the barrel once, ejecting a spent shell, then fired again. Quickly repeating the process, he fired yet a third time.

Lions roared in alarm and rampaged through the campsite with a frightening abandon. Braxton swung his light in an arc, taking in the rest of the camp. The first thing his beam settled on was the area where the Africans had set up camp. The tents were down, the canvas disheveled and shredded.

Fearing the worst, Braxton forced himself to aim the light toward Zelda's tent. Relief flooded through him as he saw the canvas structure was untouched. In fact, Injai was standing defensively at the tent's entrance, the long, sharp-ended section of a center tent pole in his hands. As the light shone on him, he shouted in Braxton's direction through the driving rain.

"Stay there, Buddy! Do not move! Father Eddie is with us. He was able to crawl over. Stay there with Kathy! Do not leave the tent!"

A lion careered past Injai, and the driver jabbed at the moving animal with a hard thrust of the tent pole. But neither the bizarreness of the action nor the danger of the situation registered with Braxton.

Dread was enveloping him as Injai's words forced a harsh realization on him. *Kathy was not there!* Where was she then? She had to be out there somewhere. Knowing only that he had to find her, Braxton pushed himself from the tent into the whipping storm and a darkness filled with berserk carnivores.

Dimly he heard Injai crying, "Buddy, no..." But Braxton was listening to his own inner voice of desperation and plunged forward. He had not gone more than three or four feet when he stumbled. Then, out of the darkness hurtled a powerful form of snarling savagery. As it crashed into him, Braxton spun sideways and forward, falling with a painfully awkward skid facedown in the mud.

He was sure a lion had hit him, but he sensed it was a haphazard collision and rolled over onto his back, instinctively bringing his arms up defensively in case the attack was still to follow. As he attempted to scramble to his feet, he did see a form coming at him. However, it was not a lion. From around the bus, heading straight for him, was a black giant that he knew could only be one man: Twamba!

High over his head the giant was holding a spear, which he swung in a wide circle, and he was screaming in alarm. As he drew closer, he shifted his huge shield to the hand that held the spear. Then, with only one arm and what seemed like no effort, the Masai picked Braxton up and ran back toward the bus.

Several more explosions sounded, and Braxton could smell the odor of spent gunpowder. Sammy stepped quickly away from the open bus doorway to allow the giant to drop Braxton beside him.

The tall warrior shouted several quick, sharp words to Sammy. The young guide nodded, lowering his weapon and responding in Swahili. Then Twamba disappeared again, and Sammy knelt beside Braxton.

"Are you hurt?" he asked, his voice filled with nervous strain.

Braxton was aware that the lion sounds were fading. The animals were retreating from the camp. He shook his head heavily. "No, I . . . Kathy . . ."

Sammy cut Braxton off as he rose to meet the others, who, led by the Masai, were hurrying toward the bus. Injai, bringing up the rear of the group, began to speak loudly before he reached the bus.

"Sammy, no warning. Lion came through the back of tent. I jumped up, grabbing pole when tent went down. Suddenly, lions everywhere. No warning. Nothing. Fire is out. No Chegee on guard. Then I saw them at his body. He was already dead. There was nothing I could do. I ran to help others. Sammy, I do not know how it happened. I . . ." Injai stopped at the bus, looking down at Braxton. "Buddy, you are all right? Why did you run out like that?"

The overhead row of lights on the inside of the bus had automatically remained on because of the open door, around which the small cluster of soaked people now stood. In the gray-green cast of light that spilled from the bus's interior, their features were dimly visible to one another. As he spoke Kathy's name, Braxton saw Zelda's expression become hollow and lifeless, while Eddie's mouth opened in unbelieving shock.

"Oh, no, Braxton," the priest whispered, making no attempt to wipe away the rain that dripped from his face. "Not the lions."

"Ed, I don't know," Braxton answered, anguish filling his voice. "She wasn't there. I woke up to all hell breaking loose out here and she was gone."

"But she was there when you fell asleep?" It was Zelda speaking now, her voice shaking.

"Yes. It...it doesn't make sense. No lions came into the tent. And she wouldn't have left. She wouldn't have gone out of the tent."

"Maybe she panicked when she heard the animals. Tried to make it to another tent or..." Eddie's voice trailed off, his weak explanation unfinished. Braxton could never remember hearing his friend sound so unsure of himself.

"Eddie, her clothes were still in the tent. All of them, do you understand? She wouldn't go out like that."

The priest suddenly frowned as a thought came to him. "There's something else. My tent had a hole in the back of it when I woke up, and no animal had been near it. It was as if it had been sliced open. Zelda, your tent was the same. I saw it when I reached you."

Zelda looked at Eddie questioningly. "Yes, I noticed it immediately, but—"

"Sammy! Father!" Injai cried. "That is why the lion is in the tent suddenly." Not waiting for a response, he ran into the darkness. Within moments, his voice shouted back to them from the area of Zelda's tent. "Cut open! The back has been cut open!"

The guide looked at Braxton. "Was yours this way?"

Braxton shook his head, trying to remember. He had glanced around the inside of the tent and it had been dark. "No, I would have noticed."

"Let us make sure," Sammy said. "Injai, Braxton's tent!" he called out.

Eddie stepped next to Sammy. "If they cut the other tents, they knew she had to be in Braxton's."

"Hapana," Injai's voice shouted. "No cut!"

Zelda wiped at the wetness on her face with an anxious gesture. "Ed, you think they...?"

The priest gave a reluctant nod. "It would explain why Chegee wasn't on guard to alert everyone. Why the fire was out. Sammy?"

The guide stared at Eddie a moment. The muscle running down the side of his face jumped erratically under his skin as his eyes shifted from the priest to the others, then back again. When he finally spoke, however, it was not to Eddie but to the slim giant who stood near them. He addressed the Masai urgently in Swahili, and without reply, Twamba turned, disappearing into the dark rain-filled trees behind them. Then as Injai returned to the bus, Sammy spoke to the others.

"We must hurry. First, quickly search this area. As with Chegee, lions do not drag their prey. If she is here, we will find her. But I believe Eddie is right. We must tear down the equipment with much speed. Have no concern for order. Throw it into the bus. By then Twamba will have returned from Gunther's camp and we will know more. Now hurry."

Injai ducked into the bus, emerging with two more flashlights, and in splinter groups they swept over the immediate camping area. Within minutes they had confirmed Kathy was not there, and following Sammy's instructions, they hurried to get the equipment down.

Assisted by Injai, Braxton worked with Eddie to dismantle their tents, while Sammy helped Zelda pull down the ones nearby. The rain was slackening now, making the work easier, but though he tried to hide it, Braxton's back was once again sending knives of pain up his spine, and he slipped in the mud while yanking at the front stake, falling sideways.

Eddie stooped over him, grabbing his hand and helping him to his feet. "You okay, Brax?"

"Yeah, I think I retwisted my back when I fell coming out of the tent before," Braxton replied in angry frustration. He shook free of the priest's grasp and, straightening with some difficulty, gathered the wet canvas in his arms. "Let's get this to the bus."

The two of them lugged the waterlogged tent over to the parked vehicle. There, with Sammy's help, they shoved it through the doorway and were dumping it onto the first two seats when the Masai warrior reappeared from the trees into the dull light.

Sammy jumped from the step well to meet the man, and turning to watch them, Braxton noticed that besides the wide shield in the Masai's left hand and the long ornamented spear in his right, the slim giant carried yet a third weapon. Tucked in his belt on the same side as the spear was a sharply honed, deadly looking, short, curved sword. The Masai looked directly at Sammy when he spoke, his expression calm and even. He showed no sign of being breathless from running and was oblivious to the light rain that splattered on his face.

Sammy listened attentively until the Masai finished and then uttered the word *"Lini?"* Braxton remembered it meant "when?" in Swahili. The warrior replied with three clipped words that Braxton could not follow, and Sammy, in a sudden flash of anger, smashed his fist against the side of the bus.

"The camp is empty," Sammy said bitterly. "Twamba says they left two, maybe three hours ago. Gunther has tricked me, Eddie. I have been a fool."

Braxton steadied himself in the doorway. "You think Gunther killed Chegee?"

Sammy shook his head. "He wouldn't have to. Once silenced by a blow, Gunther knew Chegee could not sound an alarm or tend the fire from the rain. And he knew of the lions. I found large pieces of raw meat scattered throughout the camp when I searched. It must have been left there to draw the lions. Gunther could see how all this would come about."

With the help of Zelda, Injai stumbled up to them under the weight of two more soaked tents. "What is it?" the hypnotist asked. "What did he find?"

Eddie walked over to Zelda while Sammy and the Masai heaved the remaining tents through the doorway. As he moved, Sammy shouted a command to Injai and the driver jumped into the bus, swinging into the driver's seat. He turned the ignition and the vehicle started up with a cough.

"The camp is empty, Zelda," Eddie said. "They're gone. They must have taken Kathy."

"Oh, my God. No," Zelda cried, grabbing Eddie's arm for support.

"Get in!" Sammy shouted out the doorway at them. "We are leaving!"

Eddie frowned at the guide. "Sammy. You can't leave the body of Chegee lying out there. We have to at least bury him."

Sammy shook his head. "It is no longer Chegee. It is not our way, Eddie. Burial is the white man's way. A body in the ground here poisons the grass, and the grass is life to those who live here. So is meat."

"Sammy, you're a civilized man. This is your uncle. You can't just . . ."

"It is your religion speaking, Eddie," Sammy continued, stifling the priest's protest. "As I told you before, death here has no morality. My way is the way of the savannah. Now please, get in the bus."

"No, you'll have to wait," Eddie answered in an authoritative voice. The priest reached into his trousers pocket and withdrew a small leather-bound book. "You may do as you wish, but this man was a human being and I will give him last rites."

The guide started to reply, but fell silent as he watched Eddie walk away from the doorway and over to the mutilated body of Chegee, where it lay splattered with mud and caking blood. Zelda climbed onto the bus and sat down several rows back across from Braxton, who sat slumped in a padded metal seat.

"Much as we all want to get moving, we'll have to wait, Sammy," Braxton said weakly, attempting to explain his friend's actions. He glanced over at Zelda. "Look out there. Eddie may have doubts and questions about his faith, but I don't think he need worry. If there ever was one, he is one of God's holy servants on Earth."

The other occupants of the bus turned their attention to the man who knelt in the mud over the body of Sammy's uncle. Eddie held the small book open and was lifting his hand over the inert form. The rain had stopped completely now, and in the wet mists that surrounded him, the priest appeared to be moving in a halo of light.

Eddie rose to his feet, and Sammy turned to the Masai standing beside him. The two exchanged several words and the tall warrior left them, brushing past Eddie as the priest reached the bus doorway. Sammy leaned forward, extending his hand. Eddie accepted the gesture and, grasping the guide's hand, stepped into the bus.

"Please understand me," Sammy said, keeping Eddie's hand within his grasp. "You are right. Chegee was of my blood. I have known him since I was a child and he worked with my father. And I will find time to mourn for him properly. But he is gone. I can do nothing more for him. It is your friend I must try to help now."

"I understand, Sammy. And like you, I must also do what I believe to be right." Eddie raised his free hand. It held a mud-encrusted ivory-handled machete. "I thought you would want to keep this."

With a nod of thanks, the guide released the priest's hand, accepting the slasher and shoving it under the driver's seat next to him. Then he signaled Injai, and the bus started moving with a lurch.

Eighteen

THE BUS SLAMMED up and down violently as Injai drove across a deep rut in the sodden earth, and Eddie grabbed at the nearby seat back, almost falling. Staring intently out the windshield, Sammy appeared not to notice the priest's loss of balance.

"What will you do first? Where will you go?" Eddie asked, keeping a firm grip on the metal seat.

"To the Gunther campsite," Sammy answered, raising his voice so that everyone in the bus could hear. "Twamba is already there to look for signs that will help us see the direction Gunther chose when leaving. You should all rest while you can. There is nothing any of you can do at present. For now, it is up to me."

Eddie nodded his head in agreement, then carefully edged his way down the center aisle amid the sporadic, jolting bounces of the speeding bus until he reached Braxton's seat. The news correspondent's face was ashen and he did not look up when Eddie stopped beside him. Rather, he held on fiercely to the seat in front of him, grimacing in pain every time the bus jarred his body.

After exchanging glances with Zelda, Eddie leaned over and placed his hand on his friend's shoulder.

"Have faith." Braxton stared up at Eddie and nodded without conviction as the priest continued. "She's all right. I feel sure of it. We just have to keep faith that this will work out."

"I thought you were having trouble with faith yourself," Braxton responded hoarsely. Eddie made no reply, but hurt flickered across his face, and Braxton pushed himself in his seat. "I'm sorry, Ed. I didn't mean that. It's just that...I shouldn't have fallen asleep, Ed. I still can't figure how they could have taken her from the tent without my knowing it. How could I not have...?"

The bus lurched violently, and Braxton gasped in pain, his knuckles white as he grabbed on to the seat frame in front of him.

"I thought so," Eddie said, studying his friend with concern. "You really are in pain."

Braxton eased up on his grip a little. "I know. Why the hell did I have to fall and mess my back up again? Kathy had worked on it until the pain was almost gone."

"Well, lean back and try to relax. We don't want it to get any worse. You have to stay in good spirits, Brax. I can't do comic relief—and I have a feeling we'll be needing some."

Braxton smiled, allowing his head to rest against the back of the seat, but Eddie could see the smile was only a half effort. The ever-present glint of humor was gone from his friend's eyes, an apprehensive sadness replacing it.

"I took your advice, Ed," Braxton said in a quiet, hushed voice. "I followed my feelings and jumped in with both feet, telling her exactly how I felt, or rather, how I was growing to feel about her."

The priest nodded. "And?"

A genuine smile flickered across Braxton's face. "And it's good. We talked, and I think it's going to be very good. We... I don't know, we just seem to hit it off. But I guess you suspected we would all along, didn't you? Anyway, it's a good beginning. I..."

Braxton's expression suddenly clouded, emotion finding its way through his normally guarded defenses. He turned his head away. Out the window, far across the grasslands, rays of light were breaking along the horizon, shining upward into the dark sky, a prelude to the African dawn.

"Jesus Christ, Ed. Why would Gunther take her like that? What the hell does he think he'll gain?"

"The grave, I imagine," Eddie replied.

"But she doesn't even know where it is yet."

"He doesn't know that."

"And when he discovers she can't take him there, then what?" The priest had no answer, and Braxton shook his head. "I can't lose her now, Ed," he whispered, as much to himself as to the man next to him. "Not now. We've only just started to..."

"We'll find her, Brax," Eddie said, placing his hand on his friend's shoulder. "Now stay put, and keep pressure off that back. Soon as we stop, I'll get you some dry things. In fact, it wouldn't hurt any of us to get into some dry clothing."

From the front of the bus, Sammy was watching them. "What is it, Eddie?" he called down to them. "Braxton is hurt?"

"It's his back," Eddie told him, glancing up. "His fall in the mud back there really clinched it."

A troubled frown materialized on Sammy's face, and he walked quickly back to them. Braxton took a deep breath and gave the guide a half smile.

"You don't look so good," Sammy said, returning the smile.

Braxton raised his head. "I'll make it. Don't worry about me."

Sammy leaned down to speak to Braxton, but just then the bus skidded to a stop, and through the dirt-streaked windows, everyone could see that they had arrived at a deserted campsite. Several feet beyond the bus were the ashen remains of a fire. Beside it, spear and shield in hand, stood the Masai warrior.

In the morning light Twamba seemed even more imposing. His tightly braided hair was tinted with red ocher, and his sturdy legs covered with red clay. Draped in a loose cotton toga, his tall, muscled body appeared ready for any unexpected danger. The many multicolored beads that hung from his neck and dangled from his elongated earlobes in oval rings glistened, reflecting the first rays of the sun.

A few feet behind the Masai was a towering giraffe. The animal's head bobbed nervously on its long, narrow neck, and it pawed the ground with its hoof as it gazed at the halted vehicle.

Sammy pointed out the window to where the Masai stood waiting. "As you can see, Twamba is here before us. You are lucky. Twamba is Laibon—a great medicine man. You saw how he healed me quickly. Rest a moment, Braxton. I will have him tend to you. He will help your back with his herbs also."

"We all better have some dry clothes too, Sammy," Eddie said.

The guide nodded. "I will have Injai bring the luggage inside the bus. Now let me learn from what Twamba has found."

Sammy hurried back up the aisle to where Injai had already pulled the metal door open, and the two of them stepped out of the bus.

"I'll help Injai with the luggage," Eddie said, leaving Zelda and Braxton.

Outside, the gangly-looking animal near the two Africans had calmed now, and it moved to stand next to the Masai.

"Look at the way that giraffe stays with Twamba—it's incredible," Zelda remarked, as they stared out the window.

"They might have something," Braxton said. "See how Twamba is pointing out over the savannah?"

"Let's see what Sammy says," Zelda suggested cautiously.

"Zelda, look at the way the man is pointing with his spear. What else could it be?"

"I know. I see. I just don't want to start getting false hopes up."

"Well, you won't have to wonder any longer. Here they come."

Although Sammy and Twamba had started toward the bus, Eddie was the first to come through the doorway, carrying wet pieces of luggage in each hand. Injai followed right behind the priest with more suitcases, and the two made their way toward the back.

Twamba propped his spear and shield carefully against the side of the bus before entering, and because of his height he had to duck through the doorway and walk down the aisle with his head and shoulders hunched forward. Now that he was closer, Braxton could hear the tiny bell hanging from the warrior's earlobe tinkle lightly.

Eddie stopped next to Zelda, offering her a bag. "Here, Zelda, you go first. Take this to the back. I'll hook the blanket up between the overhead racks so you can change."

"I'm fine," Zelda protested, taking the luggage from the priest. "Take care of Braxton first."

"Zelda, I'm not a cripple," Braxton protested.

Sammy intervened. "I wish for Twamba to look at Braxton, Zelda. Why don't you go ahead."

"Twamba found something out there by the fire, didn't he," Braxton said, unable to suppress his need to know.

Sammy nodded. "Yes, we could easily see where the vehicles went as they left. But Gunther would know that. In the rain he could not cover his departure. He would find a main road quickly, for that will make it much more difficult for us to follow."

"And then?"

"We will have to see, but with a Masai tracker to guide us, we have a chance. This is Twamba, Braxton. He will give you medicine. Then we will leave."

"*Jambo,*" Braxton said.

"*Jambo,*" the Masai answered, his eyes examining as he spoke.

"Trust him," Sammy said, turning to leave. "I have to go outside. I will return soon."

"It is bad, the pain, Buddy?" Injai asked, hovering behind Twamba, who was kneeling on one knee, gently running his hand down the back of the man next to him.

"I'll live," Braxton responded, attempting a smile.

"*Wapi panauma?*" Twamba asked.

Braxton moved his own hand to the base of his spine, responding in both Swahili and English. "*Kichwa.* Backache."

The Masai grunted with a nod and, after checking the spot Braxton indicated, turned to Injai. *"Maji!"*

Injai nodded and hurried to the front of the bus, while the Masai continued moving his hands along Braxton's spine, applying pressure at various places.

"Certainly does behave like a doctor, doesn't he?" Eddie said, watching the proceedings with a keen interest. "Maybe you should ask him his fee before he goes any further."

"I thought you didn't do humor, Ed," Braxton muttered.

The Masai spoke again, and as he did so, he opened his mouth, pointing toward Braxton's face and nodding.

"He wants you to open your mouth," Injai said, returning to them with a thermos cap full of water.

"Yeah, I remember the treatment with Sammy," Braxton answered as he watched Twamba tap some of the powdery substance from his pouch into the water.

Dressed in a dry kimono, Zelda reappeared from behind the blanket. "What's the prognosis?"

"Don't know yet," Eddie said.

"But I'm about to take the magic cure," Braxton added, accepting the cup from the Masai and glancing nervously at the fragments floating on the liquid. "Wonder what this is?"

Twamba nodded his head, obviously not understanding, and tapped his mouth.

"Might be better if you don't know," Eddie said. "Come on, we need you well. Down the hatch."

"That's easy for you to say," Braxton groaned, bringing the cup to his mouth and pouring the liquid down his throat.

"Injai!" Sammy called from the doorway.

Hearing his name called, the driver ran back up the aisle.

"How was it, Brax?" Eddie asked.

"Well, it's no Heineken, my friend," Braxton responded. "But if it makes this back ease up, I'll gladly take as many as needed." Then, smiling, Braxton handed the cup back to the Masai.

Twamba nodded, standing in his hunched-over posture. Then, tucking his pouch away, he turned, hurrying back to the doorway.

"If it works as fast as it did with Sammy, the pain should ease fairly soon," Zelda said hopefully.

Braxton shrugged. Like the others, he was looking at Sammy, who was coming down the aisle. Strapped on the guide's hip was a holster that held an ivory-handled pistol, and in his hands he carried a rifle along with several boxes of ammunition. Injai, bearing more weapons, followed the guide.

"Twamba's medicine is good—you will be fine soon," Sammy said, dropping the boxes of shells on the seat in front of them. He offered the weapon he held to Braxton. "Here. Keep this with you."

"No, thanks, Sammy," Braxton said, holding up his hands defensively. "I wouldn't know what to do with it."

"It is not hard, as I told you." Sammy took Braxton's hand and placed the rifle in it. "Even though your back is bad, you may use this. Point it carefully where you want to shoot and, after releasing the safety here below the shell chamber, pull the trigger. Be certain the stock is tight into your shoulder so the kick does not change your aim or make your back feel worse."

"Sammy, I think it would be better if the weapons remained stored under the bus," Eddie said evenly. The authoritative ring was once again in the priest's voice, but this time Sammy was having none of it. He turned to face Eddie.

"What do you believe will happen when we find Kathy, Eddie?"

"I don't want weapons involved, Sammy," Eddie replied firmly.

"Couldn't we get the authorities involved once we find her?" Zelda asked, siding with the priest.

Sammy shook his head. "As I told you, Gunther pays these authorities well. I know, Zelda."

"But this is kidnapping!"

"You have no proof of that. And Gunther will make certain it can never be proved. I worked for him, Zelda. That is why I know we must be the ones who find her. And I also know we must be prepared. Hear me, Eddie! In a fit of rage, Gunther beat me senseless and left me to die. I tell all of you, if Frank Gunther and Dog Bassett have taken this woman, they have weighed the risks, decided the reward is worth it, and you will have to fight to get her back."

"We'll find another way," Eddie said, refusing to yield.

Braxton closed his fingers around the gun Sammy had offered him, taking a box of ammunition from the seat in front of him with his other hand. "It holds more than one shell, Sammy?"

"Yes. You will see when you look at the chamber. There is a law limiting automatic weapons to two shells, but I have removed the plug. It will continue to fire every time you pull the trigger."

Eddie's face flushed with anger. "Braxton!"

"No, Ed! Stop kidding yourself. Everything changed when they took her from us. One person is dead already. Sammy's right. We'd better be prepared. That's the reality."

"Braxton, talk sense. I'll give you a reality. You think you could actually fire that gun at someone? Try to kill someone?"

"In all honesty I don't know, Ed," Braxton answered quietly. "But I think Gunther could. And *will*, if he has to. He sure as hell isn't going to apologize and hand her over when we pull up to his camp."

Braxton pushed off the top of the ammunition box, then flipped the lever that allowed the shell chamber to open. Eddie stared at him in disbelief, his words an explosion of frustration.

"Is this what it's all about then? Is this why we made the trip? So that it could end like this?"

Braxton looked up at his friend. "Ed, the reasons have all changed. They've taken Kathy."

"And we're going to try to find her, but does that mean we have to sink to their level? Braxton, I thought you had more sense than that."

"Look, Ed," Braxton suddenly spat, his face coloring. "I didn't ask to get involved in this. You came to me. And now I've gotten so tied into Kathy that the only thing I know for sure is that I'll do anything to get her back. Now, we're wasting important time. We'd better get started."

Sammy had been standing quietly as the men argued, and now he turned toward the priest. "Eddie?"

"All right. Let's go. We can talk as we ride. But I'm not giving in on this. There will be no guns used."

"Oh, come off it," Braxton said angrily. "You know why you get depressed, Ed? You know why you're so upset lately? Because every so often, no matter how hard you try to believe otherwise, the truth seeps

through. And the truth is we're a sorry goddamned lot
that you priests try to shepherd. You said it yourself.
We've been killing each other since Cain. It's a damned
world, my friend. We're all sick. Every goddamned one
of us. Filled with swell qualities like hate, greed, and
rage." Braxton rose to his feet, grasping the top of the
seat in front of him for support, his voice filling with
emotion. "You want to know if I can use the gun, Ed?
Let me tell you something. If that slimy bastard
Gunther or that psychopath named Dog has touched or
harmed Kathy, I'll try to blow their heads off! All right?
I'm no hero, Ed. I'm just an average guy who's found
himself in the middle of an asinine trip. But, by God, I
mean what I say. So, you see, there it is. Furthermore,
I'll keep my gun, if it's all the same to you. Now let's get
the hell out of here!"

"No!" Eddie shouted in Braxton's direction, his own
voice filling the bus's interior. "I will not accept that,
Braxton! Yes, we're flawed. Yes, it seems that needless
death is always with us. I've buried enough people who
have died of disease and starvation in the past few years
not to have to be reminded of that. Just as I am all too
aware that it always seems to fall to the priests and
women to mourn for all those who kill and die. But if I
did not believe there was hope, I would not have become a priest. I know I'm having my own doubt, but I
will never accept such pessimism. And I will never,
never accept killing as justified. I don't care what the
reason!"

"Okay, fine, Ed," Braxton fired back, his voice still
tight with emotion. "Start coming up with some clever
way to handle this when we do catch up to them. And
while you're at it, you'd better do some heavy praying,

Father. Pray that Kathy is still okay—if and when we find her.''

Zelda had turned in her seat with the intention of trying to calm Braxton and Eddie, but it was Injai who brought the heated words to a halt. Without warning, after a signal from Sammy, he shoved the bus in gear, and the vehicle jerked into motion, throwing Eddie into the seat across from where Zelda sat and dumping Braxton back down with a grunt of pain as his spine jarred against the hard cushion.

"Sorry, Father...Buddy," Injai called back, "Sammy told me to move."

"It would be good to stay seated," Sammy called to them, propping his own rifle next to him as he sat down behind the driver. "We will be moving quickly. Hold on. It will be a rough ride."

The group heard the guide's words, but it was Twamba who grabbed their attention. Though they had seen the Masai do the same thing from a distance days before, they still watched in astonishment as Twamba climbed up into a seated position on the sloping spine of the giraffe. They were still staring out the window in amazement when Injai turned the wheel of the bus to follow after the Masai who, spear held high, gave a high-pitched wailing cry and rode off into the distance on the galloping giraffe.

Nineteen

IT WAS HOT inside the spacious tent, a light breeze offering little relief from the sweltering heat of midafternoon. But more than the humidity was causing Dog Bassett to perspire as he sat on a small camp stool just inside the entrance of the tent. Though his face wore its usual inscrutable expression, Dog was acutely aware of a turmoil swirling inside him as he stared across the space that separated him from the still blanket-wrapped woman who lay near the far wall.

Dog Bassett knew that besides being unattractive, he had a face that conveyed very little; just as he knew that his considerable bulk caused a certain amount of fearful apprehension in people he encountered. More than once while trading in the underground market, he had used these attributes to his financial advantage. And the fact was he didn't consider himself to be an overly emotional man. Nor did he think he was oversexed, for that matter. When the urge for a woman came over him he took care of it, short and simple. While women weren't attracted to him and sometimes he had to pay, there were other times when he found willing partners. But never had he let it get the best of him. Dog made it a practice to never let anything get the best of him. Which was why he was having trouble understanding the need hammering inside him now as he stared at Kathy Sullivan.

Maybe it was because Gunther had talked about the attractiveness of the woman from the very beginning. Or maybe it was the flashes of her naked body he had seen, or the feel of her body struggling against him when he pinned her with his legs while Gunther gave her the needle. Whatever the reason, Dog Bassett knew the urge to have the woman he was supposed to be guarding was pretty damned strong, and it was bothering the hell out of him.

For many long minutes he had been able to restrain himself. But now, unable to resist at least a look, the massively built man stood and crossed over to where Kathy lay. She was still unconscious, but as he stooped down on one knee beside her, Dog could see that the heat was affecting her. Beads of perspiration had gathered in tiny pools on her forehead and along her hairline.

"It's the blanket," he muttered quietly, seeing the way the heavy material was wrapped tightly around her and tucked under her arms. Dog brushed a clump of matted red hair away from her face, and as he looked down at her, he could feel his heart begin to race. Gunther had been right about her, no question: She was one beautiful woman.

Telling himself the heat might be harming her, and that he should try to make her cooler, he reached over and lifted her limp left arm. He had intended to enjoy the tantalizing feeling that he knew loosening the blanket would bring, but free of the restraining arm, one corner of the cover slid down, leaving him staring at Kathy Sullivan's completely naked body. As he took in the beauty of what he saw, Dog realized he was doing a fair amount of sweating himself. Unconsciously sucking in his breath, he lifted the blanket completely away and swept his eyes over the feminine form in front of him.

She was even more captivating than he had imagined, and for several long seconds, he did not move. Transfixed, he stared down at her, unable to stop. Unable to stop staring at the way her slender, creamy white throat melted into the curve of her shoulder. The way her full, round breasts had settled into delicate, red-capped mounds that shimmered slightly with the even rise and fall of her chest. The way her form narrowed to her trim waist, which in turn widened again to her slender hips and the smooth spread of her thighs. And yes, the way her waist melted downward in soft, white curves of flesh that disappeared beneath—

"Having yourself a look, are you, Dog?"

There was no question that Gunther's voice had startled him, but Bassett wasn't about to let him know that. Slowly he lowered the blanket over Kathy Sullivan's body, hardening his facial expression before turning toward the entrance.

"She was perspiring badly, Frank. I thought I should loosen the blanket to allow her more air."

Frank Gunther stood framed in the tent opening. He held a native robe across his arm and his smile was laced with mockery. "Why, sure, Dog. Damned thoughtful of you. And while you were at it, you decided to have a little peek, is that it?"

"I haven't seen any rhinos, Frank," Bassett answered flatly. "A deal's a deal. I just thought I'd take a little preview."

"If this works out, you won't need to sell illegal rhino horns ever again, Dog," Gunther said, the smile remaining as he walked over to Bassett. "And you don't have to tell me if I was right; I know I was. I got a couple of quick shots of the lady's lower region of delight when we picked her up. Anyway, I brought this robe for her. Thought maybe if we show her we're not such bad guys and let her put something on, we'll get better cooperation." On the ground in front of them, Kathy moaned lightly and her head thrashed back and forth several times. "In any case, it appears you've had your last looks for the time being. She's coming around. Let's move back to the entrance. We'll get off to a lot better start when she wakes up if she doesn't realize you've been over here checkin' her ass, don't you think?"

Without replying, Bassett followed Gunther back to the entrance, where they watched as Kathy slowly regained consciousness.

"You sure we lost her people?" Bassett asked quietly.

"Dog, I wish you'd stop insulting me. My guess is they're still recovering from that pride of lions—if there's anyone left to do the cleaning up. But even if there is, I'm telling ya, I did such a good job of covering our tracks, *I* couldn't find us. And I'm the best damned tracker in Kenya." Kathy stirred again, and Gunther pushed back the tent flap, motioning for Bassett to leave. "Now go on. Wait outside. Let me deal with her alone and see how she's going to take this."

Somewhat reluctantly Bassett nodded, taking one last look at the woman on the ground, then disappearing out the tent entrance. Gunther closed the flap after him and turned his attention once again to Kathy—only to find her looking straight up at him with a wild, frightened gaze.

Gunther smiled reassuringly and sat down on the camp stool next to the entrance.

"It's all right, Kathy," he said easily. "How do you feel? Okay?" When Gunther spoke, Kathy emitted a short squeal of fear. Pulling the blanket tightly around her, she moved backward slightly. "Take it easy, kid. It's Frank Gunther, remember? Relax. You're okay."

Comprehension began to light up her eyes, but the fear was still there, along with caution.

"Kathy, it's Frank Gunther. Okay?"

The slightest of nods.

"That's better. Now everything is going to be fine. And I want you to understand that you are safe."

This time she edged away from him a little more.

"I know. This is a little confusing for you right now, but the main thing to realize is that nobody is going to hurt you. You're going to be fine. There's no reason to be frightened."

Gunther got up and took a couple of steps across the interior of the tent, smiling his best white-hunter smile, but Kathy cringed, shrinking away from him.

"Stay away from me," she said in a harsh whisper. "Where is Braxton? I was with Braxton? Where is he . . . and the others?"

Gunther cleared his throat and pushed his hat back on his head, his voice filled with sympathetic understanding. "They're not here, Kathy. That is something you're just going to have to accept. I know it's difficult. And I don't want you to be frightened, because no harm will come to you. I give you my word on that. All we want is a little cooperation."

Kathy did not reply. Frank could see her mind was now beginning to clear, that she was grasping the reality of her situation. At first he thought she was going to cry, but then a look of hard determination settled on her face, and she pulled the blanket tighter to her, staring hatefully back at him.

"Where are my clothes?" she said finally.

"Well, we had to leave in kind of a hurry, Kathy, and I didn't have a chance to pick them up. But I knew you'd be uncomfortable, so I brought you a robe." Gunther offered the garment he held in his hand. "Here. You can put this on. Kikuyu robe. Not the best, but it'll have to do for now."

Kathy did not reply but continued to glare at him, and Gunther smiled, dropping the native robe next to her. "Well, anyway, it'll be here when you decide you'd like to have it."

Kathy's eyes followed him as he stood again, and then she spoke, her head shaking in disbelief. "Why? Why are you doing this?"

Gunther nodded. "Good. Let's get right to it. I like that. Okay, simple question deserves a simple answer. It's the grave, Kathy, my dear. You're going to take me to the grave. Actually, this whole thing doesn't have to be unpleasant at all. You show us where to find the grave. We get what we want. And everybody comes out all right."

Kathy's eyes widened in disbelief. "What? You kidnapped me because you thought I could take you to the grave! You must be out of your mind!"

"No, I don't think so," Gunther said with a smile of assurance. "I know it's got to be there, because you people wouldn't be doing this if it weren't. And Dog assures me there are people out there who would be willing to pay through the nose to get their hands on the bones of the first man and woman. So that's it, Kathy. My guess is this could be worth a million, maybe even more if we can find other stuff there besides bones. You know, primitive personal items that might have been buried with the bodies. Stuff like that. Dog assures me that if the grave is real and the contents well preserved, the right person will pay us damn near anything we ask to be in possession of such a rare find. And that was just too good an opportunity to pass up.''

''And what do you have planned for me, Mr. Gunther? Once you have what you want I get my head kicked in and am left to die on the open plains like you did to Sammy?''

Gunther shook his head. ''Not a chance. I told you. No harm is going to come to that pretty little head of yours. We leave you in an isolated spot that is safe but gives us a chance to leave the country, and then we're all home free.''

Kathy shook her head. ''Gunther, what in God's name makes you think I can lead you anywhere?''

''Because I watched you smack that map, little lady. They're all keyed in to you. You're the one who's got the goods, so don't try to tell me any different. And I know you're concerned about other people's welfare, so I'm sure you'll help us out. Now listen to me, because I want you to be sure to understand what I'm saying. I know damn well what I've gotten into by taking you the way we did. And I don't plan on losing on this one. You understand? I'll do whatever I have to do to get to that grave. I said you were safe, Kathy. But I can't guarantee what might happen to the others you were with. The truth is they're a pretty defenseless lot. And this is a wild country. Anything could happen. And if you get it into your head not to help us, I can make sure something pretty destructive happens to them. Those friends of yours could vanish from the savannah without a trace. And don't for a second make the mistake of thinking I couldn't. On the other hand, if you find it in your heart to cooperate, I could go out of my way to make sure nothing happens to them. Once we have what we want, I can arrange that they find you. Because by the time any or all of you make it back to Nairobi, I'll have the goods and be nothing but history in the country of Kenya."

Kathy's attitude seemed to shift as she listened, and it was obvious she had decided on a new tack when she replied. "Frank, listen to me. If you'd stayed around to talk to us more, you'd know that what you ask is impossible. We're not even sure of the location yet. We need to do more hypnosis sessions. And that is impossible without Zelda. This is insanity. You talk about bones and rare relics. We don't know if anything will be there even if we do find the location of the grave. Don't you understand? It might all be for nothing. You can't do this."

"Hey, look around, lady. I've done it. And I'm sure you'll understand if I don't exactly believe you," Frank added with a knowing smile. "There's no way you people would go to all this trouble if you didn't know something was going to be there."

"Frank, you're wrong! You have to believe me, damn it. I'm telling you the truth. I can't take you anywhere!"

Gunther adjusted the hat on his head. "All right, I'll tell you exactly how it is. I'm going outside. And while I'm gone, my suggestion is that you deal with two things. One, you'd better put that robe on. I saw the way Dog was looking at you before, and I think we'd all be a lot better off if you were in some clothes. Second, before nightfall, you'd better do some heavy meditation or whatever it takes for you to know where we're supposed to go next, because in terms of your friends' safety, there are hundreds of ways to die out here on the open savannah and almost all of them can be made to look like legitimate accidents.''

Having issued his threat, Gunther turned and walked out of the tent without waiting for a reply, the center flap closing noiselessly behind him.

Twenty

KATHY WAS FULLY CONSCIOUS NOW, and she sat unmoving, clutching the blanket to her as she attempted to grasp what was taking place. It was unbelievable, but they had actually kidnapped her.

The urge to cry welled up within her again, but she fought it down, as she had when Gunther confronted her. No, damn it. There would be no tears. In spite of the fact that her situation seemed hopeless, she would not give up.

She grabbed the robe Gunther had left at her feet and pulled it over her head, ignoring the horrible odor that came from the rough fabric. She swept her eyes over the interior of the tent and tried to collect her thoughts. She had to think. Concentrate. Obviously, she couldn't hope that the others would find her. Gunther would have made sure of that. So whatever she did, she was on her own.

Okay, what were her options?

"Not very many," she murmured to herself, staring at the entrance. There wasn't much doubt in her mind that Dog Bassett's powerful hulk was right outside the tent's main opening.

Okay, forget the entrance. What else? A weapon. She needed something that she could use for... For what? Against Gunther or Bassett? Well, maybe she wouldn't stand a chance, but at least she'd feel better if she tried.

Then her eyes settled on the bottom edge of the canvas behind her, and snatching up the blanket, she quickly crawled toward the rear of the tent. What were the odds that someone was outside the back? Slim. Still, she had to move very carefully. Quickly but carefully.

There were three metal stakes across the back. She had taken down one of Gunther's tents that first morning when they left Nairobi. That time, in order to pull the stakes out of the ground, she had used a section of the rope to give her leverage, and with supreme effort, the long, pointed metal shafts had come out of the ground.

Fixing the end of the blanket around the top of a stake should work the same way as the rope had. And if she could just get the rear center stake out without anyone noticing, she would have accomplished two goals: a space would be opened for a possible escape, and the metal stake with its jagged point would give her a weapon. It wasn't much, of course. But it was something, damn it. And as long as there was the slimmest of chances it would work, she would try.

Slowly, making certain the canvas stretched along the ground did not move, Kathy pushed the end of the blanket under the bottom of the tent next to the stake. With her fingers she dug into the dirt until she touched the metal. Then she grasped the blanket and eased it around the buried shaft, working it until it caught on the rope hook at the top of the stake.

She then gripped the sides of the blanket with both hands, squatted and, gritting her teeth, pulled with a strong, constant pressure.

Nothing. It didn't move. Then she knew why. Of course. Her direction was wrong. Because of the way it had been hammered in from the outside, she was pulling against the angle of entrance.

Sweating profusely now, Kathy glanced at the still flap that covered the entrance of the tent, then moved beside the stake. Positioning herself at the edge of the canvas yet being careful not to touch it, she squatted again and, taking a deep breath, pulled.

The stake gave. Just a little, but there was movement. Her heart beating with excitement, Kathy wiped at the perspiration dripping into her eyes and, with a muffled grunt, yanked the blanket. And the stake gave, sliding from the earth in which it was buried with a suddenness that dumped her sideways. Instantly she scrambled to her feet, then crouched near the loosened stake. Her hand was sliding under the canvas to grasp at the loose stake when Dog Bassett lifted the tent flap and came through the opening.

"Do you mind waiting a minute?" Kathy demanded angrily, snatching the blanket up to cover herself. "I had to go to the bathroom."

Dog shook his head, placing his considerable bulk down on the stool next to him. "Sorry. Frank said not to leave you alone. Do what you have to do. It doesn't bother me."

"I've finished, thank you," Kathy replied, making sure the blanket covered not only herself, but the area around her. As she glared at the man on the stool across from her, she desperately searched with her hand beneath the canvas. It had to be there, damn it. Where was it?

"Did Frank tell you the terrible mistake you've made?" Kathy said as her hand scraped with agonizing slowness over the dirt. "Did he tell you I don't know where the grave is?"

The man said nothing, his cold eyes simply lingering on her, so Kathy tried again, her voice filled with urgency. "Mr. Bassett, please. Help me. I know it was Gunther. I'll tell them you aren't involved. Please. I don't know where it is. You've got to believe me."

"You can call me Dog, if you want to," the huge man said, coming to his feet. "Everyone does."

Then two things connected at the same time. Kathy suddenly realized that Dog Bassett was telling her he liked her, and the fingers of her right hand touched the cold metal of the tent stake.

A tiny thrill coursed through her as she greedily closed her fingers around the long shaft and very, very slowly pulled her arm back inside the tent until her hand and the stake were at her side beneath the blanket.

She shifted the stake in her hand until she held it at its base, the point away from her like a knife. She smiled tentatively.

"All right . . . Dog. Please, help me get out of here. Please. I don't trust Gunther. You know I'm right—that this is crazy. You're not afraid of Gunther or what he would do if you helped me, are you?"

Bassett walked over and squatted down in front of her. Suddenly, for the first time since Kathy had known him, he half smiled. "No, I'm not afraid of Gunther," he said.

"Then help me, Dog, please," she pleaded, reaching forward and grabbing his arm. The action had been an unconscious gesture, but the moment Kathy touched the man in front of her, she knew she had made a mistake.

It was as if the contact set him off, somehow. She could see the change that came into his eyes. Her blanket slipped a little with the movement, and the man's gaze had shifted below her neck, where the loose-fitting

robe revealed a deep cleavage that disappeared between rounded swells of pale flesh. Bassett's breath
caught and Kathy released his arm, pulling the blanket
to her.

"If I help you, how would you help me?" Dog said,
the stupid half-smile remaining on his face.

"I...would pay a reward. I promise. We have money.
Plenty of it. Help me, and I'll see that you get as much
as you want."

"It's not your money I need," Dog said. And then he
raised his hand, touching Kathy's hair before sliding his
fingers loosely around her neck. "I see you put on the
robe. It looks good. But then anything would look good
on you."

And suddenly Kathy realized with an ever-increasing
horror that, terrible as he was, she had been better off
bargaining with Gunther. With the hunter, she had at
least been safe until he had what he wanted. But what
Dog Bassett wanted was in his eyes, and she could sense
the urgency of his need as his hand tightened around the
back of her neck.

"No, Dog. Please. Gunther will be back any second.
You have to get me out of here now. Please."

But Dog Bassett was no longer listening. As Kathy's
pleading became more insistent and she began to protest, the memory of her naked body struggling against
him when he had held her down between his legs came
flooding back to him. Bassett didn't think about what
Gunther might do, nor did he care about any reward.
All he could concentrate on was satisfying the fiery need
within him. One hand remained around her neck, as the
other hand reached forward and drew the blanket away
from her.

Emitting muffled sounds of fright, Kathy twisted in an attempt to avoid the man's clutching grasp, but her reactions were blurred by anxiety and fear as his thick hand closed over her breast, clamping down on it.

Gunther! She had to alert Gunther! With the thought came her voice, and she started to scream, but Dog's hand moved to her mouth, cutting off the sound before it could tear from her throat. Frantic now, Kathy squirmed to free herself. She brought up her knee, driving it toward Bassett's groin, but he turned, and she smashed harmlessly into his thigh.

And then he was pushing her downward. Oh, God, he was so strong. So horribly strong. She was going to lose. She was no longer able to stop the horrible swirl of events that had dragged her to this awful moment. And with one last attempt at defending herself, she focused her remaining shreds of energy on the metal stake she held hidden beneath her.

And then, suddenly, in a remote corner of her mind, Kathy realized that she was not crying. No, as she grasped the metal weapon tighter in preparation to strike, and as she fought against her attacker, something was happening to her: she could be pushed no further. After all the weeks of torment and doubt and fear, she had reached the saturation point.

She would be pushed no more, damn it! Whatever the outcome, she had had enough! Yes! She would be frightened no more! Yes, you filthy son of a bitch! Enough!

Slowly she inched the metal stake out from under her, all the while lashing out at the man bearing down on her with her free left hand, scratching and forcing him to contend with her attack while she waited for the right moment to strike.

Finally, he struck her. The blow was hard across her face, snapping her head sideways. Kathy knew she was hurt, but she could not concern herself with how badly.

She forced her body to go limp, simultaneously turning her weapon so the jagged point was upward. At her lack of resistance, she felt the man relax for just an instant, and he reached down and pulled up the robe that covered her. In that instant, summoning every last ounce of strength left in her, Kathy brought the stake up, back, and then savagely forward, aiming the blade at Dog Bassett's ugly, brutish head.

Dog saw the metal shaft coming at him and dodged, jerking awkwardly with a gasp of surprise. But the reaction was not fast enough, and Kathy's chopping swing connected. The dirt-covered point glanced off the bridge of his nose and buried itself deeply beneath his right eye.

Kathy felt the weapon sink into flesh and heard the man utter a sudden outcry of pain. Without pausing, she again pulled her weapon back and swung it forward with a vengeance. Again she connected, this time sinking the jagged end into the man's fleshy cheek.

Dog wailed in agony as blood dripped from his face, and his hands shot up to cover his punctured eye. With all her might Kathy struggled to pull free, and finally she was out from under him.

Not even pausing to consider who or what might be waiting for her, she grabbed at the loose canvas behind her and lifted it, crawling with her elbows and knees beneath the tent wall.

As her head emerged outside, a faint hope ignited in Kathy. There, not more than ten feet beyond the tent, were the vehicles. She scrambled to her feet and ran.

Ran for all she was worth toward Frank Gunther's Cherokee.

From within the tent, Dog Bassett's screams of rage caused her to run even faster. Off to her left she saw the driver named Dingo jump up in excitement and point in her direction as he shouted "Bwana!" over and over. And from the opposite side of a central campfire, she could see Gunther turn and then reach for the pistol at his waist as he headed after her.

Faster! She had to move faster!

Then she was there. Her fingers closed around the metal handle of the Cherokee's door. She jerked at the latch and the door swung open. She didn't look again in Gunther's direction. She knew the hunter would be covering the space that separated them in huge strides.

Lunging forward, she fell into the driver's seat, dropping the stake and using both hands to pull the door closed after her and hammer down the tiny button that engaged the lock.

Then Gunther appeared, ramming his body at the door. Tearing at the locked latch. Clawing at the half-open window. But Kathy was still in motion, grasping the window handle and rolling the window up even as Gunther's hand sought to force entry.

With a final yank of the handle, Kathy tried to catch his fingers, but he extracted them just in time as the window settled into the ridges of its cushioned frame.

Kathy scooted across the seat. The other side! He was headed around the car—but not fast enough. Knowing the location of the mechanism now, she locked the door and closed the window as he came at her. But this time, it didn't stop him.

His snarling face raged at her through the closed window. Snatching the hat from his head, he wrapped it around his closed fist, and suddenly his arm reared back, then came hurling forward with a burst of speed that drove it crashing through the Cherokee's window. Splinters of glass sprayed inward, and Kathy screamed, jerking herself away from the shattering blow until she was backed against the locked driver's door.

The hand was groping through the window for her. No, it wasn't going for her. What then? It clumsily pawed the dash, reaching... *The keys! He was going for the keys.* His fingertips touched them, attempting to close over them. Oh, God. If he got the keys, it was over!

Then Kathy remembered the stake. Snatching it up from the seat next to her, she struck out with it once again, this time driving the point into Gunther's searching hand.

Emitting a cry of pain, Gunther yanked his hand away, and now it was Kathy's fingers that closed over the key in the ignition.

She wasn't thinking. Only reacting. The starter ground with the turn of the key, and the engine caught. Dingo had reached the Cherokee now, and crawling through the opening of the tent from which she had escaped, Kathy saw the awful bulk of Dog Bassett emerging.

She lifted her bare left foot off the clutch and jammed the right one down on the accelerator. Tires spun in the dirt, then caught, and the Jeep jumped forward. She tugged at the wheel, aiming for the figure of Bassett, who, his face covered with blood, one hand covering his wounded eye, had struggled to his feet and was running to block the oncoming vehicle.

Responding to her movements, the Jeep veered toward the hulking figure, and he dodged sideways just in time as the Cherokee shot past him. She jerked the gear shift toward her, clutching again, and with a grinding of gears, the Jeep's motor revved wildly and gathered new speed.

Kathy glanced in the rearview mirror. Gunther had dropped to one knee and was holding his pistol straight out, supporting it with his other hand. She heard the crack of the gun as it fired, and off to her left, a clump of dirt exploded in the air. His aim had been off. Another clanging sound reached her as a bullet tore into a fender. No, that wasn't it. The tires. He was aiming for the tires.

She jammed the shift away from her again, throwing the Cherokee into third, and pushed the accelerator to the floor. The steering wheel threatened to spin out of control as the vehicle bounced over the terrain with ever-increasing speed, but Kathy held on to it with all her might.

Gunther and the other two figures were receding from view now. She shifted to fourth gear and checked the rearview mirror one last time. It was hard to tell for sure, but she thought she could see Bassett and Gunther shouting at each other as the white hunter pointed out toward the direction in which she had driven.

Kathy stared out at the bumpy savannah in front of her, pushing the Cherokee as fast as she could. Still managing to keep the vehicle in control, she put as much distance as possible between herself and her kidnappers.

Then finally, as she looked out at the shrub-covered, straw-colored emptiness that stretched into the distance, emotions forced their way to the surface and Kathy felt her body shaking against the seat of the Jeep as tears blurred her vision.

She tasted salt from the tears that streaked down her cheeks, and within her, the voice of futility fought to be heard. Yes, by some stroke of dumb luck she had gotten away, but what had she really accomplished? They were sure to follow, and she was driving wildly in a direction that might be taking her even farther away from help.

With that thought came an ache of fatigue, reminding her how tired she was—how very, very tired of it all she was. And for a few fleeting seconds, she actually considered stopping. Just slamming on the brakes and, with an admission that it was all finally too much for her to bear, simply stopping and accepting that she had reached the end.

But the moment passed, and she didn't stop. From somewhere deep inside her, something urged her on— the same force that had driven her forward through the hypnosis sessions, the same force that had brought her here in the first place.

So now Kathy gripped the steering wheel with a hard determination and pushed on. In spite of the doubt and fatigue and pain that racked her body, she would not stop. Not until she had found what she was searching for—not until she had reached what she knew for her would be the beginning.

Twenty-One

FRANK GUNTHER hadn't been entirely accurate when he told Dog Bassett he was the best tracker in Kenya. He might have been good for a white man, but there were probably two dozen Africans who, being natives of the country, were better than Frank. And one Kenyan in particular was so skilled in his ability to read the land on which he moved that even those of other tribes spoke of him with an awe usually reserved for the figures of legend. Had it been any other man pursuing Frank, the hunter's evasion tactics probably would have worked. But the critical factor Frank Gunther did not take into account was that it wasn't just any man who tracked him under the blazing Kenyan sun. It was Twamba.

Led by the tireless Masai, Sammy's bus and its passengers continued, hour after hour, moving doggedly forward. Though none of the occasional travelers they encountered had seen the Gunther group, after a momentary stop to inspect the ground and a nearby bush, Twamba always remounted his giraffe and unhesitatingly waved them on. That was the way it had gone all day. And sometimes, for short intervals, Twamba would disappear from view on the galloping giraffe, only to reappear minutes later with a signal for Sammy to have Injai turn the bus in a new direction.

Those riding inside the bus were hot and travel weary now. Optimism continued to wane as the long hours passed, and hardly anyone spoke.

Although he fought against it, the herbal medicine Twamba had given Braxton seemed to force his system to relax, and he found himself dozing off, only to be rudely awakened again when a particularly rough bounce of the bus slammed his back against the hard seat. The others in front of Braxton were tired too, but sleep eluded them. They simply stared out the bus windows, automatically scanning the horizon for the Masai who led them. Sooner or later they knew Twamba would come back to them and either admit defeat or indicate that Gunther was just over the next ridge. However, as the tired faces watched Twamba disappear from view once again, there was a third possibility about to occur that none of them had considered, and it would send the Masai racing back toward the bus.

AS SHE HAD BEEN DOING incessantly while she drove, Kathy Sullivan checked the rearview mirror again. Still nothing. If only it would stay that way, but she knew it couldn't. They would have to come after her. Too much had been committed for her to be allowed to drive away.

How long had she been driving? Minutes? Had they started after her immediately? She had partially lowered the window next to her, but in spite of the crosscurrent of air through the broken passenger window, it was still suffocatingly hot inside the Jeep. Trickles of perspiration inched their way down her forehead into the crevices of her eyes, causing her vision to waver in stinging blurs. Her arms ached from trying to control the Cherokee, and she could feel blisters forming on the bottoms of her bare feet where she repeatedly shoved them against the pedals. Still, she pushed the Jeep on, driven by the fear that the next time she checked, the space in the mirror would be filled by Gunther bearing down on her.

Gritting her teeth against what now threatened to become overwhelming fatigue, Kathy adjusted her grip on the steering wheel and eased the accelerator down a little more. She refused to think about how long she could keep up this pace. She only knew she would not allow herself to quit until her last shred of control was gone.

For a moment, Kathy wasn't sure she saw anything. Then her vision locked on a movement to the right, and her heart raced with alarm. Gunther? No, as the figure drew closer, she was able to see it with more clarity, and her fright eased. It was only an animal, a tall, sprinting giraffe coming toward her from the side. Despite her frightened, exhausted state, curiosity sharpened her focus and she stared in startled amazement at the on-coming animal. The giraffe carried a man on its sloping back.

Then it came to her. Twamba! Yes, it was the Masai Sammy had gone to find. Twamba. His long legs were draped around the animal's shoulders, one hand grasping the elongated neck, as he galloped alongside the moving Cherokee. Then, giving a loud cry, the Masai raised the spear he carried high into the air, and the giraffe swerved away from the Jeep, turning back in the direction from which it had come.

Kathy slowed down to stare after the departing animal. The man did not look back but disappeared into the distance, his tightly woven braids bobbing against his head and his loose toga flapping in the wind.

Kathy allowed the Jeep to slow down even more. Finally she had made contact with someone, although not in the way she had expected. What had the shout meant? And why had he ridden away? Had Sammy contacted the Masai and sent him to search for her? Or was this a chance encounter? Actually, it didn't matter. There weren't a lot of choices open at the moment.

She spun the wheel to the right and pressed on the gas pedal. Her heart racing, Kathy knew she might be making a critical mistake, but she couldn't keep driving blindly forward forever. And if she followed the man, maybe he would lead her to other people. Once she was with people, Gunther wouldn't dare attack her.

Suddenly the giraffe came galloping into her field of vision again, only this time its rider was not alone. Behind him sped a long, rectangular-shaped touring bus. For several doubtful seconds, Kathy would not allow herself to believe her eyes, but by then the vehicle was too close for there to be any doubt. Her heart pounded even more furiously—but with joy, not fear!

She slammed the brake to the floor, and the Cherokee lurched forward, the tires skidding across the terrain before coming to a stop. It was the bus approaching her! Through some miraculous stroke of good fortune, they had found her. She was saved. Maybe Eddie had been right, after all. Maybe they were moving under a protection of some kind.

Kathy flung her door open. Twamba was closer to her now, and he was shouting loudly and waving his spear wildly overhead. And the bus? It was stopping. It swerved sideways in a cloud of dust, braking to a halt. Kathy started to leap from the Jeep, her arm already raised to wave at the occupants of the bus, when one last time, out of habit, her eyes glanced to the rearview mirror.

There it was. Far behind her, like some kind of dreaded plague appearing out of nowhere, a Volkswagen bus was coming into view. Now she understood the native's shouting. He had been trying to warn her. She had stopped too soon.

There was no time to try to restart the Jeep. If she fumbled, she was lost. She leaped from the Cherokee, pain shooting up her ankles as her bare feet hit the ground. She threw a quick look over her shoulder at the VW speeding in her direction and ran. Ran toward the familiar figure of Sammy emerging from the open door of the bus. As she ran, the fact that Sammy was holding a gun registered with her. Then something else became clear. Injai had swerved the bus sideways as a defensive tactic. She would be picked up, but not by them. There was no time. It would be the Masai on the giraffe who carried her. Twamba was to bring her to them.

No ONE could have been more surprised than Frank Gunther was to see Sammy's bus in the distance once they had finally closed the gap between themselves and the fleeing woman. Then he saw the giraffe and immediately understood.

Twamba! Shit! No wonder Sammy had been able to follow him. However, surprise was all Frank felt at seeing the bus and the Masai, nothing more. To his professional self, these new factors were negligible, merely additional elements he would deal with. The important thing was getting the girl back, and get her back he would.

The first one to stop was Twamba. Sammy would be no problem. The stupid asshole had already made a major tactical error by halting the bus too soon. He should have driven right up to the Jeep instead of counting on Twamba. Frank had no intention of letting that giraffe escape again.

After shouting for Dingo to ease up on the speed a little, Frank pointed to Kathy and the giraffe bearing down on her from a short distance beyond.

"I'm going to take out the animal, Dingo. Hold it steady!" Frank shouted. He was no longer looking at his driver but bringing his eye to the back side of the scope mounted atop his rifle. With professional calm, Frank led the animal, who now filled the scope's window, with the barrel of his rifle, pushing off the safety with his thumb. Then, still leading the moving target, he squeezed the trigger. The rifle cracked once, and far in front of them, the giraffe faltered clumsily and pitched forward. Gunther stayed in his firing position without acknowledging the successful hit. "Okay, Dingo. Step on it. I've got the Masai in my sights. Let's get in there."

"You bet," Dingo shouted. The bus jerked as the grinning driver jammed the clutch down and shoved the VW into a higher gear.

"Easy, goddammit," Frank growled, grabbing the window frame for support.

"Look, Bwana! Twamba comes to his feet!" Dingo shouted, gripping the steering wheel tighter as he drove.

Frank brought the scope two inches to the right, centering on the unmoving image of Kathy as the Masai came up to the woman and lifted her in his arms. "Yeah, I got him. Watch the bus for me. They're piling out the door now. If they start for her, let me know, and I'll fire a couple of rounds that way to scare them.

Now steady, Dingo. Hold the wheel steady. I've got Twamba. I'm going to shoot his leg out from under him. When he goes down, get us in there. Pull the door open, and I'll grab her. Once she's inside here, those folks at the bus are all finished."

The white hunter tightened his index finger against the trigger as the scope held the long, kicking strides of Twamba's sinewy legs.

"Here we go," Frank muttered, and once again squeezed the trigger.

AT THE FIRST SIGHT OF TWAMBA riding back into view, Braxton had crossed the rear seat to the window to see why the Masai was shouting with alarm. To his relief, the action hadn't been that difficult, which meant the concoction Twamba had given him must have started working.

Suddenly everyone was pointing and shouting. As Injai swung the bus sideways on Sammy's command, Braxton saw it too. A Jeep was speeding toward them. It was the Cherokee that belonged to Gunther. But it wasn't the hunter behind the wheel. The figure was too small, the hair too long. A rush of energy coursed through him as he recognized who it was. Kathy! The driver was Kathy!

"It's her!" Braxton shouted. The Cherokee screeched to a halt several feet in front of them.

"I see," Sammy answered. "But she is not alone. Look beyond the Jeep!" Braxton looked farther out and saw a Volkswagen bus speeding across the grassland. Twamba had already turned his long-necked steed and was galloping back to Kathy as Sammy, grasping his gun and pulling open the bus door, shouted in Swahili to him. Sammy then yelled back into the vehicle's interior, "Stay here! Twamba will bring her to us!"

"Sorry, Sammy," Braxton said, already on his feet and holding his rifle tightly in his grasp, "I'm coming with you."

The young guide started to protest, but his response was cut off by Zelda's scream of alarm. Out beyond them, Twamba's giraffe stumbled awkwardly, its neck snapping back and its towering body pitching downward. Kathy, who had been running toward the giraffe, drew back in horror, blood from the wounded, plummeting animal splattering across her.

Watching the giraffe go down, Braxton pushed all thought out of his mind and simply reacted. The woman he loved was in danger and he had no choice.

Everything was happening very fast, and though he was aware of what was going on, Braxton's own movements seemed isolated from what he saw. With a deliberateness of purpose, he turned and shoved the barrel of his rifle through the window, snapping off the safety. Ahead, Twamba had miraculously come to his feet again and was crossing to Kathy. Sammy, followed by Eddie, flew out the bus door and was racing forward. Behind Kathy, the VW was closing in fast.

Braxton brought the gun butt to his shoulder, sighting along the barrel at the approaching vehicle. The VW was close enough now that he could see the men who rode inside it. He could also see that the man behind the driver held a weapon which was raised to fire like his own.

Twamba was at Kathy's side now. The giant warrior scooped the smaller woman up in his arms and spun around, barely breaking stride as he headed back toward the bus. Sammy and Eddie stopped their forward advance and shouted urgent encouragement to Twamba.

Braxton kept his face against the steel barrel of the weapon, concentrating all his effort into keeping the moving VW in his sights. He could make out the figures inside with greater clarity now. And he could clearly see that the man in the safari hat behind the driver had his own rifle out the bus window. Gunther! He was leading with the gun prior to firing. He was going to try to shoot down Twamba before the Masai could reach cover.

"Sorry, Ed," Braxton said in a barely audible murmur. Then, pulling the butt of the rifle tightly into the crook of his shoulder, he squeezed back the short, curved stub of metal his index finger was curled around, waiting only for the smacking recoil to register against him before firing the automatic weapon again, and then again, and again and again.

This was not the first time Braxton had held a gun. Still, he was no marksman, and his first shot missed the moving target he was aiming for completely, as did his second and third. But the odds stayed with him, and on his fourth try, Braxton finally hit home.

That was why Frank Gunther missed the Masai. As he pulled the trigger, the slug from Braxton's fourth shot pierced the driver's side of the Volkswagen's windshield. The safety glass didn't shatter but rather splintered outward in a series of veinlike cracks from the round hole the bullet had made. The shot missed the two occupants in the vehicle, exiting harmlessly through the roof, but the exploding sound of the impact directly in front of Dingo's face so startled the driver that he simultaneously jerked the wheel and ducked. Frank's shot went wild as the VW veered sideways.

"Hold that wheel steady, goddamn you!" Gunther bellowed, swinging his weapon back toward Twamba.

But Braxton was still firing, his shots ricocheting off the metal car frame, and Dingo, totally panicked, didn't even acknowledge Frank. Wide-eyed with fear, the young black driver jammed the gas pedal to the floor and held it there, his hands frozen on the steering wheel.

The Volkswagen shot forward with a loud revving sound, and Frank immediately saw the danger. His driver was in a state of shock, and they were hurtling toward an almost certain collision with the Jeep, which was stopped dead ahead.

"Dingo, turn the wheel!" Frank yelled, scrambling forward. "Turn the wheel! You're going to smash us up, you stupid asshole!"

Then there was no longer time for talk as the Volkswagen careened crazily toward the Cherokee. Seconds away from impact, Frank dropped his rifle and lunged for the steering wheel.

With a forceful swing, Frank knocked Dingo aside with one arm and grabbed the wheel with the other. But Dingo's hands remained locked in position, and as the image of the Cherokee filled his vision through the cracked windshield, Frank grabbed the wheel with both hands and gave it a sharp, savage turn to the right.

There were two reasons why Frank Gunther had chosen the VW bus as a passenger carrier for safaris. One was that the body frame sat high on the wheelbase, which gave his clients better positions from which to view the game as the bus moved across the grasslands. The other reason was that it had fuel injection. Experience had taught him that dirt and grime being what they were out on the open savannah, the vehicle's carburetor inevitably became fouled and caused breakdowns. The VW's fuel injection system eliminated the problem. Unfortunately, during the crucial moments after he had control of the wheel, both of the characteristics Frank admired in the Volkswagen worked against him.

While traveling at such an accelerated speed, the high rectangular wheelbase made it impossible for the vehicle to veer off at the kind of sharp angle the steering column demanded of it. Frank's sudden turning of the front wheels did stop a head-on collision, but it also, in a stunning feat of vehicular balance, forced the entire left side of the VW to lift into the air, the wheels rising a good foot off the ground; and the bus's tilted front fender slid across the side of the Cherokee with a long, rasping scrape. Then, free of the Jeep but still half tilted in the air, the bus swerved in an arc on its two right tires for some fifteen feet, before flipping into the air. It rolled completely over three times and finally came to a crashing halt on its side.

Dingo could not have moved even if he had wanted to. The impact had jammed the end of the steering column halfway into the driver's chest and thrust his head, face first, through the windshield. Broken shards of glass protruded into his neck, face and now toothless mouth from the jagged hole where his skull had smashed through.

That left Gunther the only one alive when the vehicle came to rest. Though disoriented and injured, he forced himself into action the second the bus came to a stop.

More than just the urge to get out of the wreck drove him into motion. He heard the motor of the VW still running, and that sound meant the fuel injection system was continuing to work. After the crash, there had

o be broken lines, and the system would be pumping a
teady stream of gas onto the red-hot engine.

Frantically aware that he was inside a ticking time
omb, Frank grabbed his rifle with one hand and
ushed on the passenger door located directly above his
ead with the other. The door didn't budge. Wasting no
ime, he straightened his body, shifted his feet for a
etter foothold, and drove the butt of the rifle through
he side window of the door. As it happened, Frank's
hift in position had brought his right boot over Din-
o's upper spine. A short pop sounded as he heaved
imself upward, the additional pressure breaking his
river's neck. Frank didn't even notice. The window
hattered, and after knocking off some of the jagged
dges of glass, the hunter reached up and pulled him-
elf through the narrow opening.

Frank had been absolutely right about the danger,
nd his upper torso was clear of the overturned vehicle
hen the explosion occurred. Small snakes of flame had
hot across the underside of the bus following the gas
nes, and the thrust of the explosion was inward, which
n turn blew everything inside the bus outward. With a
last, pieces of flying metal, debris, parts of Dingo's
ody and an escaping Frank Gunther flew through the
ir in a blaze of light.

Kathy, who was now safely at the bus doorway, and
he others had watched in amazement when the pursu-
ng Volkswagen bus suddenly veered off, flipped, then
rashed. Now they stared in mute silence as the last
ieces of debris from the explosion settled to the ground
nd the billowing smoke reached a height that allowed
hem to see the shattered wreckage.

"Whooee!" Injai shouted in glee, jumping out of his
eat behind the wheel to greet Braxton as the corre-

spondent walked by him. "That was some shooting, Buddy! You stopped them cold. Guaranteed!"

Eddie watched as Braxton rushed from the bus and gathered Kathy into his arms, then he looked back at Injai.

"Braxton?"

"You bet." Injai smiled. "Buddy hit their windshield dead center and that was when they went out of control."

At Injai's words, Sammy glanced at Braxton but the guide's attention quickly returned to Twamba. After the explosion, the Masai had run back to his fallen giraffe. Head bowed, the giant warrior was kneeling beside the unmoving beast, stroking its long neck.

"Oh, that poor man's animal," Kathy said softly, lifting her head from Braxton's shoulder.

"It is more than an animal to Twamba," Sammy said, his voice suppressing emotion. "Twiga was a loyal companion and friend. Twamba loved his Twiga more than anything on earth."

Zelda had come running from the bus to embrace Kathy, but before she could speak, Injai drew everyone's attention again to the smoldering wreckage.

"There is still movement out there, Sammy," the driver said, pointing slightly to the left and in front of them. "Looks like a big man. I would say it is Gunther."

Sammy gave the driver a sharp nod and cocked his rifle. "Stay here," he said to the others near him. "I will check on this."

"Sammy," Eddie said quickly.

The guide gave the priest a look. A muscle twitched in his face, but he made no reply before turning and walking in the direction Injai had indicated.

Even before he got there, Sammy could see that In-jai had been right. It was Gunther. The guide allowed his grip on his rifle to relax a little, however. There was no danger. If anything, the man had merely been moving in pain.

Gunther was still conscious though, and when Sammy came close enough for the hunter to see who it was, he made every attempt to get up off the ground. His body was too shocked with injury to respond, however, so he lay there, scorched and bleeding, his face smoldering with hatred as Sammy came to a halt beside him.

"Told you that goddamned Dingo couldn't drive worth a shit," Gunther snarled hoarsely. "This wouldn't have happened with you behind the wheel."

Sammy said nothing. His jaw muscle was twitching erratically, and his hands opened and closed several times on the stock of the weapon he held.

"So what do you think you're going to do, shoot me?" Gunther snorted with laughter, then began to cough heavily, wincing in pain. "Fat chance! Forget it, Sammy boy. You don't have the nerve it takes to shoot a defenseless man—even if you hate the son of a bitch as much as you do me."

Sammy shifted the rifle so that the end of the barrel pointed directly at Gunther's forehead.

The hunter laughed again. "Okay, hotshot. Prove me wrong. I've already messed up most of the day. It'll round everything out for me."

"*No*, Sammy," Eddie said, stepping up beside the guide. "You must not do it."

"I instructed you to stay with the others," Sammy replied, keeping his eyes on Gunther.

"Sammy, you cannot kill this man in cold blood."

Sammy glanced at the priest. "Go back to the bus, Eddie. This is not your affair."

"Come on," Gunther growled. "If you're going to shoot me, get that high-and-mighty black asshole of yours in gear and do it. Or get the hell out of here and leave me alone."

Sammy glared down at his tormentor, and his voice shook with rage. "I do not wish to hear any more from you, Gunther."

With a furious surge of vengeance, the guide swung the end of the weapon into the air and brought it forcefully down again, smashing the shining steel barrel into Frank Gunther's head.

A loud cry of agony broke from Gunther, and small pools of blood slowly bubbled from the wound on his forehead and ran down his face in tiny streams. Shaking with rage, Sammy lifted the end of the rifle and would have struck again, but Eddie caught the barrel and, holding it firmly between his hands, broke the momentum of the swing.

"No more!" Eddie shouted.

With an incoherent cry of anger, Sammy spun around to face the priest. Unflinching, Eddie tore the rifle from Sammy's hands and threw it several feet beyond them. Sammy took a step toward the priest, his hands clenched in tight fists.

"Enough, Sammy," the priest said quietly now, meeting the guide's eyes. "Let it be. If you do more to him, you only hurt yourself."

Sammy stood very still for a moment. Then, with a cry of fury, he whirled back toward Gunther and delivered a savage kick into the hunter's midsection. Ignoring the choking groans that Gunther emitted as his body curled in pain, Sammy walked past the priest to the spot where his rifle lay.

"Now it is enough," he said.

After retrieving his weapon, Sammy strode quickly back to the group of people clustered near the bus. Kathy had moved behind Braxton now, her hand examining his lower back.

"How serious is it?" she asked him.

"He will be fine," Sammy answered for him. "Twamba has given him medicine. Our concern is for you. They did not hurt you?"

Kathy shook her head, though it was obvious she was attempting to minimize what had happened. "No, there were some touchy moments, but I . . . I'm okay."

"Thank God you're all right," Braxton said, wrapping his arm around her. He lifted her chin and looked into her eyes. "I was pretty crazy with worry, Kathy. I don't know what I would have done if we hadn't found you."

Unable to reply, Kathy bit at her lip, her eyes filling with tears as she snuggled into the security of Braxton's comforting embrace. After a few moments, Braxton pointed in the distance to Twamba. Spear once more in hand, the Masai warrior had turned from his fallen giraffe and was walking back toward the group.

"I'd say we're stacking up quite a list of debts to your friend Twamba, Sammy. We never would have gotten to Kathy without him. Not only that, but whatever there is in his potion, it's good stuff. The pain in my back is definitely easing. Listen, I saw there was a little problem out there between you and Ed. Is everything all right now?"

"Yes," Sammy answered, turning so that his answer reached the others as well as Braxton. "But there are unanswered questions. Dog Bassett is not here."

"I hurt him pretty badly with a tent stake when I escaped," Kathy said. "Gunther probably didn't take the time to wait for him."

"But he is not dead?"

"No, he'll live—unfortunately," she replied, shivering at the memory of the huge man hovering over her.

Sammy nodded. "As will Gunther. We must decide on our future actions with much haste."

"Don't we have to report this?" Zelda asked. "Someone is bound to find the wreck even if they haven't seen the smoke already. I mean the driver was killed and Gunther is out there too."

Sammy shrugged. "It was an unfortunate accident. Gunther is the one who shot game illegally. Let him explain it if people come by. I tell you now that if you do not wish to be detained by long periods of questioning, we must leave quickly."

"I . . . I feel so badly about the animal, Sammy," Kathy said as Twamba walked up beside the guide. "Could you tell him how sorry I am."

Sammy turned and translated Kathy's message to the Masai. When he had finished, Twamba shifted toward Kathy and replied in short, clipped speech.

"What is he saying?" Eddie asked.

Sammy spoke to Twamba again, then answered the priest. "Twamba says there is no need to feel sorrow. Twiga died during an act of courage. It is a good way to die. And he asks if Kathy is the woman of visions I spoke to him about. I told him yes."

As Sammy translated, Twamba left the guide's side and crossed over to Kathy. For a moment he merely looked at her. Then he lifted his hand to her chin and turned her face from side to side, studying her with his steady, unwavering gaze. Finally he released her, spoke a few words in Sammy's direction and walked to the bus. Grasping the ladder, he climbed quickly up to the roof rack and sat down, his spear held upright, its base resting against the metal roof. He turned his head to shout a command to those on the ground, then once more faced front.

"Get inside the bus, everyone," Sammy said, ushering the others to the door. "Twamba says we go now."

"Wait," Zelda cried, stepping in front of the doorway. She turned to Braxton, who stood ready to escort Kathy onto the bus, and raised her hand in objection. "Please, I think we should... reconsider. I... I honestly didn't think it would ever come to something like this." She gestured to where Eddie knelt near the wreckage of the Volkswagen. "We should have listened to you, Braxton, and I'm sorry. I'm sorry because Kathy has had to suffer and people have died and it could have been avoided. And... much as I wanted to follow this through, I think that what's happened to Kathy—and now this violence—is enough."

Kathy took a step away from Braxton toward the hypnotist. "Are you saying that we should give up, Zelda? You can't mean it."

Zelda nervously shifted her hefty weight from one foot to the other and nodded. "Yes. I... I think you've been through more than anyone should have to bear. Enough is enough, Kathy. I'm sure Braxton agrees."

Kathy turned to the man next to her, her voice small and hesitant when she spoke. "Braxton?"

"What do *you* want to do, Kathy?" Braxton said quietly. "You know what you've had to suffer. Do you still think the quest is worth it?"

Kathy did not answer immediately. She looked up from the small group around her to the top of the bus, where the Masai sat. Twamba was staring down at her, his eyes steady and penetrating. The giant warrior held Kathy's gaze for several long seconds, then waved his spear again for them to follow.

"We're going on," Kathy said evenly. "Come on, you heard Sammy. Twamba wants us to get in the bus."

"Kathy..." Zelda said doubtfully.

"No, Zelda," the young woman answered. "We're not stopping. I know it's your guidance that brought us here, but it's through me that we've tapped into all this, and ultimately it falls to me to decide. Yes, I've already suffered more than I ever thought possible, but I'm not stopping, Zelda. I can't."

"Braxton," Zelda said, shifting to the news correspondent for support. "You were so insistent before. Tell Kathy you agree with me."

Braxton stepped forward and took Kathy's hand in his own. "If Kathy says we go on, Zelda, I think we should listen to her and get aboard." Not waiting for the hypnotist to reply, he turned from them and shouted, "Come on, Eddie. We're going."

The priest rose from his kneeling position in front of the still smoldering wreckage and hurried back to the bus. Sammy had followed the others inside and stood at the door waiting.

"What about Gunther, Sammy?" Eddie asked. "He's still alive out there. You can't just leave him."

"Gunther stays," Sammy said.

"He might die."

"Hear me, Eddie," Sammy answered softly. "Gunther left me on the savannah and I survived. He will also, I have no doubt. Bassett will come for him, or others will soon arrive. But I care not either way. I am finished with him. The bus is leaving as Twamba wishes. I agreed to guide you, and Twamba has agreed to help us find what Kathy sees in her visions." He nodded to the driver to start the bus, but Injai hesitated, looking at the priest.

"Get in the damned bus, Ed," Braxton ordered from his seat beside Kathy. "Gunther was going to shoot Twamba and probably Kathy too, you know. But through a quirk of fate, the impossible has happened and we've stopped him. Like you said, things seem to be continually pushing forward in spite of us. Besides, Zelda's right. Someone has undoubtedly seen the smoke and is headed this way."

"Zelda, surely you don't think we should just ignore all this and drive away, do you?" Eddie asked in disbelief.

The hypnotist drew a deep breath and nodded. "I don't see that there's much choice, Ed. Not if we intend to go on. And that is what Kathy wants to do."

"Eddie, you heard Sammy," Braxton said. "The Masai's going to help us. You know how you were telling me to have faith before. Well, for better or for worse, this is it, my friend. You want to know why these things happen, right? Well, damn it, let's go find out one way or the other. We're going after the biggie, Ed. Since it's the reason you came, I suggest you get on the bus—and let's go find that grave!"

Eddie glanced back over his shoulder, his face filled with doubt. Then, without another word, he climbed up into the bus and moved past Sammy and down the aisle. As Eddie lowered himself into a seat, the guide nodded again to Injai, and this time the driver pulled the metal doors shut and shoved the bus into gear.

Twenty-Two

"WHERE ARE WE HEADED, Sammy?" Braxton called up to the front of the bus as they rumbled away from the abandoned Cherokee and nearby wreckage.

"We will continue farther south as that is the direction Kathy first desired," Sammy told him. "It will bring us close to the Tanzania border. If I decide it is necessary, I will cross this border and come back into Kenya from another route."

"Surely you don't think there's still a possibility of us being followed," Eddie said.

"Yes," Sammy answered, turning soberly to the priest. "I would say we should assume that to be true."

"But you saw Gunther's condition. And Kathy said Bassett is badly injured also."

"Do not underestimate Gunther, Eddie. I would not have let him live. But you decided it would be otherwise, and so he must be considered dangerous. I tell you this: As long as Gunther breathes, he will try to bring revenge on us." Sammy moved passed the priest and down the aisle, addressing his next question to Kathy. "How long had you been driving the Cherokee before we came upon you?"

Kathy frowned. "No more than a few minutes."

Sammy nodded. "Then Bassett is not that far away. You say he is injured. How badly did you injure him?"

"I...I'm not sure. I struck at him, stabbing his face. I think I hit an eye, but I don't know how badly he was really hurt."

"How did you get away, Kathy?" Zelda wondered, leaning toward her with concern.

"And how did they get you out of our campsite in the first place without our knowing it?" Braxton asked.

Kathy turned to Braxton first. "I had slipped outside the tent for a second to go to the bathroom and they grabbed me, knocking me out with a needle. It happened so fast there was nothing I could do." She looked at the hypnotist, who had been joined in her seat by Eddie. "Escaping was...well, I was just lucky, I guess. When Gunther wasn't in the tent, Dog Bassett tried...tried to attack me. I had pulled one of the tent stakes out before he came in. I just swung at his face over and over as hard as I could when he came at me. And when he screamed, grabbing at his eye, I went out the back of the tent and jumped in the Cherokee. Still, it was very close. Gunther almost was able to stop me as I drove away."

"Sounds to me like you got yourself out of quite an ordeal," Zelda said admiringly.

Kathy sighed. "I still can't believe I'm actually away from them and safe." Then suddenly she frowned, looking toward the front of the bus. "I just realized. Chegee isn't here."

"No," Braxton said soberly. "Lions got him, I'm afraid."

"Lions. How terrible."

"Yes, we've had quite a time of it ourselves these past few hours," Eddie told her, avoiding Braxton's eyes. "Did they attempt to talk to you while you were there?"

"Yes," Kathy said, her expression becoming troubled at the memory. "It was the grave they wanted. They were convinced that the contents could bring them huge fortunes on the black market. I had no idea what I was going to do, since *we* don't even know where it is. I even told Gunther that, but he couldn't believe we would come this far without knowing where the grave was."

"I can understand that," Braxton said with a dry smile. "I've been a little amazed by that myself."

From above them came the ringing sound of metal against metal—three sharp blows—followed by a shout.

"It's the Masai," Eddie said, glancing upward. "He must be smacking the end of his spear on the roof."

Injai had already looked at Sammy and, on the guide's instructions, was slowing the bus to a halt.

"How bad was it...with Gunther and Bassett, Kathy?" Braxton asked quietly, as the others glanced out the windows to see what had caused the Masai to strike the bus roof.

"Bad enough," she said, leaning her head against him.

"Kathy," Braxton began, closing his arm around her, "when I woke up to find you gone, I...I've never felt such cold fear in my life. I don't know what I would have done if I had lost you."

Kathy raised her face and kissed him softly. "Well, I'm back. And I'm going on, in spite of what's happened...maybe even because of it, to help justify all I've been through. And I don't plan on letting you out of my sight again, Brax. You sure you want to be stuck with me?"

Braxton smiled. "I've never been surer of anything in my life."

Injai swung the bus door open for Sammy, and the guide stepped out to meet Twamba, who had dropped to the ground before the vehicle had completely stopped. Everyone turned to watch Sammy and Twamba, but it was Zelda who spoke.

"No wonder Twamba got excited. Look at that."

Before them was the shoreline of what appeared to be a wide lake, which extended out on both sides in a much wider arc than the one Twamba made with the sweep of his spear as he spoke to Sammy. However, it was not the size but the color that drew everyone's attention. The lake's entire surface was a glistening red.

When the Masai finished speaking, Sammy stepped back onto the bus.

"We will stop here for a while," the guide said.

"Why here?" Eddie asked. "Where are we?"

"Close to the border," Sammy told him. "What you see is Lake Natron. Most of it is in Tanzania."

"I don't care how persuasive you are, Eddie," Zelda said, with a look at the priest, "you're not going to talk me into swimming in that water."

"No," Sammy agreed. "It would not be wise. The surface temperature is 150 degrees at least. Natron is a soda lake, made up of sodium carbonates."

Eddie frowned. "But why are we stopping here?" he repeated, pointing out at Twamba, who was walking down to the lake's shore. "What is the Masai up to?"

"As I told you, Twamba is Laibon and has the gift of prophecy," Sammy explained. "Natron is its present color because when it rains during the dry season, as it has lately, water collects on the thin crystalline surface, causing millions of tiny organisms to come to life, which turns the entire lake red." He gestured toward the Masai, who had stopped at the edge of the ruddy expanse.

"Unlike you and I, Twamba does not understand these things. To him, the great redness is a blood sign of warning. He insists on casting the sacred stones to understand the red warning and perhaps see what the future will bring."

Eddie, as well as the others, had turned to listen to the guide. "I know you, Eddie, and the others may not believe in gifted ones like Twamba," Sammy went on, "but I must allow this before we can continue."

"I'm beginning to believe anything is possible, Sammy," the priest answered. "May we watch?"

"Yes," Sammy said, motioning for them to move out of the bus. "It will also give you an opportunity to exercise your legs."

"Okay," Braxton said, standing. "Come on, Kathy. Let's find out what Twamba comes up with."

The group stopped a short distance from the spot where the tall warrior sat. Zelda, Eddie, Sammy and Injai clustered on one side of Twamba, while Braxton, his arms protectively around Kathy's shoulders, moved to the other side, all waiting in silence for the Masai medicine man to offer his blood visions near the edge of the red lake.

The giant sat cross-legged, his long legs tucked under each other, his back ramrod straight. To his left was his shield, at his right lay the ornate spear, and in front of him, he had placed a brownish-white pelt of fur.

Intoning a strange, melodic cadence, the Masai reached to his belted waist and unfastened an animal-skin bag, bringing it high in front of him as his song grew louder. Slipping his fingers into the pouch, he withdrew several rounded stones, which he also held high above his head, continuing his vocal litany more fervently. Then, abruptly, Twamba's vocalizations stopped, and with a short sweep of his right hand he pitched the stones onto the fur. Bringing his hands to his knees, Twamba stared down at the stones he had thrown. And as he stared, his body became absolutely still.

For several long minutes he sat like that, stock-still and staring. Then, again with sudden abruptness, Twamba rose to his feet. No one spoke as he turned to face the small group before him. He gathered up his shield and spear and walked over to them.

As he came nearer, they could tell there was a change in the Masai. His usually calm expression was now vividly charged, his eyes wild with excitement. He stopped in front of them, but rather than addressing Sammy alone, he moved his gaze over all of them, resting it lastly on Kathy. Then he raised his spear into the air and spoke. The words were delivered in short, clipped phrases in a high pitch, and as he spoke, the Masai moved his hands and body to emphasize his narration. And at the end of each utterance, he paused to allow Sammy time to interpret.

"Twamba insists I tell you of his words. He speaks of a time long ago," Sammy said in literal translation. "A time before even the Masai tribes came to rule the great open plains. A time when there was only one tribe. That of the early ones.

"Legends tell of how these early ones were ruled by two who were older than all others. Two that had none before them. Two who were the first. And it came to be after hundreds of years that the great male leader of the old ones breathed no more. And with mourning hearts, the early ones brought this most hallowed one back to his birthplace so that his soul could cross through the land of spirits to the other side."

As Sammy spoke, Braxton could feel Kathy tense, and he leaned forward, looking at her questioningly. Kathy was listening to Sammy's words, but she was no longer watching the fluid pantomime of the Masai. She had shifted her gaze to Zelda, and the hypnotist was staring back at Kathy with wide-eyed understanding.

"It is said that the land was different in the days of the early ones, and a great river flowed across the land. It was this living arm of water that guided the early ones to their goal when they brought the old one back."

"Oh, my God," Kathy whispered.

Sammy stopped speaking for a moment, as they all turned to her.

"What? What is it, Kathy?" Braxton asked in concern.

"It's her dream, Braxton," Zelda said in astonishment. "The legend the Masai is telling us is very close to the dream Kathy has had over and over since she began the regressions."

Twamba had stopped his narration, and he frowned at Sammy. After hearing the young guide translate the hypnotist's words, the Masai continued with even greater animation.

"Twamba says that there is a place where legends say the early ones finally arrived. It is a sacred place of mystery where those who are about to die have come to find a final resting place since the beginning of time. Even today it remains a sacred haven, drawing to it the sick and feeble of the savannah. He tells of seeing...an opening there...that has appeared from nowhere. He cannot be certain, but suggests that it is possibly the place you seek."

Kathy shook her head slowly in wonder, and her voice was barely more than a whisper when she spoke. "The

final irony. The answer we've been seeking so desperately comes to us not through hypnosis but from one
who is of this land. The man who hears and sees what
is hidden from others. Tell him yes, Sammy. We would
like to see this place. Can he take us there?"

Sammy turned again to Twamba. He spoke slowly,
motioning to Kathy and translating her words, then listened to the Masai's reply.

"Twamba says the holy place of which he speaks is
near what the white man has named Oldoinyo Sambu.
I know of this place. It is a land of lava that surrounds
an extinct volcano."

"Of course," Eddie said, his own voice catching with
excitement. "It's perfect. Lava. A volcanic eruption
that spewed lava would have preserved perfect fossils
for thousands of years. Zelda, Kathy's right. This could
be it! This could really be it!"

The hypnotist was watching Kathy closely, and she
nodded at the priest's words. "What do you think,
Kathy? I think it sounds like your dream, but it could
be coincidence. We know that most creation myths have
similar elements of two people from whom all others are
descendants. Do you have any feelings about this place
Twamba suggests? Or should we have a session?"

Kathy shook her head. "We've had a session and the
answer didn't appear. I don't know or feel any more
than you do, but I think we must believe what is given
to us. If there were ever a sign to follow, this has to be
it."

"If it makes a difference to your decision, I have
heard of this place Twamba tells us about," Sammy
said. "His words that it is a place of death are true.
Many know of the strange power that draws animals to
this ancient graveyard. Though it is illegal, poachers

sometimes raid this holy ground of the natives for skins and other animal parts to sell to tourists. But this is the first time I have heard of the legend that Twamba tells of the early ones."

Suddenly Twamba moved closer to them, and in a loud voice pointed with his spear toward the stones he had thrown.

"Twamba says there is more you must hear," Sammy told those around him, still keeping his words matter-of-fact. "Twamba sees death in this place. Much death. The sacred stones have told him there is great bloodshed ahead if you go to this place. All who are here may die! But if you feel you must go, Twamba will try to help you. He is a mighty warrior and will prepare himself to serve you."

Sammy paused then, for Twamba had stopped speaking. The Masai lowered his spear and stood directly in front of Eddie. Looking him in the eye, as was always the Masai way, Twamba spoke again, holding the spear in offering to the priest.

"Twamba says you are to take the spear, Eddie. Many days ago the spirits instructed him to forge it, but he did not know its purpose until now. It was made for you. It is yours to use during the blood time that approaches."

Eddie's mouth opened in amazement. He looked at Sammy and then back at the Masai. *"What?"*

"The spear is yours, Eddie," Sammy reiterated.

"Don't be ridiculous," Eddie sputtered. "I don't want his spear. Tell Twamba thank you, but I cannot fight. I am not a warrior. I am a man of peace."

Sammy translated the priest's words for Twamba. The Masai nodded to Eddie, took back the spear, then spoke again, only this time there was a new harshness to his voice.

"Twamba says the spear is yours, Eddie. He has foreseen it. And in the end, you will use it. If you do not, it is certain all will die!"

When Sammy finished the translation, Twamba turned from the group and walked back to where his sacred stones lay scattered across the fur. Uttering a great cry, the Masai raised the spear and then jammed its point into the ground, releasing the shaft and standing beside the quivering weapon. With a twist of his hands, Twamba unfastened the tie at his waist and shrugged the loosely hanging toga off his body, his tall, sinewy frame naked but for a loincloth in the fading afternoon sun.

"What is he doing?" Eddie asked apprehensively. "Did I offend him?"

"No," Sammy answered. "He must prepare himself for the great battle that lies ahead. That there will be need for him, he is certain. He has seen it in the stones."

"Even so, why should he continue to help us if it means putting his own life in jeopardy? He certainly doesn't have to."

"Yes, from Twamba's viewpoint, he does. You must understand that for a Masai warrior there is no higher calling than to help those who are in need of his service."

Eddie looked back at the Masai. From one of his pouches Twamba had taken a red powder with which he covered his hair and face. Then, in another skin pouch, he dipped his fingers into a wet, sticky substance that he proceeded to smear on his arms, legs and body.

"The powder is ocher," Sammy said in answer to the questioning expressions around him. "It is to ward off evil spirits. Twamba covers himself with fat from a slaughtered Masai bull. This will give him a fierce appearance to frighten his enemies."

As Sammy spoke, Twamba turned his now gleaming body in a circle, spitting heavily in each of four directions. Then, raising his voice again in song, the Masai began a driving chant, at the same time twisting his body to the movements of what appeared to be a ritualistic dance. Around the narrow spear shaft he jerked and contorted himself, ending each gyrating circle with an enormous leap into the air.

"Spitting is done by Twamba to clear the air of evil thoughts," Sammy explained. "He now sings 'Eng Kijuka,' the boastful song of the Masai warriors. With this and the dance, he will rid himself of all impurities caused by laziness."

"Good Lord, look how high he leaps," Zelda exclaimed. "He's almost clearing the top of the spear."

"The dance not only builds courage, but also flexes and limbers the body for battle," Sammy explained.

"So now what?" Zelda asked, drawing attention away from Twamba's battle dance. "You say you know where this place is, Sammy?"

The guide nodded and withdrew a map from his hip pocket and spread it on the ground. "So you will be clear," he said as the others stooped to view the map, "this is our position." He pointed to a spot above the dotted line that ran across the bottom to illustrate the border. Then he moved his finger upward, stooping before he reached the center of the map. "Nairobi is here."

Leaning farther forward than the others, Kathy raised a tentative index finger, bringing it to rest on a black dot situated near the area Sammy had first indicated.

"Is this Oldoinyo Sambu that you mentioned?" she said quietly, reading the name next to the dot.

"Yes," Sammy replied, moving his hand over the map. "As you can see, it lies exactly on line between the volcanos of Shambole, here, and Lengai, here. Kilimanjaro is to the south of them, here."

"It is close, isn't it," Kathy said, continuing to stare at the map.

"Yes," Sammy agreed. "Not too far from Natron. It is very near the spot you first indicated that night in Westwood. There is a great bluff that was sliced in two by rift faulting. It is a wild and magnificent place to see."

"What do you think, Kathy?" Zelda asked, moving next to her and helping her to her feet. "Still have a positive sense that this is the way?"

"Yes, we're close, Zelda," Kathy said, a distant quality to her voice. "Don't ask me how I know, but I do. We must go toward there. Toward Oldoinyo Sambu."

Eddie was standing again also, and he joined his old friend next to Kathy. "And what are your thoughts, Brax? Twamba's prophecies of blood sound anything but promising."

Braxton gave a half smile and shook his head. "My thoughts, old friend? A jumble of confusion, apprehension, and amazement—along with a strong belief that this whole affair is completely beyond us and our understanding. But maybe that's the way it's been right from the beginning. I'm still not convinced we'll find the grave of Eve, but I have taken a few small steps in your direction and believe something that can't be readily explained is going on. So, what the hell. I'm not going to fight what obviously cannot be stopped. I go for whatever Kathy decides. That's it. I meant it before, Kathy,'' Braxton added, turning from the priest back to the woman next to him. "I'm with you all the way. Through sickness and health. For better or for worse."

"Those aren't random words, Brax," Kathy said. "Are you sure you know what you're saying?"

"Never surer," Braxton answered, extending his hand out to her. "How does it go? Till death do us part."

Kathy reached forward and took his hand, squeezing it tightly. "Thank you for coming into my life, Brax."

Braxton's expression was serious. "So, in spite of Twamba's blood visions, it's go, right?"

"Yes," Kathy answered quietly. The young woman walked over to Zelda and took the hypnotist's hand in her own. "I have to. You understand that, don't you, Zelda."

The hypnotist smiled, covering Kathy's hand with her free one and patting it affectionately. "Yes, of course I understand, Kathy. I was only trying to think of what was best for you, but I know stopping wouldn't have been any good. I doubt that I could have stopped, either, if it came right down to it. I would never be able to rest if we left this unfinished."

Kathy nodded. "There is a reason why this is happening. Of that, I have no doubt. Just as I know there is no other choice open to me than to finish."

"Okay," Braxton said, turning to the others. "You heard the lady. Everybody back on the bus and let's get to it."

"Wait," Eddie said, addressing Sammy. "Considering Twamba's warnings, you needn't continue, you know, Sammy." The priest looked at his loyal friend Injai, who stood in the doorway of the bus. "That goes for you too, Injai. There's no reason for you to expose yourself to any more danger.''

Sammy turned to the driver. "What do you say, Injai? Do you wish to stop working for me as a driver?''

Injai smiled his jovial smile. "No, you are a good boss, Sammy. I will drive until the safari is over, Father,'' he added with a nod to Eddie. Then he shrugged, turning to climb into his driver's seat. "Besides, I must go on. I have to spot a pair of cheetahs for Buddy. I have given my word to him.''

"Then there is no need for further discussion,'' Sammy said, his own face breaking into a smile as he spoke to the group. "You are brave people. In spite of Twamba's warnings, you continue because you think it is the right thing to do. This means you are also good people. And I am proud to be the one who leads you now. So, since I am still in charge, everyone into the bus, please, as Braxton asked. We must leave this place. We have been here too long.''

Zelda frowned as Injai started the engine. "What about Twamba? Looks like he's still going strong over there.''

"Twamba's preparation will continue until he feels he is ready,'' Sammy said, indicating for the rest of them to step past him into the bus. "He has told me where to find this place at Oldoinyo Sambu. And have no fear. He will find us. A Masai can travel with movements swift as the wind.''

While the group settled into their seats, Injai pushed the bus into gear and Sammy made his way down the aisle, passing out thin layers of leathery-looking food.

Zelda held a piece up after accepting it. "What is it?''

"Dried meat,'' Sammy told her. "Eat. We will need all our energy.''

"What kind of meat?" the hypnotist asked, hesitating.

"Meat to be eaten," Sammy said, smiling and moving on down the aisle.

Somewhat reluctantly the four passengers chewed the tough pieces of meat fiber while gazing out the windows, where they could barely make out Twamba's form leaping in the distance. Leaping so that he could prepare himself to protect them from the time of bloodshed that lay ahead for all, according to the spirits that spoke through the casting of the sacred stones.

WHAT TWAMBA HAD NOT SEEN in his vision and had no way of warning them about was the bloodied and bandaged form of Frank Gunther bobbing against the front seat of the Cherokee as it traveled steadily in their direction.

Every inch of Gunther's body hurt as he drove, and he knew continuing could be a serious mistake, but still he pushed himself on. Just as he had when he had dragged himself over to the abandoned Cherokee and discovered the keys in the ignition.

Iron determination had gotten him back to the campsite, where he had picked up Dog. And the same determination carried him now, even though the rough ride sent pain coursing through his body.

Frank Gunther had no intention of giving up. If his energy finally gave way, he'd just let his hatred and anger carry him until he caught up with them.

He glanced sideways at Dog Bassett, and in spite of the agonizing pain shooting through his body, he smiled cruelly. As always, even though his face was now covered with crusted blood and crudely bandaged over one eye and half his cheekbone, Bassett was expressionless.

But it wasn't simply his stoic countenance that made Frank smile; it was the sight of what Dog held in his lap.

They were Gunther's most prized possessions: two compact Uzi machine guns. Frank loved those guns more than any he had ever owned. Easy to load with a snap-in clip; lightweight and portable. So simple to use, and they almost never missed their target.

It didn't matter whether it was Bassett firing these babies with his one good eye, or himself. Either way, Gunther was going to get the people they were after. All of them.

That was how he was able to get past the pain and keep on driving. Only one thing mattered to Frank Gunther now: catching up with Sammy and his little group of travelers. Because when he did, with the help of his two steel-barreled beauties, he was going to make sure they told him where to find the grave, and then every mothering one of them was going to die.

Twenty-Three

"STOP THE BUS!"

Kathy had been staring out the window and now came to her feet without warning, stepping into the aisle, her words startling everyone out of the contemplative lull the bus's motion had induced.

"What is it?" Zelda asked, rushing to Kathy while Injai applied the brakes, bringing the bus to a skidding halt.

"We're here, aren't we." It was a statement rather than a question, directed to no one. Kathy stood unmoving, her body very straight, her head held high. There was a radiant excitement in her expression and she repeated the words. "We're here!"

"Yes, she is right—we are here," Sammy agreed, pulling on the lever in front of him, which caused the bus door to open with a loud clang. He pointed through the windshield. "Ahead is the wall of which I spoke."

Braxton stood up in the aisle behind Kathy. "Well, come on. Let's go."

"All right, Braxton," Sammy said. "But wait until I have inspected. We must use caution."

Picking up his rifle, Sammy stepped outside first and glanced quickly around. Then, assured that they were safe for the moment, he waved to the people inside, and with Kathy leading, they filed out of the bus in mute anticipation. Though Eddie frowned, he said nothing when he saw that Braxton carried his own rifle in the crook of his arm.

"It's getting darker," Braxton muttered, lifting his face toward the sky. "Can't really see that well."

"Cloud cover," Sammy responded. "Another storm approaches. We are very low here. Within a wide ravine." He pointed to the large patches of mist surrounding them. "The heat partially evaporates the falling drops before they reach low areas like this and they become hanging mists. It is called phantom rain."

"It must be an illusion because of the darkness," Zelda said, "but some of the mist appears to be rising out of the ground."

"No, you are right, Zelda," Sammy told her. "It is coming up from the ground. There are many gaps and pits in this old volcanic region, some containing hot steams that bubble to the surface. We should move with care."

"Any animals in the vicinity?"

"Oh, yes, Zelda. Especially predators seeking to feed off the weak who have come here to die. That is another reason we must move with care. Because of the ancient lava-flow formations, this area is filled with hidden caves and overhangs that are perfect for an animal to hide in, not only for protection but also in preparation to attack a passing prey."

"Like us, maybe."

"It would be wise to move with care," was all Sammy replied.

"I'm sorry I asked," Zelda said with a shudder. She turned to check on Kathy but discovered the young woman was not even listening to what was being said. She had moved away from them and stood staring off into the mists.

Braxton was standing near the bus doorway. He wrinkled his nose. "What is that smell?"

"Carrion odor," Sammy told him.

"It is the smell of death," Kathy said suddenly. As she had done since stepping from the bus, she looked at none of those around her but continued to stare into the distance. "Death is in this place."

Eddie and Zelda exchanged a quick look, and the hypnotist took several cautious steps toward Kathy. "Should we leave then? Is that what you're saying?"

Now Kathy turned to face them, and Braxton, as well as the others, could see the change. He wanted to go to her, but something held him back, and he remained where he was.

It was the eyes. Even in the dim light he knew he was looking into the same strange eyes that had stared at him that first night. And from deep inside, he felt an uneasy fear tug at him.

"There is no escape from death," Kathy said, her inflections hollow and distant. "It is always waiting, isn't it. Just as it waits for all who come here. No, we will not leave. This is the place."

Sammy seemed far less self-assured as he stared wide-eyed at Kathy. He gave a quick command in Swahili to Injai, and their driver started back toward the bus.

"What is it, Sammy?" Eddie asked.

"I am not sure. A bad feeling. Nothing more. But Injai is turning the bus around. It is not good to be closed in on all sides like this. We must be able to move quickly if—"

Injai had nodded with a smile at Braxton and was about to step into the doorway when the machine-gun fire caught him. It was a heavy barrage of explosions that lifted his body off the ground and tore across the

front of the flower-patterned shirt he wore, propelling
him backward through the doorway and slapping him
viciously against the metal stanchions that held the
lower portion of the driver's seat in place.

Braxton shouted Injai's name and leaped across the
doorway to the wounded driver. A second wave of
gunfire sounded, spraying whining bullets above Braxton's head and shattering the long, narrow window that
ran down the center of the door. Braxton flattened
himself against Injai's bleeding chest.

The gunfire stopped. A loud, commanding voice
came from the darkness behind them. In spite of the
volume, the gruff voice was immediately recognizable.

"Stay back from the wheel of the bus, Hicks! Everyone remain still. No one is to move. We got you from
above, too. Dog, show them that we mean business!"

Somewhere in the darkness above them another machine gun fired. It came from off to the right of the
small group, bullets smacking into the ground in front
of them in rapid-fire succession, the angle of contact
causing several rounds of ammunition to ricochet
wildly. A random bullet glanced out of the dirt and tore
into Zelda's left thigh, knocking her to the ground,
where she screamed in pain. Eddie started to move to
her, but the voice stopped him.

"Remain still, Eddie! Hicks, throw that weapon
you're holding out on the ground where I can see it!"

"You shot an unarmed woman here," Eddie cried.

At the bus doorway, Braxton hesitated, unsure what
to do. A moment later the dirt exploded around Eddie
and Zelda as another gun blast sounded.

"Hicks! If I have to tell you again, they're dead. I
mean it!"

"Here, take the damned gun!" Braxton shouted, hurling the rifle out in front of him and turning to the bleeding man behind him.

"Okay. Now your weapons, Sammy," the voice said. "Throw them as far as you can. And don't even think about trying to be a hero, you little traitor. Nothing would give me greater pleasure than putting about five thousand holes into your ass!"

Sammy, glaring at the shadowy figure beyond the bus, allowed his rifle to slip sideways in his hand and then threw it into the darkness. He pulled the pistol at his hip from its holster and tossed it in the same direction.

"Smart decision, Sammy boy!" the voice called out in mockery.

Eddie hollered in the direction of the bus. "Braxton?"

"Yeah," Braxton called back, lifting his head a fraction.

"How is Injai?"

Even as Eddie spoke, Braxton could hear Injai attempting to answer. As he bent over the driver, cradling his head with his hand, Braxton could see a heavy flow of blood oozing out and over Injai's lower lip.

"I'm here, Injai," Braxton whispered. "It's Buddy." Then he called to Eddie, "He's hit pretty badly. I can't see much. What about Zelda?"

"All right, let's cut the talk. You know what we want."

Ignoring Gunther's bellowing voice, Eddie again started to move to where Zelda huddled on the ground.

"I said don't move, Eddie, and I mean it, goddammit!"

"I am a priest, Gunther. You'll have to shoot me and have it on your conscience, because people are hurt here and I'm going to try to help them."

"Noooo! If anyone else is hurt, I tell you nothing!" It was Kathy's voice filling the air. A voice of screaming rage. *"Do you hear me, Gunther? Nothing! All this will be for nothing. You will never find the grave!"*

There was no response for a moment, only silence while Eddie made his way toward Zelda, kneeling beside her. Then the hunter's voice called out again, this time less strident.

"We are willing to talk!"

Sammy glanced sideways at Kathy. She was standing erect, her hair whipping wildly around her head and the native robe she wore bunching up against her in the gusts of wind that the approaching storm stirred around them. Then, taking advantage of the shifting situation, he shouted toward the bus, "Turn on the lights, Braxton! All of them. High beams and interior so that we can see each other. Then we will talk!"

Braxton reached forward and pulled out the light switch on the instrument panel. When he twisted the knob, the interior of the bus was illuminated with a pale greenish glow. Hitting the button on the floor next to the clutch, he switched on the brights. In the stronger light, he could now clearly see Injai's blood-filled mouth. He heard a faint utterance, the words garbled, but Braxton could make out what they were.

"Do you see them…Buddy? The cheetahs…are they not magnificent? Do you see them there?"

Looking out, Braxton could see the others. Kathy, standing farthest away, then Sammy, and, huddled in the spill of the headlights that reflected off the rock wall, Eddie on the ground holding Zelda.

Above and to the right of them, he could just make out the bulky figure of Dog Bassett. His head was wrapped in a crude bandage, making him look like a mummy in the reflected glare, but there was no missing the machine gun he held. It was aimed directly at the people illuminated by the headlights.

And behind the bus, Braxton could also now see Frank Gunther. The hunter's safari clothing was torn and bloodstained. His head was wrapped in tape and bandages hastily applied to cover wounds, and he leaned on a broken limb support. However, injured as he was, Gunther left no doubt that he was still very dangerous. He too held a machine gun in his hands at the ready, his finger curled around the trigger.

Braxton's chest tightened with emotion and he pulled Injai's body to him in an attempt to comfort him. "Yes, I see them, Injai," he whispered. "The cheetahs are beautiful. You are a great game spotter. The best in Kenya . . . Thank you."

Braxton watched as the body he held went limp, the life no longer within it, then gently eased it back against the seat, reaching over and closing the eyelids. The release of tension in Braxton's chest came with the emotional cry that broke from his throat.

"Injai is dead, Eddie. They've killed him!"

At Braxton's words, a deep look of sorrow came into the priest's face and his head bowed in prayer. Sammy shuddered and took an involuntary step forward.

With amazing agility considering his condition, Gunther moved forward on his staff to meet Sammy halfway. By the time he reached Sammy, the hunter had turned his machine gun sideways, and as Sammy grabbed for him with a cry of rage, Gunther brought the weapon's wire stock up and across Sammy's chin, then back into the side of his head, knocking the small man off his feet and leaving him sprawled, unconscious, in the dirt.

"Even though I'm half dead, you're no match for me, you little asshole!" Gunther growled down at the limp body. Then, using his crutch as a support, he hobbled forward until he was well into the spill of light that enveloped those before him. "Look, Kathy, I kept my word. I could have killed Sammy. But I didn't. Right? Now, I'm sorry about the driver, but I couldn't allow the bus to be moved. And the woman getting shot was an accident. You all could see that. Right? Now I've shown I'm a man of my word. So let's talk, and I promise you, no one else will be harmed."

Except for the soft muffled sounds of Zelda crying, there was a silence for several seconds after Gunther finished speaking. And although Eddie tended the hypnotist's leg, wrapping it with a section of torn cloth from his shirt to help stop the bleeding, it was Kathy the priest watched, as did Braxton from his position at the bus doorway. Since screaming her threat at the hunter, she had not moved, but stood her ground, her eyes always on Gunther.

As he watched Gunther and Kathy confronting each other, for the briefest instant Braxton thought he heard the sound of a tiny tinkling bell carried through the night air on a gust of wind. He tilted his head, but the sound was gone. Gone so quickly he could not be sure he had heard it at all.

"Come on now, Kathy," Gunther was saying. "A deal's a deal. What have you got to tell me?"

"Put down your gun first," Kathy said, her voice hard and cold.

Gunther frowned. "What difference does it make? Don't forget about Dog up there. Because I assure you, lady, he hasn't forgotten about you."

"I won't talk to you while you hold a machine gun pointed at us, Gunther."

Braxton was also frowning as he watched Gunther come to a decision. The hunter was right about Dog, so what was the point of Kathy's request? Or was she playing on a very slim hope? Had she also heard the faint tinkling sound in the wind?

Frank Gunther flashed his white-hunter smile and let the machine gun slip from his grasp to the ground, where it clattered loudly. "All right. Anything to oblige. But that's it, little lady. Last concession. Let's have it. Where's the grave?"

A flash of lightning lit the sky overhead, and Kathy did not respond.

"I said, where's the grave, Kathy? Come on, cut the shit and let's have it. There's no getting out of this one. It's over."

"Here," Kathy said matter-of-factly. "The grave is here somewhere. But we're not sure where. We still have to search for it."

Gunther shook his head. "Well, now, Kathy, my dear, I'm afraid that's just not good enough. Because nobody's going to be able to find shit in this darkness and you know it."

Gunther suddenly raised the staff that supported him and shook it with rage in Kathy's direction.

"Now I'm all through being jerked around, lady! This discussion is coming to an end right now. I'm in too much damned pain to keep talking anyway. So here's how it's going to be. I'm going to have Dog shoot one of your friends. And we're going to keep on shooting them until you decide to give us the exact location. We're already over the edge with this. Whether more die makes no difference anymore. You chose the wrong place to come to if you think I can't get away with it. This is a graveyard you're standing on. The natives don't come near this place for fear of spirits, and it ain't exactly a tourist attraction, except for the hyenas. Nobody will find the bodies until the hyenas have skinned them beyond recognition and the remaining bleached bones are nothing but scattered skeletons. So you better start talking, lady, and I mean right now...or they're all going to die. And after they're all dead, if you still can't remember, I'm going to let Dog use the one good eye you left him to see with to take another close-up look at that lovely body of yours. Now... *where* is the grave?''

At Gunther's words, the fire seemed to go out of Kathy. It was as if she had tried a last desperate bluff and lost. Where she had stood so defiantly before, she now seemed to slump. Her hand fluttered to her mouth and forehead as if in confusion.

''I told you all I know,'' she said weakly. ''I ... don't know any more. Please, you've got to believe me.''

''Gunther, for God's sake,'' Eddie called out. ''She's telling the truth. We don't know.''

''Dog!'' Frank Gunther shouted, ignoring the priest's plea and waving his stick-crutch angrily. ''Shoot Hicks in the bus over there!''

''No!'' Kathy screamed, her hand extended in pleading. ''I...''

Braxton had been standing in the doorway listening in awe as Kathy stood up to Gunther with such confidence. But when he saw her start to falter at Gunther's threats, he moved to step out of the bus toward her. Gunther's shout stopped him in midstride.

Flinching, Braxton dove for cover under the dashboard beside Injai's body. His feet still visible, he grabbed at the seat stanchion near his head and jerked his legs up. He waited. But the shots never came.

"Dog! Shoot the son of a bitch, goddammit!" Frank shouted again.

Then it came.

A bloodcurdling cry broke through the darkness behind them, and suddenly the machine gun Dog Bassett held started firing, the barrel lifting upward while bullets pinged and smacked off the rocks high on the cliff wall above. The flaming barrel continued to point toward the sky as Dog's body plummeted off the ledge above them and into the light. He bounced awkwardly when he hit the ground close to Gunther, his body finally halting in what seemed an impossible angle. The spear Twamba had offered Eddie was standing up as it had been when Braxton saw it last, only this time its glistening point was buried deep within Dog's forehead above the clotted crusts of blood half visible through the torn bandage over the man's wounded right eye.

"Twamba!" Braxton shouted. As he shifted his body to peer out, his hand brushed against an object protruding beneath the driver's seat. Glancing down, he saw the ivory handle of Sammy's slasher and closed his hand around it, pulling it out.

As he leaped from the bus doorway, carried by reflex now, Braxton saw Gunther throw his staff onto the ground and reach for the machine gun at his feet.

But Braxton was also moving. Machete held high, he ran as hard as he could toward Gunther, screaming like a banshee. As he watched Gunther fall on the machine gun, his right hand groping, an index finger curling around the trigger, Braxton poured on a final burst of speed and threw himself at the man.

Gunther was attempting to stand and careened sideways as Braxton hit him. But the hunter had the gun now, and he raised the barrel at Braxton. Though slightly off balance, Braxton swung the wide blade of the machete at Gunther's hand to deflect the shot, but Gunther too was in motion. As he struggled to stay on his feet, the slasher missed completely, slicing harmlessly through the air.

Now that he'd found his footing, Gunther clutched the machine gun, aiming to fire, when a piercing cry sounded off to one side. He spun toward it with a choking shout.

Hurtling out of the darkness, his own curved sword held high, came the giant, grease-glistening figure of Twamba!

If it had been a healthy Frank Gunther holding the machine gun, he probably would have pulled the trigger, spraying bullets at the charging Masai. But the assault of the charging warrior proved too much for the wounded hunter to deal with, and he froze, uttering a whimper of fright as Twamba crashed into him.

Braxton had brought the machete back to chest level in a final effort to somehow defend himself, when he too turned toward the cry. That was his position when Gunther's body slammed back against him. They fell together, he and Gunther, the point of the machete stabbing the hunter's back, then burying itself deeply within as they hit the ground.

Gunther made a short grunting sound, and Braxton rolled to one side. The slasher's ivory handle was torn from his grasp as Twamba grabbed Gunther by the shirt front and lifted him off the ground.

The Masai's sword was held back and cocked, ready to strike, but he stayed his hand, for he saw the blow would make no difference. Gunther's body jerked several times, then was still. Issuing a final cry, the Masai hurled the body onto the ground. The throw had such force that when the body hit the dry, hardened earth, the machete blade broke through the front of the hunter's chest with a wet crack.

Braxton came to his feet. He was tense, breathing hard, his back throbbing with pain. He stared down at Gunther's still body uncomprehendingly, then realized it was over. Twamba was already crossing to Sammy, who lay sprawled in the dirt. The Masai's movement awakened Braxton from his daze, and he turned and ran to Kathy, gathering her in his trembling arms. He hugged her for a long time until he began to feel his heart slow and his body settle, then pulled back slightly and looked at her.

"You okay?"

She gave him a nod, but Braxton could see immediately that it wasn't true. The distance was still there. She was far away, staring at him through a fog. He glanced over at Eddie, who was holding the hypnotist.

"Zelda?"

"She's all right, Brax," Eddie told him. "Bullet scraped her leg, but I was able to stop the bleeding." He smiled at Braxton. "Good job out there, Brax. It didn't look to me like Twamba would have gotten to Gunther in time. You saved our lives. How could you run like that with your back out?"

"Fear," Braxton answered. "I think I've found the miracle painkiller that will equal Twamba's drink. Cold fear drives the pain right out of you."

"And what about you, Kathy?" Zelda said from where she sat, nursing her wounded leg. "You were very brave holding Gunther off the way you did. And getting him to put down the gun was a masterful stroke. Did you hear the bell?"

"Yes," Kathy answered vaguely. "I wasn't sure, but I thought it was worth the gamble."

Braxton hugged her tightly. "You did very well. And now it's over."

The wind was strong now, whipping at their clothing as they stood there. The sky above them rumbled heavily, and a flash of lightning ignited the darkness, followed by another. Sammy uttered a low moan as Twamba helped him to his feet, and holding his face, he called out to them, "The storm is beginning."

"Sammy," Braxton shouted over to him. "You okay?"

The guide gave a short wave. "Sore. That is all. Twamba says all is well?"

"Yes, thanks to him. Your Masai is the one who saved the day, Sammy."

"I am glad, Braxton. We should all get to the bus. The storm is directly over us."

"No!" Kathy said, pulling away from Braxton.

"Kathy?"

"It is not over. I cannot stop now. Not now!" She was already turning from them as she spoke, and without looking back, she began walking slowly along the path made by the glaring bus headlights toward the wall of rock that towered before them.

"Eddie!" Braxton said, a trace of wonder in his voice. "She's going on. Look, she seems to... You don't think she really knows...."

"Yes," Eddie replied, hurrying to his feet, his eyes following the robed woman who moved ahead of them in a shaft of light. "Yes, I do."

"Eddie," Zelda shouted. "What's Kathy doing? Where is she?"

"We think she's going for it, Zelda. Look at her. I think she knows where it is!"

"Help me up. Help me up," Zelda insisted.

"Zelda, you're hurt."

"I don't care. Help me up!" She grabbed at Eddie's hand, pulling herself to her feet. Then, standing awkwardly, she slipped her arm around the priest's waist. "All right. Get me that staff that Gunther was using. I'm going with her, damn it. I didn't come all the way over here to end up missing this. Not if I have to crawl."

Making sure Zelda could support herself momentarily, Eddie rushed over to retrieve the thick stick that lay near Gunther's body, and as he gave the staff to the hypnotist, he turned toward the bus. With Twamba's help, Sammy had made his way there and was bending solemnly over Injai's body, which the Masai had taken from the bus and placed on the ground near the doorway.

"Sammy, can we get some torches?" Eddie called.

The guide looked over in confusion. "Eddie, the storm..."

"I know. We'll have to chance it," Eddie replied, running to the bus. The sight of Injai's body stopped the priest momentarily, and he shook his head, taking the dead man's hand in his own. "The death that has occurred here sickens me, Sammy. This man was one of my dearest friends. And I will pray for him. I will find time to pray for all those who have died." He placed Injai's hand gently across the dead man's chest and turned to face the guide. "But the moment is at hand. And I believe we have been brought to it by God. It can be no other way. Kathy is going for the grave and I don't think we could stop her even if we wanted to. We need Twamba to show us the way, and we will need more light."

"I will bring torches," Sammy answered with a nod of agreement, speaking quickly to Twamba in Swahili. The Masai disappeared toward the cliff wall and into the low brush that grew along it.

"No, Sammy, stay on the bus," Eddie said. "You need not come."

Sammy shook his head, wincing in pain. "I have not used caution since I agreed to lead you people, Eddie. I am not going to start now."

Braxton had left the others and run ahead to Kathy, who was moving steadily forward. "Kathy, wait," he cried, coming up beside her. She stopped and he took her hand in his. "Wait for us. Twamba will show us the way. You are not alone, Kathy. We'll all go together."

Kathy turned to face him, and for a moment, the fog lifted. She closed her hand tightly on his and leaned against him, her head resting on his shoulder. "I love you, Braxton Hicks," she said quietly.

"And I love you," he answered.

They remained like that, waiting for the others. Hand in hand, standing alone in the dark vastness of the African wilderness, while overhead the thunder broke in heavy rolls and bolts of lightning knifed their way down toward the towering cliffs that rose out of the savannah floor.

Sammy lit the crude torches Twamba had fashioned, and the two of them distributed the dry moss-covered stakes to the others. As they joined Braxton and Kathy, the tiny group of travelers all paused for a moment to look toward the mighty bluff. Then, with Twamba in the lead, they began to make their way forward.

Twenty-Four

ONCE THEY DREW CLOSE to the rocks, it became clear that they had been looking at a secondary wall and not the main bluff. However, it too was a large structure, wide enough to block from view the lower portion of the main towering rock wall. After reaching it, as Sammy had indicated, they found many odd-shaped slices and openings in the petrified remains of the ancient lava flow. Twamba chose an opening to the right of their approach, and following Kathy, the rest moved toward the gaping hole.

At the last second Braxton protectively crossed in front of Kathy and, ducking his head, stepped into the passageway ahead of her. The opening was low—no more than chest high—and very narrow, making it impossible for more than one person to pass through it at a time. It opened to the right and then curved off left, giving it a cavelike appearance while obscuring what lay beyond.

That was why Braxton was the first to see the tree. Emerging from the other side and raising his torch, he could tell he was still some distance from the bluff. In front of him, surrounded by protruding rock shelving and dark impressions that seemed much like the entrance he had just passed through, was a wide open-topped natural chamber carved out by erupting lava that must have spewed across the landscape eons before.

The beams from the bus headlights penetrated various rock openings in the first wall so that in addition to the glow from Braxton's torch, the entire area was dimly lit by strangely shaped, random arcs of light that crisscrossed through the mist-laden air. When a particularly strong bolt of lightning cracked to life in the sky above, these webs of light would sporadically merge into one blinding flash.

Twamba stood with his spear at the ready while waiting for the others to emerge through the rock opening, and beyond him, off to the left of center, was the tree. It had a wide-spreading top like the umbrella-shaped acacias so common to the Kenyan plains, but it was larger than the brush Braxton had seen along the outside of the wall. And it was unique in two other ways. Most noticeably, it stood completely alone, the only tall vegetation in view amid the dirt, loose rock and short tufts of dry, brown grass that surrounded it. And although the usual protective thorns protruded from the limbs, instead of a light brown tinge, the bark was a bright yellow.

Braxton paused until the others joined him, Sammy bringing up the rear. Then, after allowing them time to adjust to their new surroundings, he pointed toward the solitary tree.

"Isn't that a fever tree?"

"Yes," Sammy responded. In one hand he held a rifle and in the other a torch, which he raised now to get a better view. "The fever tree grows larger than most acacia. Its thorns are bigger too, with hard, jagged tips. Very bad to step on or catch against the skin."

"Anything unusual about it being here?"

Sammy shook his head. "No, what is unusual is that nothing else of any large size grows here."

"I think I see the reason," Zelda said, leaning forward on her makeshift crutch. "There's some kind of wide crevasse in front of it, isn't there? Or are my eyes playing tricks on me?"

"No, you're right, Zelda," Eddie confirmed. "See the break running along the ground? The back side where the tree stands is slightly higher than the front. It looks like a small fault where shifting earth forced the ground to break open."

"I see it now," Braxton said. "Is there a mist too?"

"Yes, Braxton," Eddie told him. "Watch the crevasse. See it there. The mist is seeping out of the ground near the foot of the tree, isn't it, Sammy?"

The guide nodded. "Yes. Could be some sort of spring underneath. That would explain why it exists when no other large growth does. If you look closely, it appears the roots grew directly from the inside opening." From where he stood nearby, Twamba spoke with clipped enthusiasm as he pointed his spear toward the tree. "Twamba says the opening in front of the tree is the one he wanted you to see. He says it has grown since he was last here."

"'…and He placed at the east of the garden of Eden cherubims, and a flaming sword which turned every way, to keep the way of the tree of life,'" Eddie quoted.

"What is that?" Braxton asked. "The Bible?"

Eddie nodded. "Yes, Genesis. End of chapter three. Seeing the tree made me think of it. That's what we're trying to discover information about, isn't it? The tree of life. The secrets of rebirth, and how it's all linked to the past."

"Ed, you've been pushing for this all along. What are you saying? You suddenly think this could be a mistake? That we may be treading on hallowed ground?"

"I don't know. The thought just occurred to me, that's all."

"Well, I see some mist, but no flaming swords, my friend." Braxton turned to Kathy. "What do you think, Kathy. Straight ahead?"

Like everyone else, Kathy had been gazing toward the tree, and she answered softly without turning. "Yes."

"Okay," Braxton said, glancing from her to the others. "Why don't we go have a look, shall we?"

"Yes," Kathy answered again, starting out toward the center of the wide rock enclosure.

Zelda shivered and Eddie turned to her. "You all right?"

"Sure," Zelda said, adjusting her crutch and straightening as much as she could. "Let's see what's in that crevasse."

There was no spoken agreement, but they allowed Kathy to lead the way as they approached the tree. Even Twamba remained behind her, moving alertly alongside them as they advanced.

Kathy was several feet ahead of them and about three-quarters of the way there when the horrible sounds began.

"Good Lord," Zelda muttered, coming to a standstill. "Did you hear that?"

Braxton, who had stopped along with the others, stared through the mists of dull reflected light into the darkness. "We all heard it, Zelda."

From within the shadows along the rocky walls of the wide enclosure, first on one side, then all around them, they heard the snarls. Beast snarls.

"Fisi!" hissed Twamba, drawing the curved sword from his belt.

Sammy had moved to one side of the group opposite Twamba. The guide pushed the safety off his rifle and motioned to the others. His eyes were wide and he spoke with urgency.

"Listen carefully to me. Twamba speaks of *fisi*. They are here in the shadows, hiding from the light."

"Fisi?" Zelda asked, repeating the word.

"Yes, it is Swahili for hyena. Of all the animals, the hyena is the one the Masai do not revere, for it feeds on the dead. They call it the beast without a heart. There are many *fisi* here hiding from the light. Lurking in the darkness around us. Too many. In packs, they are always hungry and attack the living until a victim is brought down and they can all feed."

There was a new sound amid the snarling growls. It was a crackling cry, like an animal laugh. Now, however, the sound brought only tingles of fear to those who heard it.

Sammy twisted his head quickly in several directions while Twamba brought his shield up protectively, stretching to his full height as he spat the word *fisi* yet again.

"Listen to them," Sammy cried. "Enkai help us, they are everywhere. We must go back. We must get to the shelter of the wall we came through. From there, we will try for the bus. Bunch together... holding the torches out around us as a barrier. The flames may keep them back until we can reach the rocks."

Following the guide's instructions, Zelda hobbled closer to Sammy. "If you've got any influence upstairs, Eddie, you'd better use it," she whispered, her voice shaking in fear.

But the priest had not heard the hypnotist's words, and even as Sammy called for them all to come closer together, he saw that his plan was not going to work.

Eddie and Braxton were moving away from rather than toward the others. They were headed after Kathy, Braxton shouting her name as they ran. And Kathy, farthest of all from any kind of protection, was headed straight for the tree.

"Twamba!" Sammy shouted, pointing toward the lone robed woman ahead of them. "*Haraka!* Quickly!"

Sammy saw Twamba turn to run, but then he lost sight of the Masai as Zelda's scream pulled his attention in another direction.

He could see the hyenas now. They were scurrying in darting groups toward the humans. Sammy knew what they would do. He had seen it often when a starving pack of the scavengers pursued living food. They would continue circling, lunging and snapping until one of them got lucky and caught hold of a prey. Then, with a staggering swiftness, two or three others would immediately descend on the snagged victim, dragging it away for the kill. And there were too many of them for the animals to stop there. They would soon return and the process would go on until the carnivores had killed them all. Unless they could reach the rocks.

Sammy raised his rifle. "Zelda! Stay behind me! I will fire at the ones between us and the wall! When I fire, move. Take my torch! Get behind me, and keep the torches away from your body. If they come near, swing the flame at their faces. Ready?"

Zelda, obeying instructions, limped close to the guide on her crutch, taking a torch in each hand. "But, Sammy! We can't leave them out there!"

Two hyenas, closer than the rest, snapped at them, lunging inward with their awkwardly shaped bodies. Zelda screamed, shoving the torch outward.

"Twamba is with them!" Sammy shouted. "Now do as I say or we will die!" Seeing another hyena approaching in a fast, low crawl from the right side of him, Sammy spun and fired his rifle at the beast.

IT SEEMED TO BRAXTON that hyenas were everywhere, the ugly beasts slinking out of the darkness, loping around them at a safe distance, emitting their raking cackle, then suddenly rushing at them, their open jaws snapping viciously. He and Eddie had moved along back-to-back, swinging their torches at the leaping beasts. So far it was working. But the hyenas were growing braver, veering closer each time.

Behind him, Braxton could see Sammy, followed by Zelda, who thrust the torches outward to keep the beasts at bay while their guide sighted to the rear and fired. At one point the hypnotist slipped, and a torch fell to the ground. Uttering a cry, Zelda pulled the wooden staff from under her arm, drew up her thick body and delivered a driving blow at a lunging beast. The wooden crutch connected with the side of the hyena's face, and as the injured animal yelped in agony, scampering backward, Zelda scooped up the fallen torch and hobbled forward while Sammy fired his weapon into the mists.

All the while, Braxton and Eddie continued to inch their way forward. Kathy had reached the crevasse in front of the tree. The beasts were there too, but Braxton had not given up hope, for she was not alone.

Beside her was Twamba. They had no torches, so the hyenas were circling closer and attacking with greater frequency. Still, the Masai was holding his own, deflecting them with his shield and slicing at them with his curved sword.

"We must reach them with the torches!" Braxton shouted. "I don't know how long Twamba can hold the animals off without fire."

"All right," Eddie agreed, sounding short of breath. "We'll stay back-to-back. Keep swinging the torches in full horizontal arcs, and get to the tree as fast as you can. Ready?"

"I'm right with you, Father. Good luck!"

They moved awkwardly in a stumbling, sideways run. Both men knew that to fall could mean disaster. Twamba was too besieged to save them. In fact, he had handed Kathy his curved sword to defend herself as the hyenas closed in, and now he struck out at them with his great spear.

They were almost at the crevasse when Braxton miscalculated his footing and stumbled. He had been concentrating on Kathy's safety, amazed at the way she swung the sword in vicious strokes at the snapping jaws around her, when suddenly he tripped and pitched forward, his body landing with a painful thud at the very lip of the gaping crevasse.

When he started to fall, Braxton threw out his hand with the torch to break the impact. Now as he stared through the moving flames into the yawning opening, he felt the excitement of new discovery.

Something was there!

He leaned forward, straining his eyes to get a clearer view. His vision blurred and his eyes stung from the smoke, but he knew something was there.

It had form. Shape. It was thin...skeletal.... Yet the shape was not like that of an animal. It looked like the shape of a human being.

Braxton thrust the torch deeper into the opening, lost in the overwhelming reality of what he thought he saw. It was true. Oh, God, it was really true!

He had to see more clearly, but he couldn't. The image beyond him blurred in the dancing flames, changing shape, seeming to shift and vibrate with a life of its own.

There was no forethought to Braxton's next action. It was blind impulse. An uncontrollable urge suddenly surfaced within him and he went with it. Braxton Hicks, the one who did not know his own past, the one who had been the unbeliever, had to see if he could catch a glimpse of his origins. He had to know the truth.

Shifting his body, he brought his free hand around in front of him and reached down into the crevasse, probing beyond the flames for the image that swam before him. At last he touched something. And as his clutching fingers closed around it, emotion flooding his body in surging waves, he heard Kathy screaming his name.

"Look out! Oh, God, Braxton! Behind you! Look behind you!"

Kathy! Kathy was screaming! And as her cries broke through Braxton's consciousness, he jerked his head around to look over his shoulder. It was one of those illuminated moments, when, with a lightning flash, night became day. And in that moment, Braxton could see with staggering horror that the hyenas were making a final, terrible attack.

Two were already at Eddie, having pushed him back against the base of the tree. The small priest was grabbing at the fur of one beast's neck as he smashed his torch into its open-jawed face. And several more were coming straight for Braxton, leaping at him even as he spun with a turning gasp from where he lay at the edge of the crevasse.

One hyena snagged him in midmotion and sent him lurching backward. Then another shot in from the side, sharp teeth sinking into Braxton's shoulder. Then another appeared, its fangs catching his shirt, tearing at him, trying to drag him away. Braxton closed his fingers into a fist and beat at the face clamped on his shoulder while he tried to roll to his side. But the jaw held, and another set of fangs closed on his leg.

Then, while he kicked and fought with a desperate abandonment, Braxton saw a slender hand clasped around a gleaming sword sweep down toward him and slice with a crashing blow into the head of the beast clamped on his shoulder. Again and again the sword hacked until the hyena's jaw eased and the animal fell limply away. And now the sword was slicing into the beast on his leg, and with a mighty kick, Braxton pulled free.

"Kathy!" Braxton cried, scrambling to his feet. He grabbed the fallen torch with his right hand and moved back beside the woman who had saved him. Kathy, her flushed face framed by her flaming red hair, screamed in furious rage as she wielded the curved blade of steel with both hands like some ancient Amazon warrior, striking and hacking at the beasts around them.

Then the bleeding figure of Twamba was there too, a swinging, slashing machine of fury. Bit by bloody bit as Twamba swung with his great spear, the space around the three of them began to open. It was not hope, however, but a terrible, desperate fear for his friend's life that hammered at Braxton's senses. In front of the tree, a group of hyenas surrounded Eddie, tearing at the struggling priest with an aggressive viciousness as they tried to drag him to the ground.

"Twamba...Eddie," Braxton screamed, grabbing at the Masai's arm and pointing toward the tree. "We've got to save Eddie!"

With a nod as he grasped Braxton's meaning, the Masai lifted his head and gave a mighty, earsplitting shout toward the priest.

Instinctively, Eddie turned toward the sound, and as he did so, Twamba shouted a second time. Then, holding the bloodstained spear upright in his hand, the Masai thrust his arm forward, hurling the spear across the space that separated him from the priest.

It was as if from somewhere deep within him Eddie had found a new strength, and as the Masai shouted a second time, the priest managed to pull his small, frail body once more erect, his arm reaching out and his fingers closing on the spear that came sailing to him. Now, spear in hand, he gave out a wail of his own and struck out at the beasts before him.

He was positioned with his back against the tree, and he was covered in blood. His shirt was soaked with dark blotches from the lacerations where the hyenas' jaws had caught him. And red fluid seeped from wounds on his crown where the tree thorns had cut into his head, the blood streaming in tiny rivulets over his forehead and down the edges of his face.

Even though the priest struck out with renewed strength, the beasts around him had tasted blood, and they attacked with a savage frenzy that would not be denied. As the hyenas came at him for what he knew would be the final time, he stood there in the raging storm, spear in hand, as Twamba had foreseen. The howling beasts had nailed him to the tree at the mouth of the great opening he had sought to reach so desperately, and now Father Eddie Fitzsimmons raised his face to the sky, gave out a cry for help to his God, and lifted the spear high into the air.

And the sky opened.

Attracted by the long metal rod, a ragged lightning bolt came streaking from above, shooting downward and connecting with the tip of the spear in a jolting blaze of power. For an instant, both Eddie and the spear seemed to glow, then the tree on which the priest leaned burst into flames, and the charging beasts turned in howls of fears, scattering from the fire.

With an involuntary cry, the priest hurled the spear from him, and it shot through the air, landing point first in the ground beyond the crevasse. Eddie's body reeled backward, crashed against the blazing trunk, then fell face forward at the base of the flaming tree.

And the lightning came again. Only this time there was not just one but many flashes—bolts of fire knifing downward as the sky opened to release torrents of rain, and each bolt struck the quivering spear where it was lodged in the ground. The smell of burning fur and flesh filled the air, and the howling beasts scattered through the windswept fires that raged and fed on themselves within the huge enclosure. Still the lightning came in tongues of flame that struck at the ground and walls, sending rocks and giant boulders flying into the air.

Braxton grasped Kathy close to him, trying to protect her with his body, and looked back to where he had seen Eddie fall. But all he could see was the blazing tree. Wide, high flames leaped and danced into the night sky like the wings of a majestic bird ascending into the heavens on a huge towering oval of light and fire.

Bringing his face close to hers, Braxton saw that Kathy was staring beyond the crevasse, into the flames. And he saw that the eyes were as they had been during the hypnosis: not her eyes, but the eyes of the Eve of regression; searching eyes, seeking an answer in the pulsating embryo of flaming life before them.

AS KATHY SULLIVAN GAZED into the wall of light before her, she knew that finally her search had ended. It was not hypnosis influencing her now, nor the fleeting images of dreams. This was reality. Like a great cloud lifting before her, the fog had finally cleared, and she could see into the flames.

And what she saw shimmering within the fire was not a vision of the mother she had sought for so long. What she saw was not something skeletal that shifted on a swirling flame of death and decay.

No, to Kathy's astonishment, what she saw was an image that made her heart sing. It was an involuntary response. A joyful answering. And in that moment, she knew beyond doubt that her search was ended, for now she responded not as the child, but as the mother.

It was indeed a womb of life that swam before Kathy's vision. And nestled in the center of that womb was the tiny form of an unborn child. A small, perfectly formed child, whose tiny hands opened and closed, reaching out for her, calling to her in faint infant wails of longing—as she herself had called for so long to the mother who had never answered; the mother she had never known.

SHE WAS STRUGGLING against the hands that held her. Trying to pull free, to move toward the fire.

"Please," her voice cried. "Let me go. I have to go there."

But Braxton held on with all his might to this woman he had come to love. He had lost her once, and he would never lose her again.

"No...Kathy," he pleaded. "No, that is not the way. This is the way of the dead. We are the living. Come back to me, Kathy. Please...come back to me."

As he called to her, Braxton turned her face to his, forcing her to look at him.

"Please, Kathy," he cried, as he fought to reach the woman he knew. "Please...I love you. I need you, Kathy. Hear me, Kathy. Please! Come back to me!"

And then slowly, ever so slowly, Kathy's struggling eased. Her eyes cleared, and with a flicker of recognition she relaxed in his arms, curling against him with a whimper.

His own energy expended, Braxton collapsed. And with Kathy cleaving to him, the two of them tumbled over the lip of the fault as one, into the crevasse's waiting mouth at the base of the flaming tree.

Twenty-Five

IT WAS ZELDA'S VOICE that told Braxton it had not been his time to die.

"Braxton," the hypnotist's voice called. Braxton's eyes fluttered open, squinting from the daylight. "Get Twamba over here, Sammy," Zelda's voice continued. "He's coming to."

"Kathy?" Braxton muttered, raising his bandaged hands.

"She's going to be okay, Braxton. Easy does it, now." He could see Zelda now. Her clothes in tatters, she was kneeling next to him on the ground. Braxton saw it was morning. The sun was on its daily climb toward the peak of the sky. "She's right next to you," Zelda said.

Braxton craned his head in the direction of her nod. Kathy was lying on the ground to the right of him. She had her head sideways and was looking at him when he turned. Her face was filthy, and marked with caked blood and heat blisters, but she smiled weakly at him, reaching over and squeezing his hand.

"You all right?" Braxton asked hoarsely.

Kathy nodded. "Thanks to Twamba's medicine, I'm not feeling much pain from the burns. They tell me I'll make it. How about you? Okay?"

Braxton tried to gauge how badly he was hurt, then realized large areas of his body were numb. Twamba must have administered painkiller to him also. "I'm not sure. But I think I have more than a simple backache."

Kathy held his eyes. "I...I would have gone over the edge if you hadn't been there, Brax."

"I know," he replied. "I saw it in your face. But I wasn't going to lose you again."

Kathy frowned, remembering. "Did...did you look into the flames? There, in the fire? It simply overpowered me. But you broke it for me when you forced me to look at you, and I was able to grab hold of reality again."

"What did you see in the flames, Kathy? Was it...?"

Kathy shook her head. Emotion flooded her face, but there were no tears. The time for crying was finished. "No, she wasn't there. But that knowledge has given me a strange sort of release, somehow. I finally feel that it's finished and I can stop chasing phantoms from the past. It's time for a new beginning. I...I did see something in the flames, though, Braxton. I know I did. I saw...a child."

Once again, though she had promised herself she wouldn't, Kathy found herself crying as she spoke to the man next to her. Only this time it was different. This time her tears flowed from a warm, happy emotion.

"I know it sounds impossible, but I think that's what I saw. I think I saw...our child, Braxton," Kathy said, smiling through her tears. "I think we're going to have a baby."

Braxton stared in astonishment at the woman beside him, unable to think of a response to what she had said, and she smiled even wider, a soft chuckle bubbling out of her that caused her to wince slightly in pain.

"Speechless, Braxton Hicks? Well, if it's any comfort, it was not what I expected, either."

Braxton had tilted his head, considering what Kathy had told him, and then, with a smile of his own, he returned the squeeze she had given him.

"I admit it's not something I had considered, but I don't think I would mind if it were true," he said. "And I mean that, Kathy. I wouldn't mind at all."

"Well, it certainly wouldn't be possible if you hadn't been able to bring me back when you did. Although I still don't understand how we survived. I remember we fell forward into the opening at the foot of the tree. What stopped us? Why didn't we die?"

"I think I can answer that," Zelda said, coming closer between the two and groaning slightly with her own pain as she eased herself into a kneeling position next to Kathy. "After Twamba pulled the two of you out and we were sure you would live, I examined the hole the Masai hauled you from. It sank about two feet down and then stopped, ending in a rock ledge. There was no more mist. Nothing but a hairline crack along one side to indicate that the opening could have ever been any deeper. My theory is that the lightning bolt did it. The rock slab where you were lying was still pretty hot when we finally got to you. That's where some of your burns came from. The force of the impact when the lightning hit must have shoved the rock and dirt inward, sealing the crevice. If anything was there, it's buried beneath solid rock now, which pretty much puts an end to that."

"And Eddie?" Braxton asked softly.

Zelda's expression became solemn and she looked away momentarily. "It doesn't look like he's going to make it, Braxton. Twamba was with him when you came to just now."

"There is little Twamba can do except make Eddie comfortable by trying to ease the pain," Sammy said, coming up to them with the Masai.

"Take me to him," Braxton requested, releasing Kathy's hand and half starting to rise.

Twamba was beside him instantly, shaking his head and holding Braxton down with a firm hand. The Masai too showed signs of having been through a battle, although he appeared to have plenty of strength still in reserve.

"Braxton," Sammy protested, "you must not move. You are not able yet. Please. Twamba's painkilling herbs do not allow you to know how badly you are hurt."

"Then carry me," Braxton said, "or I will try to go to him. Take me, please. I must see him."

Sammy looked at Zelda for guidance, but the hypnotist merely shrugged. Reluctantly the guide spoke to Twamba, and with a great gentleness, the Masai slipped his hands under Braxton's body and lifted him into the air.

Once up, Braxton could see the devastation the events of the previous night had wrought. The entire area had been burned to an ashy blackness. Tiny columns of smoke still rose in places from the smoldering ground. And there was another difference. Something had changed. Braxton glanced toward the extinct volcano that still towered high into the Kenyan sky, then back again, and he knew immediately: there was no longer any wall behind them.

"The entire wall is gone!" he exclaimed.

"Yes," Sammy said, moving beside Twamba as the Masai made his way across the burned crusts of earth. "It was the last series of lightning flashes from the sky.

We were huddled against the ground near this side of the rocks when it came. We were very lucky in two ways. First, that we were able to make it so close to the wall, for otherwise we would not have survived. As it was, the falling hail of boulders and rock buried everything between where the wall had stood and far beyond the bus." Sammy pointed toward the horizon. "My vehicle was there," he said, indicating an area where the rock-covered landscape rose into a jagged mound. "Now it is buried somewhere beneath that rise."

"They're all gone," Braxton murmured as he stared beyond. "Gunther and Bassett . . . ?"

"Yes," Sammy said. "Injai also. None will ever be found beneath those piles of rock. Many of the retreating animals died in the explosion of rock and are buried with them. The rest have vanished. Only we remain."

Braxton blinked, staring at the devastation. "It's unbelievable."

Sammy nodded. "The spear appeared to attract the lightning, which in turn created a path that other bolts followed into the chamber almost as if they were drawn into a funnel."

Sammy stopped walking, and as Twamba eased Braxton's body to the ground, Braxton saw that they were at the spot where the tree had been. And he saw that Zelda was right. The crevice was no longer the endless yawning mouth he had stared into, but merely a narrow coffin-length impression two feet deep in the ground.

Eddie lay next to the opening. Zelda had been right there, too. The priest was in very bad shape. All his hair was gone; eyebrows, eyelashes, on his arms, head—everywhere. And his face and those parts of his body visible through the charred remains of clothing were scorched and blistered to the point where they were unrecognizable. Oozing burns and crusted blood covered him, and if it had not been for the tiny lifting and falling of the priest's chest as he breathed, Braxton would not have believed it possible for his friend still to be alive.

Twamba placed Braxton very close to Eddie, and Braxton pulled himself off the ground, Sammy kneeling to help him as he leaned forward, whispering the priest's name.

"Eddie...Eddie, it's Braxton. Can you hear me?"

A tiny shiver passed through Eddie's body, and his head rolled toward Braxton, the cracked, bleeding lips moving to form a word. No sound came, only a plosive, nonvocal "Baaaa..."

"Don't try to talk, Ed," Braxton said. "Just know we're here and we're going to take care of you. You saved us, Eddie. When you lifted the spear, it became a lightning rod and the fire from the lightning stopped the attacking animals. You saved us all, Father. We're going to make it. And you're going to make it too."

Slowly Eddie's head rolled back and forth in a negative response to Braxton's final words, and then his eyes opened. His clear blue eyes gazed steadily at his friend. Then the priest's lips moved again and weakly, with great effort, he spoke.

"Did you see it, Braxton?" he asked. "Did you see into the grave?"

"Yes," Braxton answered. "I saw, Eddie."

"Good. Then you know. You are no longer a man without a past. You have seen where you come from, and what you are. You must write about what you saw."

The priest's eyes closed and Braxton leaned closer, his voice filling with concern. "Eddie?"

Before he could go on, Eddie's lips moved again, only this time it was to smile. Then his eyes reopened, and he continued.

"Write about it, Braxton. Will you?"

"Yes, Eddie," Braxton promised. "You have my word. Now don't talk, please. There's no need. Rest."

"No, I must tell you, Braxton," the priest answered, the strain of speaking seeming to ease as the words came rushing from him. "Oh, Braxton, I've seen. Now I have seen, and now I understand! Tell Kathy. She must not agonize. All the illness, heartache and pain is merely a casting off. Death is only the soul shedding old skin to begin anew. I see now, and am ashamed to have ever doubted. It is all a labor of preparation. It is not the end. There is more. So very much more. These are only the first signs of the great labor still to come for the new birth. We walk blindly at the edge of the Garden, painfully searching through life's wall of thorns for the way back. And it is close, Braxton. Very close. What is ahead is not the end; it is the beginning."

The priest's lips stopped moving momentarily, and Braxton leaned forward, afraid that the effort had proved too much. Then Eddie's faint smile widened and his face took on an expression that could only be defined as unqualified joy.

"And there is hope, Braxton," the priest whispered his eyes shining. "As I always knew. Soon we will find the opening through the thorns and see that our search has brought us to where we began. Oh, Braxton, we know the way, yet move in darkness. But now I know what is to come, and understand. There must not be despair. Though the cycle brings us back, it is only shifting of the soul on a great spiral that leads to the heavens. And hope sings at the window of our soul. We will learn. And we will be reborn. This time of preparation is the eve of a return to a new beginning. I spoke the truth without knowing it. My doubt clouded the meaning of the phrase I repeated so often. Tell them, Braxton. Tell them this is . . . the eve of regression.''

"Hey, hang on, Ed," Braxton began as the priest's eyes closed once again. "You can't leave me. I need you. You're all I've got."

"No," Eddie said, his lids remaining shut as he spoke in slow, halting words. "That isn't true. And you know it, Braxton, because you too have seen the light. We all have much, much more."

"Eddie, come on, I mean it," Braxton said softly. "Don't you go dying on me now." The tears were flowing freely down his cheeks as the priest's breathing suddenly became weaker and more erratic.

"No," Eddie replied, scarcely audible, "I won't do that, Braxton. I won't die."

With a final effort, Eddie brought his hands together and folded them across his chest as his lips closed in a tiny, cracked smile. And then the small, battered frame that was the priest's body simply ceased to breathe.

Crying like a baby, Braxton insisted they make the service Eddie's grave. Sammy fashioned a cross while Twamba scooped dirt over the body. And as Zelda propped Kathy up into a sitting position so she could see, Braxton instructed Sammy to have Twamba drive the cross into the place where the tree had stood. Then Braxton spoke the simplest of prayers, and his friend, the priest, was gone.

LATER, WHEN NIGHT began to fall and they were all
huddled around a small fire that Twamba had built, it
was Sammy who brought up the realities of their situation.

"Twamba says we can make it to safety," he informed them. "He will not only guide us, but also help
to find provisions for survival along the way."

The warrior had gathered several limbs of various
sizes, and together, he and Sammy were assembling a
long, narrow wooden stretcher of sorts. They had used
ropelike vines to tie two heavy branches parallel to each
other and were now lacing smaller limbs between the
two main supports.

"Kathy will be able to walk," Sammy continued as
he worked, "and Braxton, for now, will ride here. We
will place furs over these wooden crosspieces. Not the
best, but it will have to do."

"Don't be ridiculous," Braxton put in. "I'll pull my
own weight."

"Soon, perhaps," Sammy agreed, spreading the furs
Twamba handed him over the length of the stretcher-
sleigh they had fashioned. "But not yet. Twamba will
know when you are able. For now, this is where you will
ride. Now we will try it."

With that, Sammy lifted the top of the rough-hewn
wooden carrier onto a boulder so that it rested at a low
angle off the ground, and Twamba, ignoring his protest, lifted Braxton and placed him across the stretcher.
Sammy smiled as Braxton, giving in with a helpless sigh,
allowed his body to relax against the fur.

"I don't want to know where Twamba found these
furs," Braxton said.

Sammy's smile widened. "Hyena fur is as comfortable as any. It will do fine. Twamba will make rope lengths for the two of us to pull. We will manage."

"And what do we say if and when we do reach someone?" Zelda asked.

Sammy spoke without hesitation. "We tell what happened—to a point: There was a terrible storm; I lost men and the priest was killed by lightning; we are greatly saddened by the event, but there was nothing else we could do."

"Come on, Sammy," Braxton said, frowning in disbelief. "What about Gunther? This thing could blow wide open."

"No, Braxton," Sammy answered. "It will not. Remember, the bodies are gone. No one will find them, believe me. Gunther and Bassett are not our concern. We know nothing about them. The wilderness is a wild and dangerous place. Things happen. That is the attitude to missing safaris. I have seen this official reaction many times. What happened here will remain buried forever."

"What did happen here?" Zelda asked, frowning. "I can't help but feel that we know little more than we did when we started."

"No, some things have changed, Zelda," Kathy said from her seat on the ground near the stretcher Twamba had placed Braxton on. "I'm free of some of my own personal torment." She looked at Braxton and smiled. "I think I've finally gotten it through my thick head that it's time to stop worrying about the past and start living for today."

"Kathy, I understand that," Zelda told her, "and I'm glad you've been able to resolve some of your turmoil, but I still feel a certain frustration about all this. I never got to that opening. Did we find it? The two of you were closest to it. Was it the grave of Eve?''

"Eddie died believing he'd found it," Braxton answered.

"And what about you, Braxton?"

He was silent for a moment. He tried to remember. What had he seen? His had not been an image like Kathy's, yet there had been something. In the flashing light when he had reached out, clutching at what was within, he had thought he saw someone, and with the image had come a wave of emotion. For, strangest of all, it was not a stranger he saw; it was himself.

Braxton reached over and covered Kathy's small, delicate fingers with his free hand as the memory of the vision rekindled questions in his mind. He thought about the image Kathy had seen of the child and realized that he wanted it to be true. The thought of them having a child to love and cherish gave him a feeling of deep inner peace. Of... fulfillment.

Was that what drew male and female together to bring about the painful joy of new birth over and over? A simple search for a rebirth of self in the form of a child?

Or was what he saw the Adam or Eve missing from all of them? Not a reflection of self, but the part that makes one complete.

Was that what drove everyone to avoid loneliness? To be loved? A mighty, irrepressible evolutionary urge to reach the end that had been the beginning? To mend a severed self that had somehow been rent apart at the beginning of time? Was that the answer to the mystery of what Eddie had called the "eve of regression"?

Heavy thoughts for a wounded man lying on a stretcher in the African wilderness. Much too complex to be dealt with under the present conditions. But he would attempt to sort it out. As he had promised Eddie, he would write it all down with as much clarity as possible. Perhaps then, as he and Kathy began a new life together, they would be able to talk and gain some understanding not only of what they had felt and seen, but of the reason why it had all taken place.

Of course he couldn't be positive he had seen anything. Things hadn't been exactly calm around him. And the image had lasted but a moment. The only thing he knew for sure was that the experience had changed him somehow, and intuitively he knew it was for the better.

"Well, Braxton?" Zelda prodded.

Braxton rested his head against the stretcher. "I think we're probably not going to find too many answers looking for treasures in the earth, Zelda. You were there too, Kathy. What do you think?"

Kathy's eyes were clear as she met his. "I think I'm ready to forget pursuing the ethereal and start concentrating on a real relationship," she replied. She shifted the direction of her gaze and stared up into the sparkling constellation of the Kenyan night sky.

"Braxton's right, Zelda. It's time to stop looking at holes in the ground and start looking up," she said with a smile.

High above them, a shooting star ignited in a blossom of white against the dark African heavens, then trailed off in a short sparkling tail to disappear into nothingness.

A breathtaking roller coaster of adventure,
passion and danger in the dazzling
Roaring Twenties!

SCANDALOUS SPIRITS

ERIN YORKE

Running from unspeakable danger, she found shelter—and desire—
in the arms of a reckless stranger.

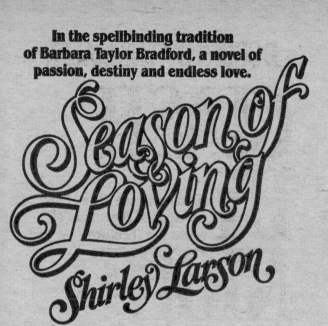
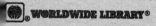

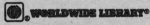

Shannon OCork

Turning Point

A novel of passion, power, wealth and deadly secrets...

A young woman is suddenly cast into a world where beautiful faces hide daring lies, shocking truths... perhaps even murder.